THE HAPPY MARRIAGE

THE HAPPY MARRIAGE

A Novel

TAHAR BEN JELLOUN

Translated by
ANDRÉ NAFFIS-SAHELY

MELVILLE HOUSE
BROOKLYN · LONDON

THE HAPPY MARRIAGE

First published in France as *Le Bonheur Conjugal*
Copyright © 2012 by Éditions Gallimard
Translation copyright © 2016 by André Naffis-Sahely
First Melville House printing: January 2016

Melville House Publishing		8 Blackstock Mews
46 John Street	and	Islington
Brooklyn, NY 11201		London N4 2BT

mhpbooks.com   facebook.com/mhpbooks   @melvillehouse

Library of Congress Cataloging-in-Publication Data
Ben Jelloun, Tahar, 1944– author.
Title: The happy marriage / Tahar Ben Jelloun.
Other titles: *Bonheur conjugal*. English
Description: Brooklyn, NY : Melville House, 2016.
Identifiers: LCCN 2015041338 (print) | LCCN 2015041424
    (ebook) | ISBN 978-1-61219-465-3 (hardback) | ISBN
    978-161219-466-0 (ebook)
Subjects: LCSH: Marriage—Fiction. | Domestic fiction. |
    BISAC: FICTION / Literary. | FICTION / Family Life. |
    FICTION / Political.
Classification: LCC PQ3989.2.J4 B6613 2016 (print) |
    LCC PQ3989.2.J4 (ebook) | DDC 843/.914—dc23
LC record available at http://lccn.loc.gov/2015041338

Printed in the United States of America
10 9 8 7 6 5 4 3 2 1

Cet ouvrage publié dans le cadre du programme d'aide à la publication
a bénéficié du soutien du Ministère des Affaires Étrangères et du Service
Culturel de l'Ambassade de France représenté aux États-Unis.

This work, published as part of a program of aid for publication, received
support from the French Ministry of Foreign Affairs and the Cultural
Service of the French Embassy in the United States.

Cet ouvrage a bénéficié du soutien des Programmes d'aide à la publication
de l'Institut Français.

This work, published as part of a program of aid for publication, received
support from the Institut Français.

MARIANNE: Do you believe two people can spend a lifetime together?

JOHAN: It's a ridiculous convention passed down from God knows where. A five-year contract would be ideal. Or an agreement subject to renewal.

—INGMAR BERGMAN, *Scenes from a Marriage*

I make my own luck.

—KING VIDOR, *Gilda*

THE HAPPY MARRIAGE

PART ONE

The Man Who Loved Women
Too Much

Prologue

It landed on the tip of his nose. It was neither large nor small. Just an ordinary fly, gray, black, puny, inconvenient. It felt good sitting there, atop that nose where it had just landed like a plane on an aircraft carrier. It cleaned its forelegs. As though it were rubbing and polishing them for some urgent mission. Nothing could bother it. It was busying itself while rooted to its spot. It weighed next to nothing, but was still annoying. It irritated the man who couldn't shoo it away. He tried to move, brush it away, he blew on it, shouted. The fly was indifferent. It didn't flinch. It was there, right there, and had no intention of leaving. Nevertheless, the man didn't mean it any harm, he just wanted it to go, to leave him alone, because he could no longer move his fingers, his hands, or his arms. His body had stopped working. He was temporarily indisposed. A kind of blackout in his brain. An accident that had occurred a few months earlier. Something he hadn't seen coming, and which had struck him like lightning. His head could no longer control his limbs. For instance, he wanted that arm right there to lift up and chase the intruder away. But it didn't move. The fly couldn't care less. It didn't matter whether he was ill or healthy, that didn't change anything, the fly carried on calmly grooming itself atop that spectacular nose. The man tried to move again. The fly continued to cling on. He felt its tiny, almost transparent legs sink into his skin. It was entrenched. It didn't want to go anywhere else. How had it even gotten this far? What misfortune had led it here? Flies were free, they didn't obey anyone, they did what they wanted, and flew off whenever anyone tried to shoo them or swat them. It's said that they have 360-degree vision. That they're remarkably alert. For the time being, the man pondered what route the fly had taken to reach him. Ah, the garden! The dogs that never stopped eating out of their bowls. The neighborhood flies were well acquainted with his house and the street corner just outside the front gate. They would flock to it from all directions, sure they'd undoubtedly find their meager fare. After having stuffed their bellies, they would wander around, flying to and fro while digesting their meal. They would hum, dive into the void and dash off in all directions. Until a human nose came into view and invited them over for a visit. Ever since the first fly had landed there, none of the others had dared trespass on its territory. The man was in pain. He felt the urge to scratch himself, to shoo it away, to get up, to move around and clean up that dirty garden where the watchman often threw out part of the trash. He even started thinking about how he would put the world to rights: if the gardener had been to school, if his farmer parents hadn't left their village for the city and become beggars, car-washers, parking attendants, if Morocco hadn't experienced two years of horrible drought, if the country's money had been better distributed among urban and rural areas, if the latter had been valued as a national treasure and the country's breadbasket, if land reforms had been justly carried out, if on that morning the watchman had had the idea to clear up that part of the garden that had been set aside as a garbage dump, if he'd gone through the trouble of chasing away those flies that gathered around that rubbish, and if, on top of that, the two men who took care of him had been by his bedside, that fly, that satanic fly, would never have been able to land on his nose and given him such a cruel itch that it was driving him—who'd had a stroke that had nailed him to his bed for the past six months—insane.

He told himself that he was at the mercy of an insect, a tiny insect. Whereas when he'd been in good health, a simple mosquito would have sent him spiraling into an incomprehensible fit of fury. As a child, he would abandon himself to chasing mosquitoes at night, when he would crush them under huge books whose covers displayed traces of blood to this day. Because they seemed just as indifferent to poisonous plants where he lived as they were to detergents and toxic waste products. His wife had even summoned a sorcerer to write some talismans and recite prayers to chase them away. But they had proved stronger than everything. They spent the night sucking the blood out of human beings only to vanish at dawn. Vampires.

On that afternoon, the fly had come to avenge the Moroccan insects the man had massacred throughout his life. The man was a prisoner of his paralyzed body, but no matter how much he cried out, shouted, and begged, the fly didn't budge in the slightest, and made him suffer all the more. Not a great deal of suffering, just a vague discomfort, which eventually overexcited his nerves—which wasn't at all advisable in his current condition.

Then, little by little, the man managed to convince himself that the fly wasn't bothering him anymore, that the itching was all in his head. He'd begun to triumph over it. Not that he felt any better, but he'd realized that he needed to accept reality and stop cursing it. His perception of time and things had changed over the past few months. His accident had been a test. He'd already stopped thinking about the fly. All of a sudden, the two caretakers who were playing cards in the adjacent room had come to check on him and the fly had immediately flown away. There was no trace of it now aside from a quietly seething anger, a contained anger that spoke volumes about the psyche of that man—a painter who could no longer paint.

I

Casablanca

February 4, 2000

I have the capacity to love, but it's all been bottled up.
—INGMAR BERGMAN, *Scenes from a Marriage*

The two sturdy men who'd carried him and then left him in that armchair facing the sea were out of breath. The invalid was also having trouble breathing and the look on his face was full of bitterness. Only his conscience was alive. His body had grown fatter, he'd become very heavy. As for his speech, it was slow and mostly incomprehensible. They often asked him to repeat what he said, and he hated it because it was both tiring and humiliating. He preferred to communicate with his eyes. When he looked up, that meant no. When he lowered his gaze, that meant yes, but a reluctant yes. One day, one of the Twins— this was how he referred to his caretakers even though they weren't brothers—thinking that he was doing the right thing, had brought him a clipboard with a felt-tip pen attached to it by a string. The man had gotten furious and summoned the strength to throw it to the floor.

On that morning, the Twins had been unable to shave him. An outbreak of pimples around his chin had made it too difficult to do so. He wasn't happy. He looked scruffy. Felt neglected. He couldn't stand it. His stroke had dealt him a devastating blow, and he refused to accept any sloppiness when it came to his clothing or physical appearance. When he'd discovered that a coffee stain on his tie hadn't been cleaned, he'd grown more sullen. The Twins had hurriedly changed it, and he was now dressed all in white, but he still grumbled under his breath.

Whenever he spoke, the Twins would guess what he was saying, even if they didn't understand certain words. They would read his facial expressions and anticipate his wishes. They needed a sharp sense of hearing and a lot of patience. When he grew tired, he would blink his eyes several times to signify that he wanted them to leave him alone. Perhaps that was when he would allow himself to cry, he who had once been so brilliant, elegant, and celebrated wherever he went. He'd had a close brush with death, but he hadn't completed his work. He took this as an insult, a dirty trick that fate had played on him, and a spiteful one at that. As he'd dreamed of dying in his sleep like his old, fun-loving, polygamous uncle, this was a constant source of grief for him. But what had befallen him was the same thing that had struck so many friends and acquaintances who belonged to his generation. As his physician had told him, he had reached a critical age. To be in the prime of life meant facing a few storms.

When the anger of the first months had subsided a little, he decided to begin smiling at those who came to visit him, a means for him to fight against the physical decline that sometimes caused the mind to follow suit. So he always smiled. There was his morning smile, which was subtle and sweet, his afternoon smile, which was impatient and curt, and the one he wore in the evenings, which in the long run turned into a faint grimace. Then, he suddenly stopped smiling. He didn't want to pretend anymore. Why should he smile? Who would he smile at, and for what purpose? The illness had changed his habits. Was it an illness or was it death?

He wasn't the same man anymore, he saw that in other people's eyes. He had lost his presence as a great artist. But he refused to hide; he wanted to be able to leave the house before too long and show his new condition in public. It would be a painful process, but he insisted on going through with it.

Curiously enough, despite his almost total paralysis he had never contemplated giving up painting. He was convinced that the evil that afflicted him was nothing more than a little episode that was bound to be temporary. Every day, he would try to move the fingers of his right hand. And every day he would ask for a brush, which they would place between his thumb and forefinger, but he was unable to keep a grip on it for long. So he would keep repeating the exercise several times each day. The moment he could grip a brush, he would start caring less about the condition the rest of his body was in.

Ideas for new paintings swarmed around in his head. His inability to paint had put him in a constant state of excitement. He was even more impatient than usual. Eventually, those moments of disquiet and intensity would give way to long silences that came coupled with feelings of defeat. His mood would change, and he would feel as though he'd fallen into a thick fog, which seemed to foreshadow some gloomy event. A sting of drool hung from his half-open mouth. From time to time, one of the Twins would gently wipe it away. This would stir him back into consciousness, and he would feel ashamed that he'd been unable to contain his spittle, ashamed that he'd dozed off. It was these little things that bothered him the most, rather than the fact he was paralyzed.

The television was on and there was an athletics championship on. He'd always been fascinated by those magnificent, supple, perfect bodies, in fact too perfect to be human. He would gaze at them and wonder how many years, months, and days of hard work lay behind each movement those young athletes performed. He didn't want anyone to change the channel. No, he wanted to watch that show precisely because of the state he was stuck in. He dreamed and experienced a strange sort of pleasure in admiring those young athletes' movements. He found himself watching and encouraging them as though he knew them personally, as though he were their coach, their teacher, their adviser, or as though he were simply their father.

His mind turned to a book by Jean Genet that a friend had given him on his birthday, *The Tightrope Walker*. He'd read it very excitedly and had pictured the kind of tension that the acrobat must have suppressed with each movement he made. He had thought about drawing some illustrations for that book someday, but he'd been told that Genet wasn't an easy man to deal with and that he would probably refuse to give his consent. He would reread it from time to time and focus on a wire extended between two fixed points, and picture himself balanced on top of it, his body drenched in sweat, his trembling arms holding onto the rod, then watch himself slip, fall, and shatter all his limbs. He'd even go to the lengths of inventing a whole backstory behind that injured tightrope walker, who'd wound up like that because he'd fallen while performing in a circus. That accident was physical, not psychological. That man wasn't a vexed, anxious painter, but an acrobat who'd broken his body thirty feet below the wire.

He was pleased with the discovery he'd made. Not a single tear had slipped down his cheek. His spirit hadn't flagged. He touched his leg using his limp, heavy hand and didn't feel a thing. "We'll get better. Hang in there, sonny boy," he said to himself.

He hadn't seen his wife since their last quarrel—and the stroke that had immediately followed in its wake. He was now living in his studio, which he'd had equipped with all the things he needed in order to get by and overcome the trial of that illness. She occupied the other wing of their house in Casablanca, which was very large. The Twins had been instructed never to let her anywhere near him. But he might as well not have bothered. The distance between them rather seemed to suit her, and she hadn't shown the slightest interest in looking after an old sick man. He had wanted to take stock of their twenty-year marriage. From that point of view, the break that his stroke had imposed on their relationship had been fortuitously timed. He would sometimes see her make herself pretty to go out from one of the studio's windows that gave out onto the inner courtyard of their villa. Nobody knew where she went, which was for the best. In any case, he had decided to neither keep an eye on her nor suspect her.

In the past, when he'd been healthy, he had fled, gone on a trip, and disappeared off the face of the earth. That had been his usual response to his frustrations or their marital disputes. He used to keep a journal where he only wrote about the problems in his marriage. He didn't mention anything else in that notebook. Over the course of twenty years, the transcripts of their quarrels, aggravations, and tantrums hadn't varied a great deal. It was the story of a man who believed that people could change, overcome their defects and strengthen their positive qualities, and improve themselves through constant self-examination. While he'd never necessarily wanted his wife to one day grow docile and submissive, he had always harbored a secret hope that she would at least become loving and obliging, calm and reasonable, in short, a wife who could help him build a family life and then share it with him. It had been his dream. But he'd been misguided and he had instead oppressed his wife, forgetting to acknowledge his share of responsibility for that failure.

II

Casablanca

February 8, 2000

Every sacrifice is possible and tolerable in a couple until the day when one of them realizes that there were sacrifices to make.

—SACHA GUITRY, *Give Me Your Eyes*

As soon as he woke up, the painter asked the Twins to bring him a mirror. It was the first time in the three months after his stroke that he felt strong enough to dare to gaze upon his reflection. When he saw himself, he burst into a huge laugh because he didn't recognize himself at all and thought his reflection looked completely pathetic. He told himself: "What would I have done in your place? Kill myself? I'm not brave enough for that. Would I have refused anyone who tried to give me a mirror? Yes, that's it, that's exactly what I would have done! I wouldn't have looked at myself, so as not to realize what I've become.

I would have avoided tearing open another wound in my suffering at all costs!"

He'd never thought about suicide after suffering his stroke. His desire to live had grown stronger, and giving up would have been too easy. Even though he wasn't in good shape, he had gradually started to find pleasure in everyday things again. Dark thoughts had stopped clouding his mind, not entirely of course, but he'd become more adept at chasing them away and not wallowing in them. What would be the point in whining about it? Probably to paralyze his thoughts. His mother had taught him never to complain, first and foremost because it was useless, and secondly because it annoyed people. One had to endure one's suffering, even if it meant crying alone at night. Full of irony, his mother would tell him: "I'll have so many things to say to my gravediggers! As for the angels who guide us on the day of our funeral, they'll lift my soul all the way up to the sky. It'll be the nicest trip I've ever taken!" How could that fail to summon the image of the two angels in black suits who came to fetch Liliom's soul—played by Charles Boyer—in Fritz Lang's film? Still, he believed that the angels who came to lift his mother's soul to heaven would be smiling, welcoming, and dressed in white. He could picture them and was convinced that his mother deserved to make her final voyage in the arms of those angels described in the Qur'an.

In the mirror, he could see that his physical deterioration had been spectacular. He would have to accept that he was no longer the same man, that he no longer matched what people thought he looked like, that he would have to put up with his new face and grow used to it—this was what he would have to endure if he was ever to resume his place among the living. He felt that he'd started to resemble a crumpled-up piece of paper, as though he were nothing but a caricature of his former self. He mused wryly about how he looked like a Francis Bacon painting. He had noticed this in the eyes of some of the relatives who came to visit him. He noticed their shock as they gazed at his deformed, diseased body, which he could barely move. The shadow of death had paid him a visit and it had left its traces on his leg and his arm. But it had just been a brush with death.

Perhaps his visitors could see themselves in his place, spying their own reflection in a mirror held out to them for a few seconds, at which point they would say to themselves: "What if this happened to me one day? Is this how I would wind up, sat in a wheelchair pushed along by a healthy man? With half my body paralyzed and unable to speak properly? Maybe my relatives would also abandon me . . . I would become a painful burden for my nearest and dearest, I would become useless and boring, people never like to see other people's bodies suffer!" Then they would all rush to see their doctor and get checked up. Besides, everyone was curious to know how the accident had happened. They really wanted to know how to prevent it and avoid becoming victims of the aberrations of the machine that feeds the brain. They grew suddenly afraid when they were told that the brain was in fact a complex organ composed of hundreds of billions of nerve cells working in unison to allow for the smooth running of our daily lives. They didn't dare ask him how the whole thing had happened. They talked about it amongst themselves, went on the Internet and read everything they could find about strokes. The worst came when they found out either from the Internet or their physicians that strokes could happen to anyone at any age, but that there were still contributing factors. Hamid, one of his childhood friends, had been so shocked and distressed that he'd stopped smoking and drinking. He had shown up one day, white as a sheet, with a rosary wrapped around his fingers, and bent down and kissed his old friend on the forehead: "Thanks to you, my life has changed! I was the only one to profit from your misfortune. I was so scared that it taught me a valuable lesson!" He had known for a long time that excessive smoking and drinking could trigger that kind of illness; he had started taking care of his high blood pressure and avoided sugar because he had a history of diabetes in his family, but he'd been unable to do anything about stress, that silent and often fatal killer.

Stress—the kind of aggravation that left holes in one's vital organs. He thought of it as a machine that disrupted everything in its path without anyone noticing. Stress was his evil doppelgänger, who demanded that he worked harder and harder, underestimated his real capacities, and made him think he could exceed his limits. Stress seized hold of the heart, clenching its grip, knocking it around and impeding its normal functions. He knew all of this and had analyzed it umpteen times.

In the days when he'd been healthy, whenever he got bored, which didn't happen all that often, he would stop working and examine this frame of mind, when time came to a standstill, pausing while he harped on about his set ideas. Boredom was a byproduct of insomnia, a refusal to let himself fall down the black hole of the unknown. He would go around in circles, then let it all go and wait for it to pass. He would thus contain stress in this space, situated between his sleepless nights and the stillness of his waking hours.

In the studio where he now spent all of his days, far from the noise of the city, he asked himself how the stroke could have destroyed his body to such an extent. He was having a tough time stomaching how battered his body was, which prevented him from moving freely and doing what he wanted. He had played football on Casablanca's beaches as a teenager. He had been an excellent striker and his friends would always carry him in their arms at the end of the matches because he had scored all the goals. He might have even become a professional footballer but at the time this would have meant moving to Spain and joining one of their big teams. His parents had preferred that he took up painting instead, even if it meant he would never earn a dime. Anything would be better than living in exile among the Spaniards who hated the Moors!

He would once again observe his reflection in the mirror. He looked hideous, or better yet, banged up. He recalled the lyrics to

Léo Ferré's "Vingt Ans": "*Pour tout bagage on a sa gueule, quand elle est bath ça va tout seul, quand elle est moche on s'habitue, on se dit qu'on n'est pas mal foutu; pour tout bagage on a sa gueule qui cause des fois quand on est seul . . . quand on pleure on dit qu'on rit . . . alors on maquille le problème.*" He remembered the time he'd spent with Ferré when the latter had come to perform in Casablanca. They had drunk a cup of tea on the patio of the Royal Mansour hotel and he had observed the man's small eyes, his mannerisms, his almost permanent bad mood, but especially the overwhelming weariness that marked his face. He had always thought of Ferré as a poet, a rebel whose songs did much good for those who took the trouble to pay close attention to them.

During the first months of his illness, he had mostly kept to himself, sheltered in the safety of his studio. Surrounded by his unfinished canvases, he had relied on himself, experiencing a feeling of supreme solitude, because suffering can never truly be shared. Needless to say, he had received many a get well soon card. This had brought him much pleasure, and he'd been stunned and moved to see some people whom he barely knew find exactly the right words for the occasion. For instance, there was Serge, with whom he'd only crossed paths from time to time because they lived in the same neighborhood. Yet only fifteen days after he'd left the hospital, Serge had come to visit him and had spoken on terms of the utmost frankness. Serge had quickly gotten into the habit of visiting him once a week, asking how he was doing, and generally helping to lift his spirits. Right up to the day that the painter learned that Serge had suddenly died. It wasn't until Serge had died that the painter learned what had been eating away at him. He'd felt like crying. So much friendship and humility from a man who didn't even belong to his inner circle of friends had left its mark on him. Serge had been completely different to some of the painter's friends, who'd suddenly grown silent. They had just all vanished. Fear. The Great Funk. As though strokes were contagious! Someone had told him that one of his friends kept insisting that he didn't want to go visit him because he was ashamed of being in good health. Of course there was no reason to suppose the man was lying. But whenever invalids feel they're being abandoned, suffering instantly grows more insidious and cruel.

When he was a child, his father used to urge him to visit the sick and the dying. "This is what our Prophet counsels us to do," he would say, "we must visit those who suffer and who are waiting for their appointed hour, which is slow in coming. Visiting a dying man allows you to be both selfish and generous. Giving up your time to visit a man who is nailed to his bed is a good way to learn humility, to learn that it's the little things that really make a difference in life, and that we are but grains of sand who belong to God, to whom we will return! Those who are afraid of other people's illnesses must overcome that dread and learn to familiarize themselves with what lies ahead for all of us. There you have it, my son. These may be platitudes, but they have a kernel of truth!"

At the clinic where he'd been hospitalized following his stroke, the painter had shared a room with a twenty-seven-year-old Italian pianist called Ricardo. Ricardo had also suffered a stroke while holidaying in Morocco. His doctors and his family had been waiting for his condition to improve slightly before sending him back to Milan. Ever since he'd regained consciousness, Ricardo had kept staring at his hands. He could no longer move his fingers! And thus wept in silence. His tears flowed incessantly. As though nothing could stop them, he would shut his eyes and turn his head to face the wall. His life had fallen apart and his career cut brutally short. A woman, perhaps his wife or his friend, would spend each day at his bedside, comforting him. She would rub his fingers, caress his face, dry his tears, and then leave the room, devastated. She would leave the clinic to smoke a cigarette then return, looking sad. The woman had once sat on the painter's bed and started talking to him. He had listened to her and nodded his head.

"Ricardo is the love of my life, he had an incredibly bright future ahead of him, but his enemies won in the end. I'm Sicilian and I believe in the evil eye, it's no coincidence that jinns are almost always cruelly beaten. Jealousy, envy, and malice. I've been told that people in Morocco believe in the evil eye. It exists and I have the proof. Ricardo and I were planning to get married a month after our trip to Morocco. His parents had been against the match—you see, as they belonged to the Milanese upper classes they could hardly stand by and watch their only son marry a fisherman's daughter from Mazara del Vallo! But we had a plan, we'd had the idea to move to the United States as soon as we'd married, where his agent had told him he would always be in demand. And then the day after we arrived in Casablanca, he collapsed in our hotel room. I don't know what happened. I knew that he'd often told me about how stressed he was, about the perfectionism that he wanted to achieve, an ambition that gnawed away at him, he couldn't tolerate the slightest mistake or oversight. He would become ill before a concert, he wouldn't eat or speak to anyone, I could feel him twisting himself into knots, as anxious as a bullfighter entering the arena. What will become of us? Please forgive me, here I am talking to you and I don't even know you . . . I haven't even asked you what your name is and what you did before your stroke . . . I'm just so upset!"

He had tried to mouth some words. She had understood that he was in just as bad shape as Ricardo. An artist struck by the same misfortune, the inability to practice his art. She had lowered her gaze and tears had streamed down her cheeks.

He had observed her, without her knowing it, admiring her wild beauty: a Southern girl, dark, tall, elegant, and lacking in manners. "What a waste!" he told himself. Life had been truly unfair!

Ricardo left the clinic a few days later and was sent back to Italy. As she'd been preparing to leave, the girl had scribbled a few words on the back of a prescription that she'd left on top of the painter's bedside table, and then planted a small kiss on his forehead. She had written down their address and phone number along with a little message of hope where she wished they could meet again one day and sit around a table in Sicily or Tuscany. She had signed it "Chiara."

His new condition as an invalid reminded him of his visits to Naima, a cousin whom he'd loved like a sister, who'd been struck down by Lou Gehrig's disease at the age of thirty-two. He had watched the disease evolve, and witnessed her body's slow but inexorable deterioration, which was gradually losing its muscle mass. He'd greatly admired that young beautiful woman who was confined to a wheelchair and yet was still so brave and optimistic. She couldn't speak and was completely reliant on her nurse: a fearless lady who was so devoted to Naima that she never left her side, who not only considered herself a member of the family, but also an extension of her hands, arms, and legs.

He knew that amyotrophic lateral sclerosis was incurable. Naima was perfectly aware of that too, and begged God every day for a little more time so she could maybe see her children complete their studies or perhaps even see her two daughters get married. She prayed and put her trust in God's hands.

The painter wanted to emulate her example. Yet he wasn't enough of a believer to dutifully attend to his prayers. He believed in spirituality, so every once in a while he would invoke the tender mercies of the higher power that governed the universe. He was a skeptic who was inclined to explore the ways of the soul. An artist could not work with certainties. His entire being and body of work were plagued by a sense of doubt.

During one of the first nights he'd spent in the studio, he'd suddenly suffered a severe cramp and the urgent need to change his position in bed. But the bell hadn't worked. However much he had tried to make his thin, reedy voice audible, however many times he tapped on the bed's handrail, it had been to no avail. The Twins, who'd been sleeping in the next room, hadn't heard him. He'd been in pain, the entire left side of his body had twitched and then stiffened. A final effort to move his body had caused him to abruptly fall off the side. The noise he'd made during the fall had been so loud that it had awakened the two men, who'd rushed to his side. Luckily, he hadn't broken anything in the fall, and was unscathed aside from a few bluish bruises on his hip. Once more, his thoughts had turned to Naima, and to the terrible nights she must have endured.

Naima's illness had radically altered his outlook on the world of disabled people. He knew more about it than most of his friends. Every time he'd crossed paths with someone who was disabled, he had tried to visualize what their daily life must have been like. He would give them a great deal of attention and take an interest in their case. Good health, both physical and psychological, always conceals reality; it prevents us from seeing the vulnerabilities of others, the occasionally cavernous wounds of those who are struck down by fate. We simply walk past them, and while in the best of cases we feel a pang of pity, we ultimately continue on our own path.

Thus he had one day accompanied his friend Hamid to a meeting for parents of disabled children. Nabile, Hamid's son, had been born with Down syndrome. The painter had witnessed the desperate stories of those mothers whose life was a complete struggle due to the fact that Morocco did not have any adequate facilities to take care of these children. "Afflicted by a disease nobody cares about!" as one of the psychologists present in the room had said. After the meeting, the painter had had the idea of inviting Nabile back to his studio. He'd given him a canvas and some colors. Then he'd shown him how to use them. Nabile had been happy and had spent the whole day painting. They'd left in the evening along with his paintings, which his parents had had framed and hung in the living room of their home.

His stroke had provided him with the opportunity to reconsider everything in his life. He was completely convinced of that. Not just his married life, but also his relationship to work and the act of creating. "I would love to paint a scream like Bacon did," he said to himself, "or even fear, that certain something that makes my blood freeze or makes me vulnerable. To paint fear so accurately that I would be able to touch it, as well as render it useless, rub it out, and banish it from my life. I believe in the magic that comes out of painting and acts on reality. Oh yes, as soon as I can move my hands and fingers, I will unleash my attack on fear, a fear that is as horizontal as railroad tracks, an amorphous fear that constantly changes its colors and its appearance, a fear that will extinguish all lights. Indeed, I will catch that fear and lay it out in front of a sea whose blueness will spill over the whole canvas. I will gaze at it in the same way that I think about death. Death no longer frightens me now. But I must be especially careful not to get caught up in my style. I'll have to create a new rhythm, a music that will repel fear!"

He eyed his lifeless leg and laughed softly. One evening, when he'd been meditating on his fate, he had convinced himself that his paralyzed leg had become the sanctuary of his soul, and that this was where his liberation would begin. The soul is alive and cannot put up with what is stiff and motionless. He was happy to think that his soul had lodged itself in his leg and was working on restoring his ability to move. Sure, it was a bit of a crazy idea, but his belief in it was unshakeable. Since he could no longer paint, he spent his time dreaming and reinventing life. He liked to tell himself that he was living in a little hut from which he could watch the world go by without being seen. Nevertheless, his pain, which was still raw, and his difficult physical therapy exercises had quickly pulled him out of that sickly child's universe.

One day, when he'd gone back to the clinic for a checkup, he received a phone call. One of the Twins had given him the handset and told him: "It's Madame Kiara!" which he'd accompanied with an incomprehensible gesture. He'd immediately recognized her voice and was stunned that she hadn't forgotten him. She had asked him for news, but had quickly realized that he still found it difficult to talk. She told him that Ricardo was doing spectacularly better. They had spent some time in Italy, but had soon been able to travel to set up a new life in the United States, where Ricardo's physical therapy had completely changed him. His agent had taken care of everything. Ricardo could now move his fingers and when they sat him in front of the piano, he could still play, albeit slightly off-key, just like Glenn Gould, who interpreted Bach in his own inimitable way. His agent had immediately decided to exploit this new angle to Ricardo's style. "Producers always have their heads screwed on," she'd added, "but what we really care about is for Ricardo to regain the full use of his reflexes."

The painter had been pleased to receive news of his old roommate. He told himself that hope could be found on the other side of pain.

Once he'd returned home after his checkup, he had amused himself by imagining how rumors of his stroke had spread and what they must be saying behind his back: "You didn't know he'd had a stroke? Poor guy, he can't even paint anymore . . . now is the perfect time to buy his canvases!" Or even: "He was arrogant and selfish and now God has given him a sign: it's a warning, the next time will be his last!" Or even more cruelly: "He's completely fucked now, he won't even be able to get an erection, a tragedy for someone who loved women the way he did! . . . As for his wife, that poor lady he treated so badly, she can at least rest assured now that his willy isn't good for anything apart from pissing! There's a poetic justice to that, isn't there?" "The great seducer will now become acquainted with our solitude. I must admit we were jealous of his conquests, and after all that, his paintings even sold well!" He tried to picture what his art dealer would have said to the buyers: "Whatever you do, don't sell, wait a few months!" And what about his wife, what had she been up to ever since she'd learned the news? Would she not try to exact her revenge? No, no, he'd promised himself he wouldn't ask those kinds of questions. He didn't want to fight with her, he wanted peace, so that he could heal.

Whenever you're struck by misfortune, either through an illness or an accident, the people around you suddenly change. There are those who scurry off the sinking ship, like rats, those who wait to see how the situation develops before making their next move, and finally those who remain loyal to their feelings and whose behavior doesn't change. Those friends are both rare and precious.

He was surrounded by people who belonged to each of the three categories. He'd never deluded himself about this particular fact. Before taking up painting, he had devoted himself to studying philosophy. He had especially loved Schopenhauer and his aphorisms; those cutting remarks of his had made him laugh, and they had also taught him to never trust in appearances and to watch out for their traps. For a while, he had even resisted studying philosophy, because he had believed that painting and reading Nietzsche and Schopenhauer were irreconcilable. But he knew how to handle pencils and brushes better than anyone he knew, and his art teacher had strongly encouraged him to study at the École des Beaux-Arts in Paris. Those encouragements had helped him put his dreams of being a philosopher to the side.

And so one fine day he'd left Morocco for Paris. He hadn't even been twenty years old at the time. In his mind, Paris had stood for freedom, boldness, and intellectual and artistic adventures. This was the city where Picasso had risen to fame and glory, and he had first discovered his vocation when admiring the master's early canvases, especially those where the fifteen-year-old Picasso had painted his mother on her deathbed. Picasso had left a profound impression on him, and he had wanted to follow in his footsteps. He perfected his style at the École des Beaux-Arts and found his own voice. He had distanced himself from the great names to forge a unique style of his own, a kind of hyper-realism that would eventually become his signature. His canvases, which were rigorously precise, were the fruit of long, painstaking work. He could not create art in any other way. He'd never been able to understand how his contemporaries could splash a bucket of paint onto a canvas or doodle a few lines. He thought their hands were guided by what came easiest to them, and that was exactly what he hated the most. He detested anything that came too easily, without any effort or imagination. He had wanted his painting to be like his philosophy (which he'd nevertheless abandoned): a precisely built edifice that left no room for vagueness, generalities, clichés or approximations. This had been the foundation on which he'd erected his life. As far as he was concerned, it was about being demanding. He took special care over the projects he worked on just as much as he took care of himself. Even the state of his health had become a constant concern, not because he was a hypochondriac, but because he'd seen people close to him die simply out of negligence, or because they hadn't taken their doctors' recommendations to heart.

In his present state, his conscience—which dictated that everything be achieved to the highest standards—had stopped mattering as much as it once had. What was perfection good for if he couldn't even grip a brush between his fingers? On some days, when he felt less overwhelmed and more optimistic, he wouldn't give in to his usual despair of ever creating anything new again. He would remember Matisse and Renoir, both of whom had continued to paint well into their old age despite their physical afflictions. After all, he had avoided the worst. Hadn't his friend Gharbaoui died of cold and solitude on a park bench in Paris at the age of forty? And hadn't Cherkaoui, another painter he admired, died of peritonitis at the age of thirty-three after fleeing France right after the Six-Day War had broken out?

When he'd come to the clinic, a few days following his stroke, and when they'd brought him up to speed on his condition, he'd suddenly remembered what his mother had feared the most: becoming an object, like a pile of sand or rocks that had been dumped on one of the corners of life and was completely dependent on others. Happily, once he'd returned to his house, he'd been able to hire the Twins to help bear the burden of this new and unpredictable situation he was in. Being able to wash himself, or shave, wipe, dress, while still retaining some of his natural elegance, hanging on to his dignity and affability, that's what lay on the horizon for him. The time of impulses and desires had drawn to an end. He could no longer satisfy his sudden urges for steak tartare at a restaurant. Could no longer go out for a morning stroll to stay in shape. Could no longer visit the Louvre, the Prado or the pretty galleries in the 6th arrondissement. Could no longer dive into new dalliances, or rendezvous with new beautiful women, or have romantic dinners in Rome or elsewhere, could no longer make impromptu visits to his old friend, the antique dealer, with whom he loved to visit Parisian markets. All of these things— and many others besides—had now become impossible. He had lost his inner lightness. Now he was no longer the sole master of his life, his movements, his desires or his moods. He relied on others. For everything. Even to drink a glass of water or to sit on the toilet seat to do his business. His reaction to that was immediate, he just became constipated. He would hold it in and delay his bowel movements as long as he could. That his bowel movements were few and far between partly encouraged that approach. "Shit betrays us," he told himself. His mother had become incontinent; she would refuse to wear diapers and would then shit herself, just like a baby. His mother would stink of shit and yet he would still lean down and kiss her. Then he would call the nurses over so they could clean her up, while he would go out into the corridor to weep in silence. When your life is in someone else's hands, is it still really a life?

"Illusion travels by streetcar!" An inner voice often murmured that sentence. It reminded him of something else, but he couldn't put his finger on it. All of a sudden, as though in a flash, he saw a beautiful brunette with her hair combed in the 1950s style. She was sitting down and was propping her cheek up with her right hand, while her left lay on a man's shoulder. The man had a pitiful look to him and his arms were crossed, and his shirt collar was unbuttoned despite the fact that he was wearing a tie. It was a black-and-white image. Then, as though in a dream, he suddenly recalled the woman's name: Lillia Prado. It shone out of his memory's murkiness. Lillia Prado! But who was she? Where had she come from? He recalled an old Algerian friend who shared the same name, but who looked nothing like this Lillia. And besides, why did illusions travel by streetcar? He asked himself that question several times and then the name Luis Buñuel rose out of his innermost depths. The sentence that had come to him was in fact the title of a film shot in 1953 by the filmmaker when he'd started living in Mexico after fleeing Franco's Spain. The title the French producers had chosen—*On a volé un tram* (*A Tram Was Stolen*)—was ridiculous. They had stripped it of all its poetry and mystery. He was pleased to have solved that conundrum, it was a sign that his memory was starting to work once again.

III

Paris

1986

If a man and a woman are two halves of an apple, then two
men are quite often two halves of a couple.

—SACHA GUITRY, *Nine Bachelors*

By the mid-1980s, the painter still hadn't put down roots anywhere.
He never kept the same studio for more than a few months, traveled
without any luggage, and most of the time he'd been happy to work
with only a notebook and pencils for his sketches. His first meeting
with his future wife had utterly changed everything. A week after their
first kiss, he'd decided to spend less time in his studio and to devote
it to her instead, and they exchanged vows and swore to keep them a
month later. Those who knew them best couldn't believe their eyes.
The painter had been able to guess what his friends must have said
about him when they crossed paths in Paris: "She's too young for him,
and too pretty too!"

They had been wrong to bad-mouth them, because throughout the first two long, pleasant years of their married life, the painter and his wife were the happiest couple in the world. She'd known how to keep him happy, had quickly learned how to adapt to his mannerisms, habits, and whims. She had accepted them with a smile and would sometimes even mock him a little about them. There had been no conflicts of any kind. "Not a cloud in the sky," she would say with a smile.

He had rented a little house for her on Rue de la Butteaux-Cailles. It was a charming place: one would have thought that it was in the middle of the open countryside instead of smack in the center of Paris. They led a smooth life that was completely devoid of conflict. He still looked back on those days with a deeply felt and sincere nostalgia. His wife had been very loving then and had thrown herself into their conjugal life with a great deal of intensity. They hadn't gone on a honeymoon, but they had decided that she would accompany him wherever he was invited: exhibitions, symposiums, or contemporary art fairs. They always extended their visits by a few days in order to properly visit the country, guidebooks in hand. The painter, who'd already traveled a great deal, had found it very moving to introduce his wife to the great cities of the world: Venice, Rome, Madrid, Prague, Istanbul, New York, then San Francisco, Rio de Janeiro, Bahia . . . She would buy him everything that he liked and always brought presents back for his family. The painter, for his part, spared no expense. On their return to Paris, she would call her friends and relatives and tell them about their wonderful journeys down to the slightest detail. She would humbly tell them that she felt blessed to have such opportunities. When she would hang up, she would whisper in his ear: "You know, I'm the one who was lucky to have met you!" He thought that marrying a twenty-four-year-old woman had been something exceptional for a thirty-eight-year-old man, a privilege reserved for a select few. In his mind, never being like anyone else had always seemed like a guarantee of eternal happiness. And then, he'd thought, the time had come to settle down, start a family, and change the rhythm of his life. She was the ideal woman for that new life.

They made love often, and it was tender and natural. He would occasionally wish that she could get a little more involved in the act, but she would laugh and make him understand that she was too bashful for that. One evening, when they'd been changing channels on the television late at night, they'd stumbled onto a porno. She'd cried out, horrified by the spectacle of those unrestrained women and men with huge penises. Shocked, she had snuggled against him as though wanting him to protect her from some imminent danger. She'd never seen a porno in her life. He had reassured her, telling her that those films were transgressive and outrageous, and that most people's sexuality was rather simple. Then she'd regained her composure. At which point he'd switched the television off and they fell asleep on the living room sofa, their bodies entwined.

One day, she took the train to go see her parents, who lived on the outskirts of Clermont-Ferrand. She had asked him if he could help buy her ticket, and told him she also wanted to bring her parents a few small presents. He'd given her all she'd asked for and told her that they would open a joint bank account that very afternoon so she would never have to ask him for money again. She'd been very happy to hear this and he'd told her that everything that was his also belonged to her, and vice versa. He'd laughed, happy at how perfect their arrangement was.

She stayed with her parents for a week. The painter lived through those seven days and nights as though he'd been abandoned. It was the first time they'd spent so long apart. He had missed her terribly. He would call her every day, but had often been unable to speak to her because she had just left, or had gone out for a run . . . it allowed him to discover how deeply he was in love with her, "smitten," as people used to say in his youth. She dwelled in his thoughts, and would not be dislodged. While at his desk, he would fail to make any progress on his projects. He would imagine her in his arms, humming songs from his village, tunes that he was not especially fond of, but which he could suddenly not do without, even though he didn't really understand the meaning of those words. That was love, the kind of love that reminds you of your beloved. Tired of not bumping into her in one of the rooms of their house, he would go into the bathroom in the middle of the day just to smell her pajamas, or her perfume. On the following day, he'd even brushed his teeth with her brush. While sitting in the living room, he would be surprised to discover he'd been speaking out loud as though she were right in front of him. Unable to concentrate on his work, he would watch old films on the television until late at night. He would always fall asleep on the sofa and wake up at two in the morning and confuse his wife's face with Natalie Wood's in Elia Kazan's *Splendor in the Grass*. They slightly resembled one another, but his wife must have been a little taller, and her hair was darker.

When she finally returned from Clermont-Ferrand, there was a great celebration. He'd driven to the station to pick her up, and had arrived far too early. Little presents were waiting for her back at the house and he'd put on some music to welcome her back. Looking worried, she'd asked him if he'd missed her. That's an understatement, he'd said, he hadn't been able to sleep without her, or eat, or drink. "I was like a child in foster care!"

Two months later, she told him she was pregnant. He'd jumped for joy and had started singing to the top of his lungs until their kind neighbors came by to see if everything was all right. They had quickly agreed to have dinner together and they toasted the happy news with champagne. He'd never been so attentive to a woman before. They could spend whole hours at a stretch together doing absolutely nothing, and he would bend over backwards to spoil her. Once, she asked him for sea urchins in the middle of the night. Why sea urchins? Neither of them had ever eaten them. Because she'd read about those creatures of the sea in a magazine that day and simply wanted to try them.

They had gotten into the car and left in search of an open restaurant that would serve them that dish. They crisscrossed Paris from north to south and east to west, but their quest had been in vain. It was three o'clock in the morning, and everything had been shut for some time. As he was speaking to her, he'd realized she'd fallen asleep. Her craving must have suddenly left her. During those nine months, they'd also invented a series of games. They would improvise scenes as though they were being filmed by John Cassavetes. It was a mad, charming, and liberating game. As for Cassavetes's real films, which he dragged her to see on Rue des Écoles, she liked those a little less. They were too dispiriting, too disillusioned. She confessed to him that she preferred comedies and romantic films, and that she also had a weakness for Alain Delon. When he found out about this, one of their friends, who was a unit still photographer, invited them to visit the set of a film at the Studios de Boulogne where Delon was playing a gangster. She had carefully put some makeup on and had taken her camera with her. Between takes, the friend introduced them to the actor. He'd been very friendly and had especially been interested in the painter's wife. She had herself photographed standing next to Delon. As they'd been about to leave, Delon had shouted across to them: "But wouldn't that young lady like to be in the movies? She's very pretty, distinctive too! One can immediately see that she's got character! So, what do you say?" Taken aback, the painter had kept quiet, while his wife had lowered her eyes and murmured: "I've always dreamed of being in the movies . . ." then she'd suddenly regained her confidence and replied: "I was a model for the Sublime Agency when I was seventeen, surely you know Jérôme, Jérôme Lonchamp?" Delon had shaken his head. A crew member had then appeared to fetch Delon as the shooting had recommenced. Delon blew a kiss at her and then disappeared.

She'd gotten all excited and happy, like a little girl who'd just been given her first doll. "I must be dreaming—my wife's in love with Alain Delon right in the middle of her pregnancy!" the painter had said to himself in the taxi that took them home that night. No, it was impossible, ridiculous even. It must have been jealousy that was making him think like that. Nevertheless, he still imagined Delon meeting his wife for an afternoon of passionate lovemaking in a palace . . . he could see her in his arms, pressed against him, or even in a pool with a glass of orange juice mixed with some liquor or other in her hand. It was crazy, stupid, sick, miserable. She noticed nothing.

Over the course of the following days, she called her friends to tell them all about her meeting with Delon. She laid it on a little thick when it came to the great actor's good looks, his charisma, and his kindness. He had tried to keep his cool. It was as though Delon were suddenly everywhere: in the living room, the bathroom, their bedroom, in his head, in her head; he had taken over everything, and devoured their entire lives without leaving so much as a crumb.

After two weeks, the Delon fever completely subsided, as did the painter's jealousy. The actor was never mentioned again. Once again happy and satisfied, his wife's attentions had turned entirely toward the baby she was carrying. Happiness and sweetness reigned in their house. Marital happiness, in its simplest, purest, happiest form. The painter would caress his wife's belly and declare his ardent love. She loved to hear him say how much he loved her. It was perfect harmony.

Early one morning, her contractions started, and the painter accompanied her to the hospital and was present when the birth took place. When the nurse held out the scissors for him to cut the umbilical cord, he was so overcome by emotion that he nearly fainted. Once he'd recovered, he'd rushed to the telephone booth in the lobby to announce the news to everyone he knew until he ran out of coins. His mother broke out in ululations and made him cry. His friends and the people he worked with congratulated him. The gallery that represented him sent them a big bouquet of flowers. He danced and sang that evening after he'd left the hospital.

Their return to the house proved more difficult. Their cleaning lady had quit, and the painter hadn't had the time to find a new one. Luckily, the painter's mother-in-law came to lend them a helping hand. They threw a wonderful party to celebrate their child. The painter's mother, who lived in Morocco and hadn't been able to come, had felt left out: "I'll organize a real party for you when you visit me here," she'd said in a peremptory manner. The painter had said nothing.

Then their life suddenly changed. The baby took up all their space, and their couple life took a back seat, but the painter was still very much in love with his wife. After a month, his gallery called and asked him to get back to work. The painter shut himself in his studio and took some time before finding inspiration. The kind of cold hyper-realist drawings he'd worked on before his marriage no longer satisfied him. Whenever he returned in the evening, he would remark on how exhausted his wife looked. He would look after her, make dinner, and console her. Then it was his turn to look after the baby, and he would change him and give him his bottle. He can still remember now how long he would have to wait for the baby to burp before he could settle him down in his crib . . . He was an attentive father, he learned how to go about it and tried to bring a little joy into the house. However, his wife was depressed. It was textbook, they'd both foreseen it. The painter became even more attentive and tender. Their child made progress day after day, and this made the couple seem stronger. Life had smiled on them and the painter felt as though his work was entering a new phase.

IV

Paris

1990

I can discharge you any time I feel like it.
—Mrs. Muskat to Liliom
FRITZ LANG, *Liliom*

It was a gorgeous hand-embroidered blanket that had been crafted in Fez toward the end of the nineteenth century. It was a little worn and it hadn't endured the ravages of time. One of the painter's Moroccan friends, who was knowledgeable when it came to embroidered cloths, had offered it to the couple as their wedding present. It was so beautiful and precious he had wanted to have it framed and hang it as though it were a painting. Before doing that, he'd stretched it out as carefully as possible on a low-lying table that he hadn't liked at all— neither the wood nor its shape—but which was the sort of typical table one would find in most homes. Gracefully situated in the middle of the living room, it covered up what was an ugly piece of furniture, but had also made the room far more beautiful. The painter had done some research on embroidered cloths crafted in Fez during the previous century and had been surprised to learn that it had once belonged to the family of his maternal grandfather. It had been a part of Lalla Zineb's trousseau. Lalla Zineb had been the daughter of Moulay Aly, a professor at the University of al-Karaouine. The cloth had become priceless in the painter's eyes! Not only because it was beautiful and unique, but also because it was a part of his family heritage. Truth be told, it was the only wedding present they'd received that he truly liked. The others had been so unoriginal that he'd quickly forgotten all about them. That wasn't the case with his wife, who scattered those presents all over their house, especially their bedroom, giving them pride of place: vases, decorative plates, sheets embroidered by little hands, synthetic wool blankets, coffee sets that imitated the English style but were almost certainly made in China, bouquets of plastic flowers made to last forever, and a whole host of other trifles whose only purpose was to sit on a shelf and serve as a reminder that the wedding had been a nice party, while one wisely waited until the dust wrapped them up in two thick layers of dirt.

On his return home one evening he'd discovered that the cloth was missing. His wife had tossed it into the laundry basket. The painter fetched it out, folded it carefully, and put it in one of his closet's drawers. He thought about the dainty hands that had spent weeks embroidering that little piece of cloth, about the man or woman who'd designed those flowers and picked the colors. The painter was very upset. To think that cloth had survived two World Wars, the French Protectorate in Morocco, and the country's subsequent independence, and had belonged to three or four different families before winding up in the window display of a sophisticated antique dealer so that one of his friends could buy it and offer it to them as a wedding present! In the face of all of that, it was difficult to interpret his wife's gesture

as anything other than crudeness, at best, or, at worst, even ignorance. He had wanted to find her so he could speak to her about the
importance he attached to those objects from the past. However, he
had noticed that his wife hated lessons. She might even make some
kind of disingenuous retort like: "But what is that old rag? My house
isn't some bazaar!" At first he thought he could forgive her, talk to her
tenderly, explain himself, teach her how to admire a work of art, tell
her that one could read an embroidery as though it were a poem, that
one could decipher an old carpet just as one follows the footsteps of
an ancient civilization, and so forth.

He'd withdrawn into his study and had asked himself why that
whole affair over the cloth had so profoundly hurt his feelings. Up
until that moment, their love had always been stronger than that.
Some elements of his wife's behavior had shocked him, but he'd been
able to overcome them. But he couldn't stomach this; it just wouldn't
do. It would be impossible to forgive her. What she had done was
irreparable, and it was the first time he'd thought they could one day
separate. The evening went by and the painter didn't broach the subject with his wife at dinner. Later that night, he laughed at himself for
how angry he'd been.

Once their son was born, his wife gained a great deal of confidence
and her attitude and behavior underwent a vast transformation. The
cloth incident was followed by daily disputes. Each time this happened, he would leave the house and go for a walk around Paris. He
hated going to bars. Instead, he roamed the streets muttering to himself with his clenched fists in his pockets.

Late one evening, he stopped in front of the window display of
a television store, where the screens were broadcasting a documentary
on music from the High Atlas Mountains. The audio was muted, but
the sight of those women in multicolored robes and those men in
white djellabas tapping on *bendir* drums while others played the flute

was so intense that he was unable to avoid wanting to hear that shrill, disharmonious music that they'd played just before their marriage. It was a memory he'd tried to forget, but which resurfaced at that exact moment.

He'd never liked folk music, regardless of whether it came from his country or anywhere else. But when the planning for their wedding had been under way, nobody had wanted to take his opinion into consideration. There couldn't be a party without music and there couldn't be a great banquet without a lot of noise. Even though the painter had dreamed of a small wedding attended only by friends or at most a few relatives, he'd found himself caught in a whirlwind of hullabaloo.

Throughout that evening, despite the happiness the painter had felt at marrying his wife, he'd looked as though he'd been in a daze, which was very uncharacteristic of him. His gaze had even grown anxious when he'd met his father's eyes, who'd been bitterly opposed to the match since he could see neither the need for it nor its merits. His mother had worn her prettiest caftan, her gold belt and her finest jewelry. Yet even she had been vexed by the difference in class that her son had subjected her to. His other relatives had shared that opinion and he'd been able to read it in their tense features. The painter's aunt, who was known for speaking bluntly, had even been told to keep her mouth shut. After all, they weren't there to quarrel and cause a scandal. As for his new in-laws, the women had done their best to go with the flow. But their eyes betrayed words left unspoken. Each side wore different clothes, and employed different gestures too. Only the music, with the sound system turned up to the max, deafening everyone there, had prevented the situation from becoming explosive and turning into a disaster. Nobody present had been happy, apart from the painter and his wife. Nobody had wanted them to get married. One had to be absolutely crazy to want to bring such different worlds together.

The painter was assailed by another memory from their wedding.

That of the clove perfume worn by all the women who belonged to his tribe. The smell of it had made him feel nauseous ever since that day when he'd first smelled it as a little boy when he'd been traveling with his parents in their car. It was as though he were allergic to it, and every time he smelled it he would experience head-splitting headaches that would torture him for hours on end.

Everything about that wedding had been calculated to put him down, and yet he'd braved it. He felt a boundless tenderness for that girl he believed was free and beyond the reach of his tribe. He looked at her and covered her with kisses, holding her tight in his arms and stroking her splendid hair, which had a blonde sheen to it. He was in love. Blindly in love. No other woman on earth seemed as charming to him, even though he'd lived the life of a seducer who'd accumulated a great many experiences throughout his travels and encounters.

He would never have imagined that this wedding celebration—which he now called a wedding *damnation*—would leave an indelible stain on their life, his life. The meeting of the two families had been a clash of classes, two entirely different worlds that could never be bridged. However, he hadn't wanted to pay any attention to that at the time. He had thought that love would prove stronger than anything, just like in Douglas Sirk's melodramas, which he adored. It was films rather than books that really influenced his imagination. In times of hardship, he'd often thought of Elia Kazan's *Splendor in the Grass* or George Stevens's *A Place in the Sun*, and he had identified with the young hero who found himself caught in the middle of a confrontation between two families. Nevertheless, he knew that films were only dreams based on reality.

By the time the sun had set that evening, and despite having been told to keep quiet, the painter's aunt had been unable to restrain herself any longer and she had voiced her opinions loud and clearly to the guests around her in an incredible display of arrogance. Without mincing her words, she declared that any kind of mixing was a betrayal of one's destiny. She had employed blunt, brutal words, accompanied by grimaces, gestures, and pouts that amplified her meaning. Her contempt had been all too obvious. How could a lady who belonged to the cream of Fez's upper classes possibly accept finding herself in the company of peasants who couldn't even speak Arabic that well? How could her nephew have led himself so astray? There could only be one explanation! *He* hadn't decided to get married, it had been decided *for* him. He hadn't chosen to do anything, and someone else did all the talking for him. It was clearly a plot. The poor groom was like a lamb who'd been delivered into the hands of ignorant people who'd jumped at this unique opportunity to claim the elegance, charm, and highest traditions that were his birthright for themselves. His aunt had wanted to both wound and warn those people from the bled that even if those lovebirds had insisted on getting married, this did not mean the two families could ever come together.

His mother had remained silent throughout the party. Her sensitivity and memory had been offended by this union, but she had swallowed her anger. She had wept in silence behind her spectacles, from time to time directing her sorrowful glance toward her son, who she thought was making a fatal mistake. His mother had been known for her kindness and wisdom, and was simply incapable of speaking ill of someone or arguing. Nevertheless, she entertained simple certitudes, which were obvious.

The tone had been set. There had been no outstretched hands, or open arms, and no hypocrisy of any kind. The painter's aunt had assumed the leadership of the refusers; she didn't mince her words, even though she had purportedly only been addressing her sister, daughters, and nieces: "Look at those people! They're not worthy of mingling with us! Look at that father who never smiles and who didn't even have the decency to wear a clean suit, he just showed up in a crumbled *gandoura* and wants to speak to us as though he were our equal! As for the food, let's not even go there. It's quite obvious we don't have anything in common, we don't share the same tastes or even the same standards, we're just strangers. It would have been better if he'd at least married a Christian girl, some woman from Europe. They don't share our faith, but at least they have manners. One of my other nephews married a French woman and her family never gave us any grief. I'm sorry to be so blunt, but I speak my mind, and simply voice what everyone else in the family is thinking. This story began badly and it's going to end badly. Let's hope he eventually wakes up and the scales fall from his eyes. Otherwise she'll bear him even more children and it'll be too late. It's an old trick: each child weighs a ton, and so you'll prevent your husband from ever leaving!"

Toward midnight, having made every possible effort to shield his wife from these hostilities, he had found her huddled in a corner crying. He'd dried her tears and consoled her. Had she heard his aunt's malicious gossiping, or had the fact she was leaving her parents to start a family with him suddenly upset her? The painter recalled his sister's wedding, where everyone had cried because her husband had come to take her away forever. That wedding had taken place in Fez a long time ago, and it had lived up to the purest of traditions, which his aunt worshipped. The two families had come together then. Everything had taken shape without anything being spelled out; everyone had known their role by heart, and the play couldn't have failed because everything had been planned and calculated in advance, the ritual had unfolded without any hitches, the families had mingled and there had been no bad surprises, and nobody had made any inappropriate or tasteless speeches. Whenever anyone had made the slightest slip, there had always been someone who'd intervened and restored the balance.

Yet on that day, the painter knew why his wife was crying and could not answer him. The attitude both families had adopted had rekindled a feeling of rejection that she'd believed she'd overcome once she'd started living with the painter. The memories of those unbearable humiliations she'd suffered during her childhood due to the modesty of her background, as though a secret wound had suddenly ripped open again.

The painter had told himself that he should have defended her more. That he should have laid the ground before their marriage. Told her that he loved her regardless of what anyone in his family said, which he couldn't have cared less about. He could have easily proven to her that their love was stronger than any bump in the road they might face. But he hadn't taken those precautions, believing that his love was so obvious and visible that it would silence those malicious tongues. This marriage was like screaming his love from the rooftops, shouting to anyone who would listen that he loved that girl from the bled, publicly declaring how proud he'd been to defy a whole social caste for love.

Alone on the street, his fists in his pockets, his mind dwelled on those old stories as he vainly tried to find the means to bring their arguments to an end and recover the essence of the love they had for one another.

V

Marrakech

January 1991

It would be terrible to have to depend on you in any way.
—Marianne to Isak Borg,
her seventy-eight-year-old father-in-law
INGMAR BERGMAN, *Wild Strawberries*

One day, when they'd been traveling around southern Morocco, they had passed through the village where she'd grown up before moving to France. He'd found his wife had suddenly become happy again, in a way in which he hadn't seen her in quite a long time, her movements were carefree and she'd become sweet and generous. She'd been friendly, had spoken to him of the beauty of the light, and the kindness of the people who lived in those remote regions. She'd suddenly reminded him of the young woman he'd known before their marriage and whom he'd fallen in love with. Upset, he'd even considered settling there, since that part of the world worked such wonderful effects on her mood! He hadn't been wrong because, by rediscovering her roots, his wife had found the reassurance she'd been looking for, allowing her to relate to others positively, rather than negatively or dejectedly. She'd spent hours talking to the women of the village, who'd told her about all their problems. She'd taken notes and had proceeded with a sociologist's meticulousness, promising those women she'd return and help find solutions to their dilemmas. She'd brought clothes for the women she knew, which she'd carefully selected, as well as toys for the children and a parcel of medicine, which she'd given to the only young girl in the village who could read.

The painter had looked at his wife while she performed good deeds and had been happy. The sky had been a spotless blue and the nights bitingly cold. She had snuggled against him to keep warm, but also because she'd felt her man belonged to her. She'd held him, pressing him against her with all her strength as if to tell him that she would be with him forever. For a moment, he wondered whether she'd brought him there so as to cast a spell on him. After all, didn't she believe in sorcery just like all the other women in the village? He'd banished that unenlightened idea from his thoughts.

He would have liked to make love to her that evening in order to put a seal on their reunion, but they hadn't been alone in the room. Children were sleeping next to them. She'd kissed him tenderly and whispered in his ear: "My man, you are my man . . ." then she'd stroked his chest for a long time.

They'd woken up early the next morning, and had a traditional breakfast. The coffee had been undrinkable, and the mixture of chickpeas grilled with some coffee beans had left an unusual taste in his mouth. He'd asked for tea, which had alas proved too sweet. Afterwards, they'd left the village to go for a walk on the road that led up the mountain. They'd held hands. She'd felt carefree, lighthearted. He'd told her that one day they would make a similar journey, to his native city of Fez. She'd told him she would like that, but on the condition that they didn't go see his family, and especially his aunt, the memory of whom was quite traumatizing for her. He'd refrained from making any comments, fearing that the slightest slip would spoil that blessed moment that he'd wanted to draw out as much as he could. He hadn't seen her so calm for months.

They'd walked for a long time and forgotten all about time. Having reached the top of the mountain, they'd come across a shepherd playing the flute. It had looked like something out of a picture book. They'd rested for a while next to him. After he'd left with his herd of goats, they'd found themselves alone once again. She'd kissed him tenderly on the lips. He'd wanted to have her at that exact moment, and had scanned the surroundings. Then she'd noticed a little cabin. They'd entered it, thrown themselves down on the hay, and undressed. They made love slowly. They had to come back there, he'd told himself, since his wife had been completely changed by the experience.

They had stayed in that cabin for a long time and had fallen asleep. As was the local tradition, the shepherd brought them fresh whey and some dates. It was their way of welcoming guests. The sun was setting. It was getting cold. The shepherd asked them a few questions about their life and told them that he'd never left the mountain, so was curious about what life was like in the city. Nevertheless, he had a little black-and-white television that was fueled by a gas cylinder. That window on the world pleased him a great deal. It allowed him to travel even to France, the country where his father and uncle worked.

They'd stood to leave, fearing the night would overtake them. The nights were long and dark in January. The shepherd had been pleased by their unexpected visit. To thank him, the painter had offered him his sunglasses as a present: "You need them more than I do! You're always out in the sun, you must protect your eyes!" The thought of wearing fashionable sunglasses had seemed to make the shepherd mad with joy. He put them on immediately and said he could see the mountain and the valley in a different way, claiming that even his sheep had a different color to them. He'd laughed, all the while showering a thousand blessings upon them. The painter's wife had slipped a hundred-dirham note in his pocket. Then the shepherd had kissed her hand, which had been embarrassing.

During their descent, their tiredness made itself felt, but it had been a good kind of tired, the kind that would lead them to their bed, where they would fall asleep immediately. They had been hungry and had dreamed of a piece of buttered bread, just like in Paris. But the lady with whom they'd been lodging had prepared couscous with seven vegetables for them. They'd stuffed themselves like foreign tourists. He'd had some difficulty stomaching rancid butter. Yet her eyes had ballooned and she'd told him: "It's good, darling. It's very good for your health, for your eyes, the memory, the imagination, and your creativity!" He hadn't had the time to do any sketching, but everything had left a strong imprint on his memory. He would often think about the very specific color of the sky there; he'd asked himself how he would replicate its effect on the canvas later. The sky in the south had nothing in common with the one in Casablanca, which was whitish, and even less so with Paris's, which was rather gray. There, in the deepest depths of Morocco, far away from all the pollution, the sky was a soft, subtle blue. Contrary to what one might expect, Delacroix had never painted anything while in Morocco. He'd merely taken some notes and drawn in his notebooks. It was only on his return to France that he'd found that country's colors and figured out how to reproduce them in his paintings.

The following day, they had taken some pictures of the village. The children had rushed toward them to pose so they could be in the shot. The women had refused to let themselves be photographed. They said they were afraid the machine would capture their souls! One of them had even turned their back to them. She'd laughed and said: "I'm very attached to my soul!" She'd worn a flower-patterned robe. It looked like a scene out of one of the paintings of Jacques Majorelle, the painter of Marrakech.

It was finally time for them to leave. They had said goodbye to everyone, climbed inside their car, and taken the road to Agadir. They'd spent the night in a pretty hotel on the beach. The painter tried to picture the city as it had once looked. Before the earthquake of February 29, 1960. He had seen one of his primary school teachers cry when it happened. The teacher had lost his entire family.

Agadir had been entirely rebuilt since then. There were rows of hotels that stretched out into infinity. The city now devoted itself only to tourism. Its soul had been buried. In 1960, the painter had only been six years old, whereas his wife hadn't even been born yet. He had kept a vivid memory of that distraught teacher alive in his mind. His father had been so dismayed that he'd even doubted the goodness of God. People had spread rumors that the earthquake had been a form of divine retribution. All of this had left a fuzzy impression in that six-year-old boy's mind. But the memory of that catastrophe had accompanied him for the rest of his life.

They had walked around the city's various markets. People in Agadir were very different to the Marrakechis. Their natural sense of dignity commanded respect. But would he have been able to live in a city that had been rebuilt as though it had undergone several rounds of plastic surgery? Nothing spoke to him there. He'd remarked to his wife that she looked sad. They went back on the road early the next morning, before her mood could grow somber again. She had taken over at the wheel and started driving very fast. He'd observed how adroitly she'd learned to handle that big car. It was as if the person next to him had transformed into a woman he didn't know, a woman who was determined and fearless.

The police stopped her for speeding. The painter was almost relieved that she'd been pulled over. At first, his wife had tried to bribe them. Then one of the two policemen had given her a lecture. Then his wife had spoken to the policeman in Tamazight, and he'd replied in the same language. He gave her back her license and told her to drive carefully.

The painter had been dumbstruck. It appeared that tribal solidarity was more powerful than any highway code.

VI

Casablanca

March 24, 2000

I've come on behalf of someone who doesn't exist anymore.
He said he would meet me in these deeply moving places, but
he will not be coming!
> —Louis Jouvet, introducing himself
> to the housekeeper, who opened the door for him
> CHRISTIAN-JAQUE, *A Lover's Return*

The painter was dozing, his head rolled forward, his legs heavy, his hands pressed against one another.

He slowly opened his eyes. The Twins were playing cars while sitting on the lawn. His wheelchair was equipped with an SOS button, a bell, but he didn't want to bother them. He'd heard them laughing and swapping jokes. He'd never been able to play any kind of game, not cards, not bridge, and not chess either. With the exception of football, he'd never excelled in any sport. He'd once played a game of tennis, but his friends Roland and François had made fun of him. One of them had said: "You're playing like one of the characters in Antonioni's *Blow-Up!*" While the other had added: "Your aerial game is so perfect you don't even need to hit the ball!" He hadn't been able to concentrate on his game. He'd spent the entire time thinking about his paintings. The painter had devoted his entire life to his work. He had taught a little, but then had spent the rest of his time doing nothing but painting and sketching. Nonetheless, he enjoyed watching sporting competitions on television. He loved the challenge at the heart of sport, how those athletes aimed to be the best in their field, by sheer force of willpower, hard work, and dedicated passion. He liked to remind his children that he had achieved his success step by step. He had climbed the ladder one rung at a time and had never fallen into the trap of going after what was easiest, nor had he been swayed by fads or trends, or the social life and gossip that ended up blinding even the best.

He had first exhibited his work at the high school in Casablanca where he'd taught. He'd had a hard time convincing the principal, but he'd known how to speak to him. The principal was an old friend from college, a man who held good social standing. He had married according to his parents' wishes, his two children attended the French Mission, he spent his holidays in the south of Spain, and he aspired to build a house on credit. His name was Chaâbi, and he'd been nicknamed "Pop"—short for "popular." A week after the painter had talked to him about having his work exhibited in the school, Chaâbi had come to tell him some news, as if he'd been the one who'd come up with the idea: "The ministry will be very happy to support this initiative, especially these days when strikes and riots abound: you deal with the students' rebelliousness through your art! It's surprising, I can see no risks and I can even predict there is a promotion in store for you!" As it happened, that was the first time many kids from working class neighborhoods had ever seen any art, especially contemporary art. Before the exhibition opened, the painter had organized several after-school meetings where he'd talked for a long time about his work in the hopes of making the students more receptive to art and teaching them how to look at a work. He'd played them a short film by Alain Resnais on the life of Vincent Van Gogh, and another by H. G. Clouzot that showed Picasso at work. They'd appeared interested, impressed even.

Over the course of the following years, many other painters took his lead. The experiment had yielded conclusive results. Thanks to him, painting had made its way into schools, and painters who rarely exhibited their work were able to leave their studios. He was proud of what he'd accomplished.

He had worked every day for thirty years, always applying himself with the same diligence, revising each painting as many times as necessary, refusing lucrative offers from many gallerists when they didn't seem serious enough. Acclaim for his work had come slowly but surely. Nothing had come easy to him and some artists, especially the mediocre ones, had tried to cause him problems and had ganged up to lay traps for him in the hopes of sullying his reputation. These had been cheap shots that had nothing to do with his work in progress. Those mediocre artists had failed, but as that stupid old saying goes, "*There's no smoke without fire!*" His father had been worried about him: "Sooner or later you'll get devoured by frustrated people. Don't show your face too often, be discreet. Never forget what the Prophet said, avoid extremes and always go for the middle ground! Look, whenever someone is under the spotlight, there will always be people who go digging around in the gutter, and if they don't find anything, they'll just make something up! The press loves it, and when you set the record straight, nobody cares, the damage has already been done!"

Thanks to his prudence and wisdom, the year the painter turned thirty a big gallery in London organized the first retrospective dedicated to his work, which was an invaluable springboard that helped launch him onto the world stage. Shows in other capitals had quickly followed. His agent had been especially happy; he'd called the painter from his office in New York and spoke in his broken French: "You see, it only takes a Jew to make an Arab a lot of *argent*, you see, *mon ami*, we've sold everything, the price will go up and up!" That same year, he was awarded the Prix de Rome, and had been able to spend a year in the Villa Medici and get to know Italy. His dazzling success hadn't compromised his modesty or altered his behavior. His parents were proud of him, women admired him and surrounded him at all turns. He continued to work just as he'd always done. Implausible rumors made the rounds, then evaporated, as all well know they do. A Moroccan newspaper accused him of profiteering by exploiting his country's beauty . . . A Libyan newspaper called for his work to be boycotted: "This is a painter who sold out to the Zionists, whose agent is a Jew, and who exhibits his work in galleries that belong to Americans who support Israel's criminal policies!" So many bad memories flashed past his mind, but they didn't affect him. He knew there was a price to pay for success. His father had often told him: "Victory has a thousand fathers, but defeat is an orphan."

He was rational in all spheres of life, which contrasted sharply with the sumptuousness and extravagance of his hyper-realist paintings. The portraits he did from time to time, which were always executed in the strictest classicism, were the canvases that most closely resembled who he was as a man. Yet when it came to the rest of his paintings, he tended to vary the sources of his inspiration, and prove that his art wasn't based on chance, but rather was the result of his thorough command of technique, which was the only way to transpose reality into a medium. He had a deep-seated aversion to schools that were either self-proclaimed or invented by art critics. As far as he was concerned, these were nothing but boxes where radically different artists were arbitrarily put together. He didn't belong to any movement or school. When they asked him too many questions, he would simply tell them that he belonged to the Adoua School, which was a primary school in Fez frequented by the sons of Fez's bourgeoisie, where he'd been enrolled by his father after completing Qur'anic school. That was where he'd learned to write and draw. Their teacher had been passionate about painting, and had often showed them books with re-productions of Van Gogh or Rembrandt. Some of the other children had laughed, but those reproductions had awoken a burning curiosity in him, which he still carried to this day.

Light was scarce in the medina of Fez. When the weather was good, he would go up to the rooftop of his parents' house and sketch whatever he saw. It had been difficult at first and he would tear up his sketches and start all over again so he could reproduce as accurate a portrait of the city as he could manage. All the houses looked alike: they were cube-shaped and fit together like the jagged pieces of a jig-saw puzzle. He had to go beyond those appearances and re-create an atmosphere. Aged ten, he'd dared to show his teacher a drawing that he'd thought had turned out well. The teacher had encouraged him and had given him a box of colored pencils at the end of the year.

Drawing had been a form of escapism for him, allowing him to experience the world in a different way. One of his neighbors had been a very pretty deaf-mute girl called Zina. Neither of them had known sign language, so he'd communicated with her through his drawings. He had spent whole afternoons making drawings for her so he could tell her sweet things and allow her to dream. He'd drawn portraits of her entire family for her. It played a decisive role in the development of his future technique. The desire to communicate with her had obliged him to become a creator. Once he would return home, he would draw stories for her that he would offer her the next morning. He'd been very sad the day when Zina's parents had left Fez to go live in Casablanca. She had promised she would send him her new address. He'd waited a long time, but had never heard from her again. The memory of Zina made him smile, since she was definitely the first girl he'd ever fallen in love with, when he'd been just ten years old . . . After a few months of fruitless waiting, he burned all the drawings he'd ever made for her so he could forget the whole story. Now he regretted having done that, but he comforted himself with the knowledge that they'd probably been poor drawings . . .

He looked at the alarm clock that lay on the rolling table where he used to store his brushes and colors when he could still paint. 11:45 p.m.: time for his injections and medications. Imane, his nurse, a brunette who moved gracefully and whose eyes were full of kindness, entered the room and immediately started looking after him. Always discreet and affable, she came to see him three times a day. He called her "Faith," which was what her name meant in Arabic. This amused the young woman and made her smile. She'd been recommended to him by one of his friends who was a doctor: "This is someone you'll have to spend a lot of time with, so as long as that person is competent, you also want them to be nice and even pretty. It's important to surround yourself with people who are easy on the eyes! As I know that you like women, this one won't displease you, especially since your relationship will be purely medical. She comes from a good family and is probably still a virgin. At least there are silver linings after the accidents in our lives!"

He would impatiently look forward to each of Imane's visits. It was a special moment because he found her presence soothing. She took to her work seriously and yet was still sweet. One day, he asked her if she had a boyfriend. She smiled and said: "Next time, during my break, I'll come and tell you all about me, and if you like, I can read to you in both French and Arabic!" The painter thought it was an excellent idea. It would be a good opportunity for him to plunge back into Baudelaire's essays on Delacroix, whom he loved a great deal, and discover what the new biography of Matisse had to say. Once she finished her work, Imane had slipped away as quietly as she'd come.

•

When it was time for lunch, his two assistants carried him to the dining room where they fed him like a baby. It was the most unbearable time of day for him. The doctor had told him he would recover the use of his right hand within a few weeks. It was just a matter of time and patience. But nothing had happened yet. He ate very little, not so much because he wasn't hungry, but because he didn't want to go through the ordeal. To see himself so clumsy and weakened made his spirits sink. He took every sip like a dehydrated old man because he was afraid he would swallow askew. It was a problem he'd inherited from his father, and it happened to him very often, which could be fatal in his situation.

The bathroom still hadn't been modified so that he could use it by himself. It was Eid al-Adha, and the country had come to a standstill. The plumber was waiting for his workers to return from their villages in the countryside and get back to work. The mason couldn't be reached. The painter had disappeared. The feast of the sacrifice was an opportunity for millions of Moroccans to eat meat, and nobody wanted to miss out on it. It was a holiday that small and medium-size businesses feared the most, since all economic activity simply ground to a halt. The timing of the holiday had been terrible for the painter, too. After lunch and a brief pit stop in the bathroom, he took a long rest. He needed it, since the mundane activities of life cost him a great deal of effort.

As they were laying him on the bed so he could take a nap, the painter recalled a conversation he'd had not long ago with his oldest son: "Where do you want to be buried, Dad, in France or in Morocco? Do you want to be wrapped in a white shroud or put into a coffin while wearing a nice black suit? Do you want people to visit your grave, or do you not care one way or the other? In any case, you won't know anything, won't know who comes to see you or not, so I guess it's all the same to you, eh? I wouldn't want you to be cremated, I've seen that in films, it's terrible. Regardless, I think cremation is against Islamic tenets, isn't it? Well, I've asked you a lot of questions, but you know that I want you to live for a long time, a very long time. I love you, Dad. But please let me know about your choice of country and the shroud, all right?"

The painter had replied: "There's nothing to think about, my son, I'll be buried in Morocco. But no black suit! What bothers me is how dirty our cemeteries are, you saw them when we went to visit your grandparents' graves, how disgustingly unhygienic they are. There were empty bottles and plastic bags everywhere, as well as dead cats, dog droppings, beggars, charlatans . . . in short, the dead are not respected during their eternal sleep. You'll probably say that the dead have nothing to do, and you'd be right, but they deserve our respect anyway, it's a matter of principle. In any case, my son, the important thing is to remember those who are not of this world anymore. Because whenever you remember someone, they're not really dead, they remain alive in our thoughts and our memories. So whether you come visit my grave or not doesn't really matter, but if you completely forgot all about me, that would be bad. In the meanwhile, live your life!"

Remembering those words, the painter fell asleep, at peace with himself.

VII

Paris

August 1992

I'm no longer the same man who first came in. How time
flies! I don't like tulips. The flowers I'm going to offer you
now are Parma violets. One day I would like anemones.
—CHRISTIAN-JAQUE, *A Lover's Return*

A year and a half had passed since the trip to Morocco, where their
bickering had come to an abrupt halt. They had continued to get
along on their return to Paris. He'd managed to paint, had looked
after the children, and spent quality time with his wife. That getaway
had allowed them to recover their equilibrium, and their fights had
begun to seem like a bad dream. Thanks to the trips he'd made to
exhibit his work, the painter had been able to spend some time away,
and this had certainly contributed to their newfound harmony. She
never held his absences against him, since this allowed her to spend
some time on her own, too.

One day, the artist had received an invitation to attend a Southern artists' conference that was to be held in China. He'd dreamed about visiting that country, which he'd known little about, but which fascinated and intrigued him. He'd happily accepted and had begun making preparations for that trip with a youngster's enthusiasm. It was August. When he'd set foot on the ground at the airport in Beijing, he'd discovered a sky as white as a monochrome painting, but it was a whiteness that seemed a little heavy, a little disquieting. He'd searched for a cloud, or a sliver of blue, but it had been in vain. The Chinese sky was utterly unlike any other on Earth. He felt a migraine brew inside his head. He'd put that down to the air-conditioning and the humidity in the atmosphere, but the headache wouldn't leave him be, despite all the painkillers he took, which usually worked their effect. Everything seemed strange. He didn't understand what was happening. He attended a reception at the Moroccan Embassy where he saw a few familiar faces, in particular an old classmate from high school who was now the embassy's commercial attaché: "Don't try to look for any landmarks," he told the painter, "everything here is different. In any case, it's very difficult to leave embassy circles, everything is closely monitored here!" The painter nevertheless accepted an invitation from the cultural attaché of the French embassy, who knew his work well. He'd taken him to a popular restaurant where the food was prepared by a family. The painter realized that one could eat better Chinese food in Paris than in Beijing. That night, he hadn't felt well, his head had been spinning, his vision had gone blurry, and his ribs had felt sore. He thought he'd caught a cold. He no longer wanted to be in that country, where everything was secret, rigidly controlled and surveilled. He found it impossible to visit an old Chinese painter whom a Spanish friend had recommended he go see. A simple address clearly wasn't enough in China. Eventually, the painter had given up on his quest to meet that man. They told him: "Ah, you too want to see him! Everybody wants to see him, but unfortunately, nobody knows where he lives . . . There are plenty of other painters in this country, not just him, if you like we can arrange for you to visit the best painters in China. They're great people, and while they're not known in the West, their talent is indisputable!"

He was feeling ill, but thought that leaving the country would be enough to heal him. After a week, he was able to change his return ticket and arrived in Paris in bad shape. He had a dull pain between his lungs and rib cage that refused to leave him. He went to the pulmonary department at the Hôpital Cochin downtown, where he was given some strong antibiotics. His condition didn't improve at all. Quite the opposite, he got worse—and he was admitted to the ER as he started choking. He came close to dying, although he hadn't stared death right in the face, but instead smelled a strong odor that was like a mixture of bleach, ether, and cooking fumes. Death had to go down several hallways to strike its intended target. They'd given him oxygen, and he'd spent several hours in the ER's waiting room because they hadn't had any available beds in the department he needed. At night, he'd been transferred to the tropical disease ward where they had a spot for him. A lucky turn of events for him. Purely out of coincidence, a young doctor had asked him: "Have you recently traveled to Asia?" The painter had nodded. All of a sudden, he felt as though the stench of death had withdrawn, and that the shadow of death had flitted away. The young doctor, who had an air of mystery about him, had asked him: "Did you eat any raw shellfish?" The painter had then remembered seeing a shrimp in the salad at the family restaurant where he'd eaten. "You've got a parasite that exists only in Asia, which only affects shellfish and attacks the lungs. I think you've got pulmonary distomatosis, or paragonimiasis, after the parasite called paragonimus." The doctor had immediately given him a couple of tablets to swallow. "If you can't sleep we'll give you some sedatives and sleeping pills," he'd said, then he'd disappeared. That night was one of the most terrible in the painter's life. His mattress was covered in plastic on top of which they'd put some coarse sheets. It gave off an unbearable heat. It tortured him, but they couldn't change his bed. So he decided to sit up, although he did so extremely carefully to avoid pulling out the oxygen tubes that were allowing him to breathe. He felt as though fire were coursing through his body, that his skin was burning and his hair was falling out. He felt once again that his end was in sight, which allowed him to understand why people said death was the disease, because death in itself was nothing, and what preceded it was far worse. He remembered what his mother used to say whenever she had a bad night: "This will be one of the nights I tell my gravedigger about!" He laughed because as a child he hadn't understood how a dead person could still speak, especially to the person digging their grave. And what would she have told him anyway? That she slept badly, had suffered from anxiety, cold sweats, that she had a feeling of impending death with its string of sufferings and uncertainties?

Unable to sleep or take his mind off his pain, he'd written down his impressions in the notebook he usually used for his sketches. In the hours between vigil and sleep, it was as though a voice had dictated those words to him:

> *The night of September 27th and 28th. A searing heat is setting my sore skin on fire, and this is more unbearable than the disease itself. A long ordeal. This night is like a waiting room in a cave where people are tortured. I sweat, I choke, I open the window, I'm afraid of catching a cold. I wait for the morning in front of a plastic-covered sofa that is incredibly ugly. The patients who spend the whole day here stretched out on their beds must be unable to sleep at night. Arrangements should be made to fill their time, activities or games should be organized, entertainers or mimes or clowns should be brought in, just like they do for children.*
>
> *The infernal bed where I tried to sleep in every position known to man gives off these burning waves that transform*

into nightmares before my body succumbs to fatigue: our home was ransacked by children who spilled buckets of colors everywhere, on the furniture, the bed, the library. I see someone kneeling while cutting red, yellow, and green sponges. All throughout, the children ignore my presence and splash about in the puddles of colors. Even though I cannot see the face of the kneeling man, I start hitting him so hard that I wake up drenched in sweat. I jump up in bed and almost fall off. I can't stand my skin touching this evil bed anymore.

I sit on the sofa, which I cover up with my clothes so my skin won't touch the plastic. I doze off. I dream again. I'm in Casablanca, at the Hotel Riad Salam. I hail a taxi. The driver goes really fast and doesn't care that I slam against the window every time he takes a turn. He's in a real hurry, he doesn't listen to me, doesn't turn around, he must take me to where I told him I want to be dropped off. The doors are locked. We arrive in Casablanca's medina and the guy throws me into a courtyard where some young men seem to be waiting for me. The first man who looks at me is bald and doesn't have any teeth. He stares at me for a long time and I hear: "That's it, now you're gonna pay." Then he leaves me in the hands of the others, who all look aggressive. I don't recognize anyone in that crowd. A guy in a brown sweater says: "Why don't you write in Arabic? Now you're gonna pay!" Then I reply: "But I'm not a writer, I'm a painter, you're making a mistake." But nobody believes me. I hear them say: "We know who you are, we've seen you on TV, you speak to us in French." I try to reason with them, to defend the right of those who write in French even though I'm not a writer, but I can feel their hatred. They want to try me and to immediately sentence me to death. I sense that I'm lost. I tell them: "I've come to Casa to exhibit my paintings." They laugh, then they yell: "He wants to run away from us, to pretend he's a painter so we won't judge him; that's easy, because painting is neither French nor Arabic." . . . At that moment, a gray-haired man arrived. I felt as though I knew him. He suggests postponing the trial until I have been properly questioned. I escaped being lynched . . . This man doesn't speak to me, he turns his back to me and leaves me in a corner where children are arranging a table, chairs, and torture instruments . . .

The painter woke up at five in the morning and cursed that infernal bed where he'd fallen asleep.

Dawn was breaking, he pulled out the oxygen tubes, turned the water on in the shower, and watched it run over his body, which was turning gray and black. He wasn't dreaming anymore, he was hallucinating.

That stay in the hospital, where he'd had such a near brush with death, had strangely left the painter feeling calm and collected.

The illness had left him very enfeebled, and the side effects caused by the parasite took a long time to vanish entirely. Nevertheless, the painter went on with his life and left the house when he wanted, as if he wasn't ill anymore. He would walk to his studio, which was situated in the 14th arrondissement, quite a distance from his place. He had a commission from Barcelona's City Hall to commemorate the Universal Declaration of Human Rights, but he was having trouble getting started. One morning, when he'd woken up more tired than usual, his wife had driven him to his studio. During the drive, he'd softly asked her if she could come pick him up around five o'clock. Quite unexpectedly, she'd blown up at him: "I'm not your chauffeur and this isn't your taxi. You know, I've been your nurse for over a month now! Who do you think you are? Do you think the universe revolves around you? You're taking advantage of the fact that you're sick, so don't count on me anymore!"

They'd been on Rue d'Alésia at the time. The painter had flown into a rage and had retorted: "If that's the case then I'm happy to walk." She'd suddenly slammed on the brakes and opened the door. He'd climbed out of the car and had walked to his studio on his own.

That incident definitely capsized their married life. Clashes followed and neither of them resembled their former selves anymore. He had his share of responsibility in that whole affair. His weakness, his naïveté, his illusions, and then that eternal hope that she would one day change. To avoid bickering with her, he'd begun to flee the house for secret rendezvous with more loving women, women who admired him both as an artist and as a man. He found a great deal of comfort with those women and a kind of sweetness that he really needed. Those secret relationships helped to keep him balanced and avoid abruptly leaving his house. The children were happy, they loved him and cuddled him. Henceforth, his happiness would take place in different places and different times, but never in the same place, there was never any continuity. He thought he could reconcile all these differences and lead a double life without ever jeopardizing that oft-mentioned equilibrium.

Things were going so badly between them that he convinced her to go to couples' therapy with him. "I'm not crazy! If I've consented to go with you, it's to show your psychiatrist how crazy, perverse, and monstrous you are!" is what she'd hit him with just before their appointment. She'd looked at him with eyes full of resentment in the waiting room.

The psychiatrist had explained how the sessions would work before beginning. She hadn't cared about any of that. She had launched into a tirade in front of that stranger about the horrors of their married life, comparing the painter to an ayatollah who wanted his wife to live in purdah, sought to prevent her from leading her own life, gave his children's money away to his brothers and sisters, traveled all the time for his work; he was basically a ghost husband . . . "He's never there! After our children were born, I was forced to assume two roles, those of the father and the mother. I do everything I can to make sure they still love him, even though he's literally abandoned them, but he doesn't care; he always uses the excuse that he has to go work in his studio, that he has to travel for his exhibitions, and so we never see him. And when he does come back, he's always in a bad mood, he shouts, screams, and hits the children!"

He gave the psychiatrist his version of events, which was a lot simpler: "For some time now we haven't had the same idea of what married life should be like, nor the same philosophy on education; her family interferes too much and makes her choices for her, and I'm not allowed to say anything about it. What she's told you really doesn't match reality. I'm sorry, she's not playing the same game here, she refuses to examine herself, while I've come here because I have doubts and because I'd like us to have some couples' therapy!"

She canceled the following session and reproached him for having exploited the situation in order to criticize her family, which she couldn't stand at all.

A month later, the painter went to see the psychiatrist on his own. He was a chubby guy with an olive complexion who wore red-framed spectacles. He had dandruff on his shoulders, which snowed down from his full head of hair. He'd given the painter a knowing look that seemed to say: "I knew you'd come back!" He let the painter speak and then interrupted him.

"—I'm going to let you in on a secret, something I've rarely done and which is hardly professional. My name isn't Jean-Christophe Armand, I'm just as Moroccan as you or your wife. My name is Abdelhak Lamrani and I was born in Casablanca. I attended medical school in Rabat and specialized in Paris. I had wanted to practice in my own country, in Morocco, but there are too many misconceptions about my field over there. Too many people think that going to see a psychiatrist means you're crazy. But let's get back to your case. Your wife didn't come here because she wants to change things. She came because she thinks you're deranged, while she's in perfect mental health. She's completely wrong, of course, but I'm unable to help people who aren't yet ready for therapy. For that reason, couples' therapy isn't advisable at this present moment. So, what should I advise you to do? Divorce? Separate? Resign yourself? Run away? You're going to have to be the one to make that choice. It's yours and yours alone. The problems will always be there. People never really change. That's not my opinion, it's the wisdom of the ancients. Good luck."

VIII

Marrakech

April 3, 1993

Three bourgeois women swap stories of their hallucinations:

> —I lifted the lid and saw a great precipice and the
> limpid waters of a stream.
> —Before sitting down an eagle flew over me!
> —The wind hurled dead leaves in my face.
> —LUIS BUÑUEL, *The Exterminating Angel*

The painter had always promised himself he would one day retrace Delacroix's footsteps in Morocco. The spring had been bathing the country in its light when he'd decided to buy a plane ticket for Marrakech. He'd brought pencils and brushes with him, just as he'd done as a young man. No other luggage. He got himself a room in a little hotel not far from Jamaa el Fna square and telephoned one of his friends, who was a writer and lived in the medina. The writer immediately invited him to come over. He introduced the painter to two cultivated women, who were also staying in town for a while. One of them was in her fifties, and she was slender and a chain-smoker. The other was clearly a lot younger, and what was more, she was pretty and voluptuous. She didn't talk much, but the other one talked for her. The first was called Maria and the other Angèle. There were at least thirty years between them. Maria worked for a multinational company and was always traveling. The painter had liked talking to her almost immediately, as she knew a lot about Morocco. When they'd parted ways, they'd agreed to meet the following day at the hotel where they were staying. The women wanted to give him a book they'd written, *The Origins of Indian Art in Latin America*, which was bound to interest him. Maria was from Argentina, while Angèle was a Catalan living in Guatemala.

He asked to speak to Angèle the next day at the hotel, but it was Maria who answered. He thanked her for the book and suggested taking them to visit a village in the South, which they didn't know about, but would surely like. However, they had to catch a plane the following day. They exchanged addresses and promised to meet up the next time they passed through Paris.

That evening, he'd tried once again to reach Angèle, who seemed embarrassed by his approaches and had answered the phone rather tersely. He cut the conversation short and regretted calling her in the first place. Ten minutes later, she'd called him back: "I'm out on the street and can speak freely. We'll write to one another as soon as I'm back, all right? I understand French but I can't speak it that well!" He'd replied: "My written Spanish isn't great, but I can try to speak it!"

His instinct hadn't been wrong. There was a chance something might happen between them. A fling, an adventure, an affair, what did he know? . . . He felt available, open to any propositions, even the most extravagant. He was trying to free himself from his wife's clutches. They hadn't slept together for several months. He felt as though he'd already left her spiritually, even though things were just as they'd always been. He rented a car, abandoned his idea of following Delacroix's footsteps and headed toward his wife's ancestral village. He'd kept his room at the hotel in Marrakech in case he changed his mind again. He still nursed both terrible and wonderful memories of that little village in the middle of nowhere.

He got lost several times before coming across the sign that read "Khamsa." The village was called that because it had five trees, five mosques, and five thousand inhabitants.

A horde of happy children greeted him on his arrival at the entrance of the village, crying, "M'ssiou! M'ssiou!" Some of them were barefoot, while others had a wounded look in their eyes. They answered him in Arabic and made fun of his Northern accent. But he'd thought about them. He pulled notebooks, pencils, and neon pens out of his bag and handed them out. He asked them to show him what they'd drawn the following day.

His wife's aunts and uncles welcomed him, but they looked very intimidated. They didn't know what to do in order to please him. Recalling his last visit there with his wife, he'd purchased some medicines in Marrakech and he presented them as a gift.

They thanked him and asked him for news of his wife. The painter assured them that everything was well, that she was looking after the children and the house and that they were happy . . . It was the first time he'd been there on his own. He felt that he should go there more often, because things there seemed different to him. He found the people there humble, generous, thoughtful, and kindhearted. He told them that he was just passing through, and that he wanted to go up the mountain to draw and take some photos. One of them volunteered to accompany him and help carry his belongings. He was a bright-eyed young man who spoke a little French but not a word of Arabic. He wasn't even twenty years old and his name was Brek.

Throughout their climb, Brek constantly asked him questions about "Clirmafirane." It took the painter some time to realize the young man had been talking about Clermont-Ferrand. There was something crazy about hearing the name of that boring town being spoken high up in those mountains. The sky was a deep blue, the views amazing, and the horizon almost stretched out into infinity. Two years earlier, Brek had led a French couple who had been visiting the region on a hike. They had promised him that they would do their best to secure him a visa so he could work for them in their house and look after their garden.

While the painter had been drawing in his large sketchbook, Brek had suddenly said:

"You know, my cousin, your wife had also suggested I go to France. I gave her some passport photos, my passport, and other documents. She told me I could go there soon. That's why I know so much about Clirmafirane, is that where you live?"

"No, we live in Paris, in the Thirteenth arrondissement. It's very different from this place."

"She told me you have a big house and that I could look after the garden."

"Ah, good!"

"Yes, I will be your gardener."

"Are you a gardener?"

"No, but the people from Clirmafirane told me the same thing. I'm up to the task. I know how to pull out weeds, dig, water the plants . . ."

"But you're going to get married soon. Are you going to leave your wife behind and emigrate?"

"No, my cousin said that my wife could work for you in the house. She said she would get a visa for her too."

Which was exactly—or almost—what happened a few months later. On his return to Paris after opening an exhibition in Germany, the painter had been surprised to find that a very young woman had been set up in one of his children's bedrooms. She was very shy and couldn't speak a word of French or Arabic. When he asked his wife why she'd never spoken to him about it or asked for his opinion, she'd answered very aggressively:

"I know what I'm doing. This girl got married very young and I've brought her here so she can go to school, and so she can help me to look after the kids from time to time. As for you, you're never here, and you don't know what goes on here when you're gone, you don't know how much there is to do. You're trying to piss me off, is that it? Find something else to do . . ."

"But you just presented me with a fait accompli!"

"Just like you've done!"

He kept his mouth shut, but he saw the extent of the damage that very day. The poor peasant girl was completely out of her element. He found dirty toilet paper strewn all over the floor of the bathroom next to her bedroom. The toilet seat had been completely soiled because she'd stood on top of it and crouched on her haunches because she didn't know that you could sit on it. Nauseous, he'd left the house. He didn't say anything to his wife, preferring that she find out on her own. On his way out, he'd peeked into the girl's room. She'd scattered all her belongings on the bed and had spread the duvet on the floor to sleep at night. The next day, he'd seen her doubled over and red-faced. She'd confused the jar of mustard with jam and had swallowed a huge spoonful of it. He'd also found a metal cap from a bottle of Coca-Cola that had been riddled with holes. She must have tried to open it with her teeth . . .

That evening, he heard her cry in her room.

The girl went back to her village a month later. The painter felt relieved. But two weeks later, another girl took her place. This new girl had just finished high school and had begun to study biology. He hadn't been told about her arrival either. Any kind of discussion or protest had been useless. He only asked his wife a single question: "And what about the gardener, when is he coming?" She hadn't answered him.

•

The village of Khamsa looked like a dry red spot from the mountain's summit. There were no oases in its surroundings, nor any greenery or shrubbery of any kind. The painter had told himself that it was a cursed douar, nothing but rocks and thistles. Brek agreed. He talked a lot about the village where he'd been born: "God has forgotten us! We don't have anything! Very little water, no electricity, no schools, no doctor, nothing, nothing grows here, but we have a lot of cats and dogs who are just as hungry as we are. They come here because we let them go wherever they like. So you see, brother, Clirmafirane is a lot better than this! Do you know why Madame Nicole never wrote to me or replied to any of my letters? And what about your cousin, do you think she'll keep her word?"

When the painter thought he'd taken enough photos and produced enough sketches, he and Brek had returned to the village, where a sumptuous dinner awaited them. The tajine with mutton and olives had been very greasy. He hadn't been able to eat, and had instead eaten some couscous that was just as greasy as the tajine. He'd been ashamed to be unable to enjoy the dishes that the women had spent the whole day preparing. Fortunately, the other guests had gobbled everything up. He'd slept in the room reserved for prayers. Stomach-ache and heartburn had prevented him from getting a wink of sleep. He'd left the house early the next morning and discovered a light that was incredibly soft and subtle. He took a few photos in order to remember it. On his return to Paris he'd immediately started to work on paintings about everything that he'd seen and which had affected him during that trip.

His wife had stormed into his studio and recognized her village. The two canvases were still unfinished. She'd looked at them and on her way out she'd said:

"The money you make from those paintings will go to Khamsa. You don't have the right to exploit those poor people. They don't even know that you're profiting from their misery. You're just like your photographer friend who shoots workers in the mines and then exhibits them so he can make a pile of cash. This kind of thing should be forbidden."

Even though he didn't know whether she'd heard him, he'd said: "They're not for sale."

IX

Casablanca

1995

Some people say that you can tell what the souls of the dead have transformed into by looking at how the color of their hair has changed.

— LUIS BUÑUEL, *The River and Death*

One day, by which time they were living in their beautiful new house in Casablanca, his wife had come up to him and told him in a laconic tone: "I know you're cheating on me, and I even know with who!"

The time of suspicions had begun. She would never stop. She would spy on him and never trust anything he said, and was skeptical of every woman in his entourage. Her jealousy knew no bounds. While he'd been preparing to leave for Berlin to appear on a panel about art and literature with Anselm Kiefer, his wife had told him that the trip had been canceled.

"How is that possible?" he'd asked. "Who did that?"

"Why, I did, who else? A girl called to ask what time your flight was going to land in Berlin, it was a North African girl, someone called Asma . . . I could tell from her voice that she was a little slut, and so I told her my husband wasn't interested in that so-called symposium and that he was going to stay here with his wife, then I hung up on her."

That episode had made the painter furious. He tried to remedy the situation, but it was too late—his wife had ripped up the invitation and he didn't have the organizer's name. He was very embarrassed by it all, and he discovered how dangerous his wife could be for him. He tried to call one of his friends in Berlin but nobody had answered. It was the day before the conference. He found it impossible to cool down. He slept in the living room that night and decided he would go see his sick mother.

By the following morning, the painter still hadn't regained his composure. He was in a hurry to be far away from home. Bitter over the canceled conference, he'd pondered the situation while driving to Fez, where his mother lived. He recalled a recent dinner with friends at the Mirage Hotel just outside Tangiers. His wife had started to say terrible things about one of their mutual acquaintances. She just made things up, saying whatever came to her mind, and had accused this person of almost drowning their children, then stopped in midsentence and addressed her husband: "You're not a man, and you're even less of a husband! If you were a real man you would cut ties with that so-called friend who almost killed one of your children!" Unable to take any more, the painter had lost all control and had thrown a glass of water in his wife's face. She reacted immediately and threw a glass of wine in his face. His eyes could no longer see and he spent a few moments in complete darkness. Everyone in the restaurant had witnessed the scene. The other couple had tried to calm things down. But the violent way in which things had happened made him feel really bad, and he blamed himself for his lack of restraint. He would never again let himself go so far. His eyes welling with tears, he left to go for a walk on the beach with his friend. "When violence sets in," his friend had said, "married life is no longer possible, everything quickly boils down to makeshift repairs and lying to oneself. At that point, divorce is the only option." It was the first time he'd heard anyone use the word "divorce" in reference to them.

Whenever his wife left on a trip and he found himself alone with his children, their house in Casablanca would suddenly become calm and life would unfold without any drama. Even his children's behavior grew less petulant. The painter would observe his house and say to himself: even the walls look more relaxed. An unusual sense of calm would reign over the house, which he would have liked to prolong beyond those absences. But how would he manage to do it? When they lived in Paris and he would go to work in his studio, he would wind up spending the night there because he sensed that a storm would be waiting for him on his return home. Thus he would postpone it for a night, hoping this would lessen the tide of recriminations. His wife suspected that he wasn't alone during those nights, and she would barge into the studio in the middle of the night and then leave without a word. She started referring to his place of work as a "so-called studio," or even bluntly as a "brothel."

Admittedly, the painter had often entertained female friends in his studio, usually in the afternoon, which he preferred. He worked in the morning, and after lunch he always liked to take a nap. One of his friends in particular knew better than anyone the meaning he attached to that word. She was a young married woman who was a professor of applied mathematics. She loved those moments when she would visit the artist, whose work she knew and liked before they met. She would bring him presents, often parcels of tea with subtle fragrances; she loved him, while also loving her husband, with whom she'd come to an arrangement that allowed her freedom without the need to resort to lying or trickery. At no point did the painter feel guilty. He was doing nothing wrong, he was simply looking for some equilibrium outside of his marriage, which only functioned intermittently, depending on events that transpired in the family or trips abroad. He spent hours talking to the prof—which was what he called her—and he sometimes even confided in her. Sometimes they also made love, but this wasn't the most important component of their relationship. After a couple of years, they'd managed to achieve a sense of peace, which they'd both needed, him in particular. There was friendship, tenderness, and especially sensuality. They drank tea and talked about the exhibitions that were currently showing. She knew him intimately and was able to anticipate his desires. She loved to read and would tell him which eighteenth-century writers really blew her away. That bright-eyed prof had brown hair and skin that was stunningly white. Whenever she undressed, he would ask her to walk around the studio so he could better admire her body and demeanor. She would beg him to remain dressed, then she would kneel before him and slide his pants down using only her teeth. Then she would take his penis in her hands and stroke it for a long time, kissing it and not letting it go until she'd swallowed his seed, which spilled against the roof of her mouth, and sent shivers all the way down his spine.

Despite his wife's suspicions, the painter told himself that he'd been right to suddenly decide to flee Paris and its grayness to settle in Casablanca. The city's light had left its mark on him and its effects could be detected in his new style of painting. The place where they lived was quite something. Built by a gay English couple in the 1920s, their house had a beautiful garden that looked out onto the old port and the sea beyond. Yet that splendid house grew somber every time another conflict erupted between him and his wife.

The painter had always had a hunch—or strange intuition—that he would one day fall victim to some sort of seizure or attack, or something like that. He had consulted a cardiologist friend who'd told him what he should try to avoid: stress, first and foremost, as well as arguments, constant outbursts of anger, and explosive reactions. "Be smart," he'd told him, "act indifferent, don't let her overwhelm you or manipulate you. We're the same age, my friend, so I know what I'm talking about, take a trip, spend some time away, if you feel tensions are rising in the house, then go to your studio, we need you to stick around because you're our friend, but also because you're an artist, you're widely respected and famous, you're also very talented, and your work has been recognized all over the world, so don't let her get you down . . . Good, so your EKG came back fine, and so did the stress test, you've got uncontrolled hypertension, so you need to keep an eye on that, get some exercise, be stricter about your diet, and above all, take some time off!"

The painter knew all that. His friend had merely confirmed it. He looked after his hypertension and avoided eating fatty things. He stopped smoking, except the odd cigar now and again, and he went out for a daily walk. Ever since they'd gone back to live in Morocco and had escaped Paris and his bustling life there, he'd had more time to look after his health. Each morning he went walking along the seaside promenade in Ain Diab with a friend whom he'd nicknamed Google because he was so incredibly erudite that you only needed to ask him a question to launch him into a brilliant speech that would last for the entirety of their walk. He would exercise while his friend rambled on, and this would go on for a couple of hours. Afterwards, he would take a dip in the sea and head back to the villa, where he'd set up a studio.

In the spring, his Spanish art dealer came to see him and was particularly adamant that the painter be ready for the big exhibition that he'd been preparing for the beginning of next year. He'd also been visited by two art critics who'd been writing a book on his work. It wasn't the first book that had been dedicated to his work, but it was the most important one yet, and it was due to be published in three languages to coincide with the opening of the exhibition. It was going to be a big deal. The painter was modest, but deep down he was proud and so had been flattered by all the attention; yet he betrayed none of these emotions and felt a kind of energy brewing inside him, which would allow him to complete a series of paintings that he'd planned and done some preliminary sketches for. For this series, he had decided to paint the trees in his garden. Each canvas would be both similar and different to the others, but the precision of his lines and the balance he'd struck between the real and the imaginary were truly outstanding—almost perfect, in fact. They were large canvases with neutral backgrounds where the trees were isolated and yet had been reinvented in a singular manner. He hated the expression "still life" because art wasn't something rigid or fixed. His canvases depicted life itself and there was nothing "still" about them. He'd always been wary of labels and categories. He had nothing to do with realism, that was for sure! One of his writer friends had told him how difficult it had been to write about his work, because the right words he could use to describe it were both rare and vague. So he'd had to rule out all inappropriate expressions.

He went to Madrid for a few days to buy the equipment that he needed, and took the opportunity to go see a few friends. He met up with Lola, a woman he'd been in love with before he'd gotten married. She'd changed, she'd gotten married too and had had a couple of children. He observed her, sometimes unwittingly, and had noticed how often our memories betray us. He'd remembered her as an incredibly sensual young woman with an amazing body and yet the woman he now had before his eyes was a mother who'd let herself go. It was a sad evening. He kissed her goodnight and accompanied her home. It was better never to revisit old memories. When he got back to Casablanca, his driver cum assistant—who handled all the administrative duties, ran all the errands, settled all the bills, and spared him having to cope with any practical problems, which in Morocco tended to be both numerous and absurd—hadn't been there waiting for him. Which was strange. Tony—whose name was Tony, although it was in fact Abderrazak, but whose old Italian employer had nicknamed him Tony—had never missed a meeting, was never late, was always meticulous, punctual, and showed up early. The painter decided to call him: "I'm sorry, sir, but your wife took the car keys away from me and fired me. I wanted to call but I didn't know what time your flight was landing!" The painter called his wife and she told him: "Good riddance! That parasite was stealing money from my children and was taking us for a ride. You're so naïve, he fools you all the time and you swallow all his lies. Your Tony is gone! Let him steal somewhere else. You don't really need him, he was just leeching off us, and now he can go back to work for his Italian pedophile . . . In any case, it's kind of fishy that you're so fond of him. Fine, I won't say anything else, I fired him because I found out he was stealing—your Tony is a thief!"

While she was screaming those insanities, the painter had felt an irrepressible rage swelling inside him. He could no longer control himself and people kept starting at him while making their way to the check-in desks. He hurled the bag containing his laptop to the floor and started shouting, too. He walked in circles like a madman around the airport lobby and hung up on his wife while cursing and fulminating against her. He was a wreck, and his saliva had started to taste bitter and unusual. It was a sign that something bad was about to happen. He looked for a glass of water. While drinking it, he swallowed the wrong way and started coughing, went all red in the face, put the glass down and then placed his hand on his chest. Someone had picked up his bag and brought it to him. As he'd been about to thank this person, he began to feel a stabbing pain in his chest. He started feeling really bad and his legs began to tremble, so he sat down. He was shivering, broke out in a sweat, and experienced a headache that was stronger than usual. Some airport employees who knew him rushed to his aid and used the loudspeakers to ask if there were any doctors among the travelers. A Swedish man came over right away and said: "He must be taken to the hospital right now!" They kept him under observation for twenty-four hours and then a taxi took him home the next day.

It had only been a warning. The children were at school and his wife had gone out, or maybe she'd left altogether. The painter felt greatly relieved since what could they possibly say to one another after what had happened at the airport? Not saying anything would be a way of expressing consent. So it very much suited him that she wasn't there. It would mean one less fight. She hadn't even been worried when he hadn't come home after their argument on the phone. She must have thought he would get on another flight or get himself a hotel room with one of his mistresses. Tony, on the other hand, had come to see him and begged him not to blame his wife, saying that he would continue to work for him anyway. It pained Tony to see his friend and employer in such a sorry state.

X

Casablanca

1995

Cruelty between a man and a woman is essential.
—Matsuko, the killer's wife
NAGISA OSHIMA, *Violence at Noon*

The painter was surprised to see that his wife had changed her habits since they'd moved to Casablanca. She was often out of the house, and would only come back in the middle of the night. She drank quite heavily and always said that she'd been "out with the girls!" She spent time with a group of embittered, divorced women who'd embraced feminism late in life, who met at the house of a witch whose ugliness betrayed her dark soul. She was short, chubby, had a mane of hair that made her look like a lioness, sharp beady eyes, and a narrow forehead that, according to a physiognomist, was a bad omen. She called herself Lalla, claiming that her mother had been one of Hassan II's concubines. All Moroccan princesses used the honorific of "Lalla" before their names. She talked a lot of nonsense, claimed that she'd once been a hippie who'd slept with celebrities, musicians, singers, and even a famous actor, whose photo she carried with her, saying it had been taken outside a villa in Los Angeles even though the décor clearly indicated it had been taken in the Casbah of Za-gora. She said she'd spent some time in India under the tutelage of a guru who'd opened her eyes to the mysteries of the soul; thanks to him, she'd discovered the source of all energies, both positive and negative. She would claim that the waves of energy we send out are slow to reach their destination, adding that she'd only just received those emitted by her mother who'd been buried ten years earlier. In a nutshell, she played the part of a mystic with complicated words whose exact meaning eluded her, but which she voiced confidently enough to influence minds that were ready to follow her, people who would obey her deliriums and submit to her manipulations. She ba-sically rehashed old feminist discourses from the 1960s and spliced them with her own unique brand of Eastern-mystical-mythological hocus-pocus, serving it up with a great deal of mass-market, Made in China incense fumes that she purchased in the drugstores of the El Maârif neighborhood in Casablanca. She would pretend that her Indian guru had sent her herbs that he'd picked from his own garden and that he'd laid to dry in his meditation room. She would feed them names of people she'd picked out from the pirated DVDs of Bollywood films that were sold close to the Joutia vegetable market on Derb Ghallef.

Lalla had a sense of theatrics and a knack for showmanship. Ev-erything about her was an illusion or a trick, but she still pulled it off, despite the obvious stupidity and absurdity of the things she said. The bigger the lie, the less her entourage of groupies suspected her of deceiving them. In her, those women had finally found a soul mate who understood them and who knew how to find the right words to speak to them and show them the way. Lalla had married a cousin of hers who'd inherited a great deal of money. Her cousin was gay and their marriage had been a means for him to keep up appearances, and he'd paid dearly for that. After a year of so-called married life, she'd separated from him after having extracted a few million dirhams from him, as well as the villa where they'd lived. Without any money worries, she'd had enough time and funds to surround herself with a retinue in order to make herself feel important. She claimed that she translated books for American publishing houses, but she'd never been able to show anyone so much as a single book that bore her name on the cover. Her father, who'd remarried after the death of his first wife, lived far away from her and hardly ever saw her. Lalla had tried to lure her stepmother into her circle, but the latter had quickly seen through her bluff and told her a few home truths. A few days later, Lalla had brought her father some compromising photos of his new wife that she'd digitally altered on her computer. She'd wanted to damage her stepmother's standing, but the latter had proved stronger and smarter, and she'd disproved the hoax. After Lalla's pathetic plot had failed, she'd been ostracized by her family and forbidden to set foot in her father's house. Nevertheless, Lalla had told her "girls" that her father had been bewitched by a sorceress who was robbing him blind of all his property and from whom she hoped she could one day save him. The painter's wife had taken that surreal story seriously. She claimed that the stepmother hailed from a family in Agadir and was descended from a long line of Southern sorceresses. Whenever her husband had expressed some doubts, she had flown into a rage and screamed because he'd dared to question Lalla's words.

For a while, the painter had suspected that his wife's relationship with Lalla could be a cover for a lesbian affair. He knew, of course, that his wife hated homosexuality, and that she couldn't stand women who got too close to her in order to seduce her. However, she was so enthralled by Lalla that he couldn't help but wonder. She would sometimes spend the whole day with her. She must have had some feelings for her because she swore only by her and repeated what she'd said word for word, reeling off her speeches forcefully and determinedly, emphasizing each sentence as though she were holding forth in court. The painter had tried to reason with his wife, tried to show her that Lalla was a bored, overexcited woman who needed to surround herself with an entourage to make herself feel alive, but it had all been in vain. His wife defended Lalla and wouldn't tolerate the slightest criticism. It was normal for a husband to be jealous of a woman who took up all of his wife's time, sometimes even twelve hours a day. He'd believed she would be receptive to this line of argument since she could interpret it as proof of his love. Perhaps she wouldn't break off her ties to Lalla, but it would at least induce her to have a greater awareness of that manipulator's emotional and mental state.

But no. Instead, she told him: "Finally someone opened my eyes. Lalla is the worthiest, noblest, and most honest woman in this city. She's a talented artist. It's thanks to her that I finally realized that I sacrificed my own life; from now on, I refuse to let anything upset me, I won't put up with any more humiliations from your family, or the tricks your brother and his good wife are fond of pulling, or the schemes of your sisters, who only come to see us so they can wheedle money out of us. I'm a free woman, I can do what I want. I'm going to fulfill myself. I'm going to find a way to live that doesn't involve being under the heel of a perverse, selfish monster, a coward, a husband who still acts like he's a bachelor, a hypocrite who doesn't realize he's brought children into this world. Yes, thanks to Lalla, my eyes have been opened and I'm finally going to start living my own life, and as for you, you can go fuck yourself, you and your floozies who dance around you and your filthy money . . . I sent your sister packing the other day, telling her you were traveling in Asia. She believed me and went home. She was very disappointed. I told her that it wasn't worth her while to travel all the way from Marrakech because you've gone bankrupt and we don't have any money. I think she even started to cry!"

She'd made her case, and now it was up to him to draw his conclusions. Some of his friends volunteered to talk to the painter's wife, especially since they knew of the witch's reputation. But his wife had the ability to make people believe that she hadn't only listened closely to them, but also agreed with them. So his friends had come away pleased with how their interventions had gone and had left feeling appeased. That's because they didn't know her well. His wife's defense mechanism was simple and yet astonishingly effective. She always did as she pleased and was happily oblivious to what people thought of her.

One of the painter's friends suggested that he try to seduce Lalla in order to drive a wedge between them. But the painter didn't have the nerve to take part in such a farce. He wasn't an actor. He left that kind of thing to his enemies and rivals.

Lalla's relationship with the painter's wife continued to be close, much to the despair of their children, who were beginning to realize how suspect that friendship really was. They'd complained to their father about it, who de-dramatized the whole affair so as not to worry them. One day, Lalla had had the audacity to meddle when they'd been planning their summer holidays with their mother. They had resented Lalla's intrusion and had asked their mother to stop seeing her. But their mother was by then completely under the woman's thrall, utterly bewitched, and had developed a debilitating dependence on her best friend.

Lalla had written some texts on "primal energy" and hadn't been able to publish them. She'd had them bound and handed them out to people who deserved her trust. She said that her thoughts were so personal that she didn't wish to share them with the wider public. She'd produced some rough drawings to accompany her texts, and the fruit of her efforts had been so ridiculous that it hadn't been worth all the fuss she'd made over them. This was how her tiny sect of acolytes financed her lifestyle. And nobody thought there was anything wrong with that.

One day, the painter had had the opportunity to watch a film that told the story of a young beautiful teacher who had started to teach at a college. The teacher was married and had two children, one of whom had Down syndrome. The teacher eventually made the acquaintance of an older professor who taught at the college, a middle-aged woman who lived alone with her cat. They quickly forged a friendship and they gradually became inseparable. The older teacher became a mentor to the younger one and guided her steps not only professionally, but emotionally too. One evening, the younger teacher succumbed to the amorous advances of one of her pupils, a handsome teenager. The older teacher surprised them in the act and started to blackmail her mentee, who didn't actually share the older teacher's feelings for her. The older teacher believed that her mentee was under her thumb, but an incident involving her cat and the child with Down syndrome finally put an end to their ambiguous friendship. Feeling betrayed and abandoned, the older teacher started a rumor that the younger teacher was a pedophile and that she was having sex with one of her pupils. A scandal broke out and the young teacher was sent to prison, but this turn of events eventually freed her from that perverse woman's clutches.

The painter couldn't stop thinking about Lalla's relationship with his wife. He purchased the DVD of the film and asked her to watch it. Which she did, but in the end she told him: "I don't understand why you wanted me to watch that film!" She clearly hadn't noticed how similar the two scenarios were, and didn't seem the slightest bit concerned. The painter smiled and decided he would abandon all hopes of ever freeing her from that evil woman's influence. Someone had told him: "You'll see, she'll get tired of it one day and leave her, you must be patient and give it a little time!"

Other problems came up and his wife's relationship with that witch took a back seat to those. He'd understood that what mattered the most was that he save his own skin, and that he leave that relationship, where he no longer had a place or any standing.

XI

Casablanca

April 2000

Dreams, life it's the same thing. Otherwise life isn't worth living!

—MARCEL CARNÉ, *Children of Paradise*

Imane wasn't just a nurse, she was also a physiotherapist. She would massage his listless legs and arms, doing so both tenderly and energetically. The painter loved those moments and could assess the progress he was making, however tiny those improvements might have been. She was even a bit naughty, and would flirt with him using her eyes, smiles, and charm. He'd grown attached to her and had been very pleased to hear her tell him her story one day, just like she'd promised.

One morning, during the time Imane would come for her first visit of the day, the painter had seen a man and a woman wearing white coats come into the house. Their faces were lined, stern, and forbidding. The woman had told him: "I'm your new nurse, and my brother is your new physiotherapist. Your wife sent us!" He'd protested by banging his cane against the floor, but the words hadn't managed to leave his mouth. It was the first time that his wife, with whom he hadn't spoken since his accident, had intervened in his life without taking his condition into account. He'd sent them away, and had told the Twins to pay them and tell them to never come back. He'd also wanted them to call Imane and inform her of what had happened, but he'd been so shocked by his wife's unexpected meddling that he hadn't had the courage to do so, and was waiting for the storm caused by that unpleasant visit to subside.

Imane's return, which he'd managed to bring about thanks to the loyal Twins, had both pleased and worried him. He wanted to celebrate it, there was a joy within him, which he could not show due to his deformed features. But his eyes betrayed him. Imane had told him how two days earlier she'd been visited by his wife, who'd spoken to her in a forceful and threatening manner. Imane hadn't wanted to get into a fight with her patient's wife and so had preferred to give him up. She'd even hoped to write him a letter expressing her sympathy and say how sorry she was. "From here on out," he'd told her, "you'll answer only to me! If my wife ever speaks to you, just tell her that I'm the one who hired you and I'm the one who decides."

Delighted, Imane had gotten back to work, humming and murmuring words that had a soothing effect on him. Which was exactly what he needed since the last bout of irritation still plagued him. What had happened to make his wife suddenly go back on the warpath? Must he steady himself against future onslaughts? He was worried. Imane decided to stay a little longer and offered the painter a cup of tea. The Twins were playing cards and turned their back to him in order to not embarrass him. It was a tea from Thailand called "the poet's tea," which had a smoky, subtle taste. Imane raised the cup to his lips and enabled him to drink it, sip by sip. She was sitting in front of him, and on seeing him happy, asked him if he still wanted to hear her story. He responded with his eyes, but stopped smiling the moment he remembered how hideous a grimace he pulled whenever he tried to do so. From time to time, Imane would get up and go to the window in order to see if the painter's wife was nearby. He understood her apprehension and reluctantly dismissed her, hoping to see her the following day. Unfortunately, Imane would have to spend the next day accompanying her grandmother to the hammam, which she insisted on still going to despite her age and frailness. Before leaving, she'd leaned over him and touched his cheek. She'd laughed and said: "It stings!" It had been two days since the Twins had shaved him.

XII

Casablanca

1998

Their marriage had become a living hell. Their home was their battle-
field, their friends were caught in the crossfire, and their families had
become arbiters, although they were hardly impartial. Nevertheless,
the painter hadn't given up hope of finding a means to bring the conflict to an end. He would spend countless hours reflecting on what
was happening to them.

So it was that one day he thought he'd stumbled onto the reason
why their marriage had fallen apart so strangely. His wife had become
two different people. Two people, two characters, two moods, two
faces coexisted inside a single body. Even her voice had changed. He

knew that every person on Earth seemed to suffer from a split personality, but the extent to which his wife did so was quite troubling. Sometimes he didn't even recognize her. He would ask her: "Who are you? A stranger? Are you the mother of my children, or have you been possessed by someone else?" She never answered him. Over the course of his life, the painter had met people who were called "temperamental," but this was something else. It seemed like a pathological condition! She would suddenly change from one state to the other, without any warning and without even noticing it. Whenever he heard her call out to him in a clear voice and say: "I have a surprise for you!" he knew the next fifteen minutes would be tough. It was her way of announcing that she wanted an explanation for something or that he was to fall victim to a well-organized attack.

Once, he'd returned home to find that the contents of his toiletry bag had been spilled onto the floor. He found his wife sitting on top of the stairs smoking a cigarette, waiting for him. At the time, he'd been using condoms whenever he made love to her. Calmly, she'd said: "Before you left for Copenhagen there were eleven, and now there are nine. So you cheated on me twice, you bastard, and you're going to pay for it. I already called the hotel, her name's Barbara, some bitch who works at the Klimt Gallery!"

Convinced that she was being persecuted—and that the painter's family was out to get her, that her husband's friends were dishonest profiteers, that the neighbors were jealous, that the people who worked in her house were trying to steal from her—she suspected everyone. She'd built a foundation of unshakeable certainties. There could be no discussions of any kind. He'd noticed that before she'd started to attack his family, she'd also tried to distance him from his friends, especially the ones he was closest to. She never lacked pretexts, and had ample opportunity to see them, so he'd always had to brace himself against her attacks.

The painter's childhood friend had been an easy target for her. He had a bad temper and he was just as unyielding and full of hang-ups as she was. She would provoke him and he would reply in a scathing manner. So it eventually came to a head, and the painter was ordered to cut his ties with the "dwarf" who'd dared to criticize her. That friend had a penchant for humor, but he never took things lightly. The painter had held steady until the day his friend had sent him a letter informing him their friendship was over. His wife had won.

Her next target had been another of her husband's friends, a wise philosopher. She'd eventually had a falling out with the man's wife, though she never managed to drive a wedge between the painter and his friend.

She'd done much the same to others, including a friend of his who owned a gallery and had been one of the first to exhibit his works. The painter had thought of this friend as a sister, as part of his family. She'd become close to his mother and they'd helped one another out on occasion. His wife had immediately accused this friend of being—or having been—the painter's mistress, which had made the friend laugh: there had never been anything between them, apart from a platonic friendship.

The painter had never meddled in his wife's affairs, a golden rule that he'd broken on only two occasions because he'd thought she was actually in danger. The first was when he'd discovered that she'd been seeing a Syrian "student." He'd tried to get her to understand that while he might indeed have been a "student," he was likely an agent for the security services. He'd explained to his wife that Syria was ruled by a fearsome police state and that he'd recently signed a petition for the release of political prisoners being held in Damascus. It would be very risky, he'd stressed, for either of them to be in close contact with this man. She'd refused to believe him and had continued going for "coffees" with the Syrian. The other occasion had arisen when a few friends of his in Casablanca had told him: "Your wife is keeping strange company these days. Do you know that she's spending time with a woman named Loulou, who has ties to black-marketeers and shady guys who pimp girls out to visiting Saudis? Your wife obviously doesn't have anything to do with that, but she doesn't understand the situation, or realize how much harm this could bring upon the two of you. She needs to break off all ties with this woman!"

He'd asked his wife to follow the advice they'd been given to the letter. She still had time to extricate herself. But she had taken all of this very badly and had shouted that he was just like every other Moroccan man: sexist and full of prejudices, letting himself be easily swayed by rumors. She was incapable of believing her husband, or confiding in him, or asking him any questions. She had no doubts. Never had any doubts. Never admitted her mistakes. He'd known that for a long time and now this was something all the people around them were starting to learn, too. Despite her husband's repeated warnings, she'd continued to see Loulou, right up to the day when the latter had made an indecent proposition that had shocked her, at which point she'd finally stopped seeing her.

For a long time, the painter had never asked himself whether his wife was being faithful to him. He'd never suspected her of having lovers, even though he traveled so often for work that she had ample opportunity to cheat on him. Still, he'd never kept tabs on her, didn't rifle through her belongings, didn't read her letters or look in her diary. She was a free woman and wasn't accountable to him. Yet he'd started to have doubts after she'd gone on holiday with a friend in Tunisia. She'd come back with an obsession: to know, read, and watch everything she could about—or by—Stanley Kubrick. He remembered that she hadn't much liked *2001: A Space Odyssey*, so where had this sudden passion sprung from? As it happens, she'd met a certain Hassan, who'd been writing a thesis on Kubrick and had shown her some of his films. Her sudden interest in the filmmaker had merely been a means to pay him homage. Hassan had given her a big book on Kubrick's films as a present. For the next two weeks, she did nothing except talk about *Barry Lyndon, Paths of Glory, The Killing,* or *Dr. Strangelove.*

She'd betrayed herself.

When he'd tried to bring it up with her, she'd dodged his questions and argued that his upbringing forbade him from having lovers. One day, he'd found some condoms on the bathroom floor that had fallen out of her toiletry bag.

"What are you doing with those?" he'd asked.

"Ah, those are free samples given out by an anti-AIDS campaign."

He hadn't believed a word, but he'd kept quiet and thought to himself: "If I open these floodgates then we'll have to spill all our secrets, and there'll be hell to pay!"

XIII

Casablanca

November 15, 1999

When I'm with you, nothing frightens me, not even the war,
although perhaps the police still do.
>   —Veronika to Boris, before he leaves for the war
>   MIKHAIL KALATOZOV, *The Cranes Are Flying*

One of the painter's close friends was a Greek named Yiannis. The
painter confided in Yiannis, who was also helping him learn Greek.
At some point in the future, the painter wanted to go live on the
small island of Tinos. Yiannis had a great sense of humor, with a special fondness for black humor, and he shot films about contemporary artists and occasionally wrote pieces for some of his country's
newspapers. He was also a Casanova, a ladies' man, even though he
had the physique of neither a Greek god nor an American basket-
ball player. He more closely resembled Professor Cuthbert Calculus,
and observed the things that happened to him with an ironic remove.

They always met in the same restaurant along with Father François, another friend of theirs, who wasn't a priest, but a poet and a great writer who preferred to keep a low profile. It was Yiannis who loved to call the good-humored, radical atheist "Father."

Like Yiannis, François had taken part in the delegation that had gone to the suburb of Clermont-Ferrand to ask for the hand of the painter's future wife. It was a trip that had been very memorable for the painter's friends, since it had been the first time they'd set foot in such exotic, desolate lands. It was where they'd discovered the evils of those banlieues, where immigrants and their children had been abandoned and stigmatized as dangerous troublemakers.

Yiannis and François had been worrying about their friend for some time now. They'd seen how frustrated and exhausted he'd become after all those arguments, clashes, and tantrums, which were growing more and more frequent. The painter had confided in them, and the two of them—independent and freethinking—were helping him free himself from a marriage that was doomed to go nowhere. And they were afraid for him, because they knew his blood pressure was out of control.

One day, Yiannis had accompanied the painter to a department store where he'd purchased a small voice recorder. Yiannis hadn't understood why he would need it for work. Perhaps in order to dictate his correspondence? But he knew that his friend never wrote letters.

"My wife contradicts herself all the time, doesn't know whether she said this or that, so I've decided to secretly record what she says so I can play it back to her."

"But what good will that do?"

"In the hopes that she will one day admit to at least one of her mistakes, so I'll then have the pleasure to record that admission and play it back to myself, so I can hear her say 'I'm sorry, I got confused,' or 'I was wrong,' or even 'You were right,' or better still 'I'm sorry, I shouldn't have,' to which I'll add 'Thank you, darling,' something which she's never said to me . . ."

"I didn't know things were going so badly between the two of you. I must confess that I find all of this quite shocking. You know, I ended up getting divorced for a lot less than that . . . I don't even have much to reproach my ex-wife for . . . in fact, I was the one who talked a lot of nonsense . . ."

The painter never had the chance to use his tape recorder. On the only occasion that his wife had admitted she'd made a mistake, he hadn't had the tape recorder close to hand. He hadn't even cared about recording her confession. He'd still been reeling from what had happened the previous day: she was driving too fast because she'd been tired and had almost had a bad accident with the whole family in the car. A truck had come at full speed toward them, and her reflexes had barely reacted in time. It had been an incredibly close call. The children had screamed, and the painter had frozen in his seat, incapable of mouthing a word. That terrible moment had been followed by a deep silence. Once they'd gotten back to the house they hadn't even looked at each other, or exchanged a single word.

Ever since that day, he'd decided he would never again get into a car with her. He didn't want that kind of life anymore. But he'd come to this conclusion so many times before that it hardly mattered. He needed to act, to react, and, if possible, to escape. What he was sure about was that a mountain of difficulties awaited him before he even got to that decision. That was the time when he'd gone back to the psychiatrist in order to strengthen his immune system, as though he suffered from a disease that gnawed away at his muscles, his mind, and his life.

The psychiatrist had told him:

"You can only hope that your wife decides to get some therapy, but as you know, only she can decide. Nobody—not her friends, and certainly not you—can show her the way forward."

The painter had smiled, and he'd told the psychiatrist that his wife's cultural background didn't predispose her to take such a step. At best, she would seek out charlatans who would recommend some cockamamie ritual, like burning incense during a full moon, or some herbs to put in a corner of their bedroom, or magical formulas written on a piece of paper that she could dilute in water drawn from the wells of Mecca, or talismans to hang off one of the branches of a hundred-year-old tree, or bury next to its roots, or another talisman to throw into the sea on a day when the waves were rough . . .

This kind of magic was common among illiterate people deeply attached to their ancestral traditions in the mountainous regions of Southern Morocco, and it bolstered their irrationality. It was one of the reasons why his wife had become a member of the sect that followed her infamous friend Lalla, who'd continued her efforts to poison his wife's relationship with her husband, but especially his family, and who encouraged her to go see those very charlatans, whether they were near or far.

One day, his wife had drunk an herbal infusion that Lalla had given her. The effect had been immediate. They'd been eating lunch with the children when she'd suddenly gone blank, as though she were on the verge of passing out. She'd gotten up, stumbled, and collapsed onto the bed, where she'd fallen into a deep sleep. With his children thrown into distress, the painter had called for a doctor, who'd run over and examined her, coming to the conclusion that her reaction indicated that she'd taken a strong dose of soporifics. The painter had confiscated the herbs in question and had grown angry.

"We don't know anything about these herbs. Who can say they're not poisoned? I'm going to wake her up and give her an enema."

He'd shaken her, and though she could barely open her eyes, she got up and said it was nothing. Then she'd had the good sense to vomit; it made her feel better, but she refused to admit she'd done anything wrong.

Later, when he'd been discussing the incident with a friend, the painter had told him about his grave concerns:

"How can I leave my children with someone who is so irrational and irresponsible?"

This question had a double meaning. On the one hand, he was right to worry, but on the other, it was simply an excuse not to bring this ordeal of a marriage to an end.

When the painter saw his wife in social settings—being friendly, looking beautiful, loved by all, praised by other men for her charm and beauty—and when he heard her speak in a suave voice, when he looked at her without her knowing it, the painter felt torn between admiration and anger. He admired her for being so sweet to others, and yet resented her for being so bitter when it came to their relationship. He'd once believed that she had a split personality disorder, but he'd realized he'd just been deceiving himself. His wife didn't have two personalities; she merely reserved the best of herself for others, while keeping the worst in store for her husband. She was making him pay for all those years when she'd suffered under his family's contemptuous gaze, something she'd also experienced with some of his friends. One day, he'd overheard a friend's wife tell her husband:

"She's pretty and young, but our friend deserves far better: a real, beautiful woman befitting his stature and status."

Needless to say, this was hard to hear; the friend and his wife were no longer welcome at their home.

One day, when he'd seen her looking very concerned about the well-being of her little brother, who'd been visiting them at the time, he'd noticed how attentive she'd been with him, giving him a glass of water with some vitamin C because he'd coughed the night before, then ironing his shirt, which she'd washed the day before, asking about his work, slipping some money into his pocket. After her brother had left, the painter had said to her:

"Why don't you treat me like I was your brother? Make an effort, look at me, I'm not a monster like you think I am, no, I'm just different from other people, I'm an artist, and I need support and understanding, I don't need you to admire me, that would be too much to ask, and besides, there are some things that one cannot ask for. Just be a little more attentive toward your old husband. He's not nasty, he's actually a good man. I too could have a cough or even angina, but you wouldn't offer me a glass of water with some vitamin C in it, it's not a big deal, but it's the little things that would make me happy. In fact, that's the weak point of our marriage: the lack of happiness! Making the other person happy and vice versa. Unfortunately, both of us have crossed a lot of lines. We don't respect each other anymore. I'm sorry about that, and I'm just as guilty as you are. I don't think I've ever been disrespectful toward anyone. I've been awkward, fickle, not as attentive as I should have been, but I've never tried to be disrespectful toward you. But sometimes your anger and the brutality of your actions have pushed me to use words I didn't even know I could use, words that have never been a part of my vocabulary. You've managed to bring out the worst in me, and I've done the same to you. I'm not accusing anybody. I've always tried to avoid conflicts, but now conflicts have rooted themselves in our marriage and replaced love and passion. One day I'll leave, and on that day I won't look back, because when I leave it'll mean that you've brought me to the brink of a precipice, and if I stay, you'll end up pushing me over. Finally, I know that on that day, you realize that you've been living with a stranger, an alien, someone that you didn't share anything with, a marriage that nothing good came out of, except for our children. We've deceived ourselves. It's neither your fault nor mine. Maybe I have a bigger share of the blame. I should have distrusted my instincts more, but it's true what they say, love blinds all men! We cannot change our destiny, and we let our illusions fool us. But yes, things will be all right in the end, you'll grow and become more mature. We're very different from each other, especially when it comes to our backgrounds. We come from two planets that couldn't be further apart. I knew that to start with, but I gambled on the chance that our love could overcome that. But deep down, we're still strangers to one another. I suffer through this estrangement with regret, while you're just tilting against windmills. By the time you realize this, it'll be too late, and you'll have destroyed everything."

That day finally arrived in the middle of November of 1999. He'd been in the middle of work when she'd burst in like a Fury and thrown his laptop in his face. The laptop had broken into two, and she had then thrown a heavy bronze paperweight at him, which had struck his left shoulder. She was hurling abuse at him in three languages— Berber, French, and Arabic—unleashing a torrent of insults:

"You're going to pay, you're going to pay, I'm going to destroy you, I'm going to ruin you, I'll burn all your shitty paintings and throw them in the trash, you're nothing but a monster, a pervert, a miserable husband, a shit father, and a cheat, you're just like your father, a loser, a two-faced bastard!"

At which point he felt truly shocked—both physically and psychologically—and was overcome by a sudden fever. His blood grew hot and began circulating rapidly, his face moved as though his skin were being stretched, the brush fell from his hand, and his arm became stiff, everything went blurry, then he'd fallen on the floor, hitting his head on a space heater, scraping his skin, which started to bleed. Worse: his eyes had rolled back in his head and he couldn't move his legs or his arms.

She panicked and called the emergency services. He was taken to the nearest hospital. He'd had a stroke. That was the diagnosis. A cerebrovascular accident. Hemiplegia in his left side, with complications on his right side too. They would have to wait before confirming the extent of the damage.

The doctor had spoken very quickly. He was very moved. He

knew the painter by reputation and had thoughtfully asked the secretary in the department not to inform the press.

His wife had asked for another bed in the room so she could sleep next to him. The doctor had told her: "It's better if he sleeps alone, just as a precaution, we'll be here, don't worry, we'll call you as soon as he wakes up."

Luckily, he couldn't remember anything about that day. It was as if it had never happened.

On the other hand, he had stared death right in the face. It had felt like being wrapped in a bluish-white vapor. He hadn't been able to think, but saw a quick, chaotic montage of images flash past his eyes. He hadn't been able to grip anything, his body had become a heavy object he was unable to command. His face wasn't his anymore. It had been replaced by a bad sketch. He asked himself if that coarse substitute was going to stick around for a long time. Only his mind was still active. He'd heard words, or rather noises made inexplicable by the vapor around him, which was growing denser and denser, and had now become a bluish-black. He opened his eyes, saw only blips, and then shut them again. He must have thought that death would recede a little if only he could open his eyes, that it would pass him by and leave him a little more time, give him a respite. Oddly, he started thinking about his latest painting, and in the midst of that very real nightmare, had told himself: "I won't be like Nicolas de Staël, I'm going to finish that painting, I'll see it through to the end. I won't throw myself out of the window and splatter into a thousand pieces on the pavement below!" See it through to the end of what? Of the madness that haunted him and that helped him to work.

But for the moment, his fate was in the doctors' hands, and they were trying to revive him.

XIV

Casablanca

August 27, 2000

Don't try to soften me with your troubles. Down here,
everyone has to cope on their own. I don't have any pity for
the sufferings of the soul.

> —Isak Borg's reply to his daughter-in-law
> INGMAR BERGMAN, *Wild Strawberries*

On that day, he received Imane in his studio. He still couldn't paint,
but he could look at the numerous paintings his illness had prevented
him from finishing, which he'd had laid out on the floor. Some people had been ecstatic to see those so-called unfinished canvases, while
others didn't pay them any attention. The painter told himself: "If I
ever decided to leave this world before my time is up, I'd make sure I
left my studio in order and then I'd give my children very specific instructions, even if I wasn't sure that they'd follow them, but you never
know. Then I'd go to see a lawyer to ensure that my daughters received

an equal share of their inheritance, just like the boys. I disagree with the kind of discrimination that women are subjected to, whereby they only receive half a share, while men are entitled to a full one. It makes me sad that theologians haven't yet changed Sharia law, which might have made sense in the Prophet's time, when women didn't work, but which has now become outdated. There we have it, I would put all my affairs in order before I left!" The prospect delighted him, as though the idea of suicide was no longer strange to him. The very act of putting his estate in order and imagining people's varying reactions amused him. He wanted to write, but his fingers found it difficult to grip a pen. He thought about recording his last testament in front of a video camera, the idea reminded him of a film starring Andy Garcia, who played an ex-gangster who retired in Denver and set up a company that recorded dying people's messages for their loved ones. Some would talk about their lives, others would give advice or impart some simple truths. In particular, he remembered a very pretty girl who was courting Garcia. "Are you in love?" he'd asked her. The question had been surprising. It was a lesson in seduction that the painter had retained in his memory.

He'd wanted to talk to Imane, but he still found it difficult to speak. So he decided to listen to her while she massaged his limbs. She was wearing a white blouse, where the gaps between the buttons revealed parts of her body. It was very warm on that day and so she'd wanted to be comfortable. Her patient was a courteous and respectful man. She had nothing to fear from him. Rubbing his right arm in order to revitalize its suppleness, she'd given him some slight caresses that had pleased him and made her smile. But her smile always had an unpleasant shape to it, which greatly upset him. He whispered: "Thank you. Excuse me, please tell me your story!" It took him some time to ensure she'd understood him. She'd taken a step back and replied: "I'll have some time today after work. First allow me to take care of your arms and legs, which is very important since I really want to see you back in shape and in perfect health. You know, I'm very fond of you. I don't know much about painting, but your colors and shapes speak to me. I'm not sure what they're telling me, but I'm glad they speak to me. You reproduce objects better than any photographer, because you can tell that your paintings are the result of a lot of work, which must have taken you a great deal of time. A photographer on the other hand is happy to just press a button . . . Good, now let's move on to the right leg, put some effort into it, that's right, you can move it, good, you're working with me!"

When she knelt to massage his feet, he could see her bosom. He didn't know whether she'd noticed him looking, but he loved to watch her without her knowledge. He'd always had a weak spot for breasts.

After she'd finished, she suggested boiling some water to prepare the tea, and then she sat next to him and told him a story, as though she were Scheherazade in *One Thousand and One Nights*.

Once upon a time there was a young girl who couldn't stop dreaming. All she knew about life was what she dreamed at night. At school she would see imaginary characters amongst the crowds, and she could see them clearly while still following her lessons in class. She had the strange ability to live in two different worlds: the real and the imaginary. But she could switch back and forth between the two with the greatest of ease. She didn't dream like the other girls of her age did.

She dreamed of climbing a pyramid on the shoulders of an Egyptian king whom she healed with her smiles and caresses.

She dreamed of conducting a symphony orchestra in a great hall filled with family and friends. Each musician would have a star shining above their head, a favor bestowed by the angels on each member of the orchestra.

She dreamed of making a solo crossing of the Atlantic Ocean but gave up on it because she didn't know how to swim.

She dreamed of being a female imam leading the prayers in a gigantic mosque and delivering a sermon that talked about the Prophet's love for women.

She dreamed of being a sparrow that would fly from branch to branch and provide answers to the shrub of questions.

She dreamed of being Scheherazade's sister and witnessing her wedding night with the prince. She would make herself smaller than usual, but wouldn't miss anything that happened.

She dreamed of running a hospital and waving a magic wand.

She dreamed of succulent Arabian dates and a bowl of goat milk.

She dreamed of not being in pain at the end of a long day of work.

She dreamed of long summer days spent under a tree surrounded by her imaginary friends while eating raisins and exotic fruits from distant countries.

She dreamed of being able to dream all the time.

But she would have to work harder for that to happen.

She interrupted her story because she'd noticed that the painter's facial features had almost regained their normal composure. He listened to her and drank her words. He told her to carry on by moving his eyes. She helped him swallow some sips of tea, wiped his lips, and then resumed her seat to continue her story.

Once upon a time there lived an angry man. This man had a kind, good-hearted nature that shameful people took advantage of.

He interrupted her by banging his hand against his chair. He formed the words he wanted to tell her in his mind: "I want to hear your story, not mine!" Imane was taken aback, and promised him she would tell him that story the next time she saw him.

But the next time she'd visited him, Imane had been in a hurry. Her grandmother had fallen and shattered her femoral neck. The painter had thought about his father, who'd passed away ten days after falling from his chair. This had happened in September. The painter had been working on a tribute for Giacometti when the phone had rung. One of his friends, a doctor, had told him: "At that age, it's a matter of days . . ." The painter had experienced an immense grief. That sudden death had sparked an intense anger that he'd suppressed despite shedding a great deal of tears. His wife's behavior had been impeccable. Although the painter's family had always underestimated her, he was stunned by how conscientiously she'd taken to her duties during the mourning period. Nobody had been able to crack any jokes or make innuendos about her lowly background anymore. He'd been happy that she'd managed to pull through such an ordeal so well.

Imane had barely had the time to give him his injections and a few massages, as well as to tell him that her real dream was for him to recover soon so that he could paint her portrait: "I'll tell you a lot of things when I'll pose for that portrait. You'll be surprised!" He'd agreed by nodding his head.

After Imane had left, the Twins had come to look for him so they could groom him. He'd muttered the word "hammam" and they'd looked at one another surprised, asking themselves if it would be an appropriate thing to do given his condition. One of them called the doctor, who told him it would be best to avoid the hottest rooms and the kind of forceful massages that were typical to popular hammams. The Twins hired out a room that was moderately warm and took the painter there in his wheelchair. He had been happy to reconnect with one of his childhood memories.

The Twins were efficient and highly capable. The painter was at his ease, and ready to be rid of a lot of dead skin. A man had come and he'd scrubbed the artist as though he were a root vegetable pulled out of the ground. Another came to give him a gentler massage. He felt good, especially after he got to his living room so he could rest. He dozed off and managed to sleep a little. He decided not to take any sleeping pills that evening. He was pretty relaxed and was able to sleep without a chemical boost. That night, everyone got mixed up in his dreams: his wife, Imane, his doctor, Ava, the professor of applied mathematics, the director of his gallery, and many others still who paraded before him for the entirety of the night. In the morning he'd woken up scared, thinking his dream had been premonitory, presaging all the farewell visits people made to those about to die.

Like all men who loved women, the painter thought about the succession of women who had loved him and whom he'd loved in his turn. He even imagined how he would one day assemble them under the roof of his house in order to tell them how much pleasure and happiness they'd brought into his life. He would thank them and kiss them for one last time. Then he suddenly asked himself: "Would my wife be there? Does she belong with those who gave me pleasure and happiness?" He didn't want to be unfair. Pleasure? Yes, she'd certainly done that. He greatly enjoyed making love to her, although they never spoke about it. That would never do. He was surprised that she'd never said anything about their sex life, except for a single occasion when she'd told him in anger: "You don't satisfy me either sexually or financially! You're impotent!"

It was curious and interesting that she'd linked money and sex in a single sentence. The painter had read Freud and he knew a lot about the subject. But to be called "impotent" had made him chuckle. Of course, he hadn't been able to tell his wife that the other women he'd been with had never had any complaints—quite the contrary, in fact. Still, from time to time that phrase would start ringing in his head like a crazy alarm clock. "Fine, maybe it's true. She isn't happy or satisfied, but I know it isn't true. That is, unless she was faking, and I can't do anything about that!"

After that incident, he'd asked himself the same old question: "Why have we never been able to speak to each other, to talk without arguing, to understand each other without wanting to smash everything around us—in short, to compromise and live together? Am I a monster and a pervert like she says I am? Am I so emotionally stunted to the point that she has to reproach me for never concerning myself with my family or what goes on in the house? I know that all of this isn't true, but thanks to her endless accusations I've wound up believing her, or at least have started to doubt myself. Perhaps that's what she was aiming for—to get me to doubt myself, to doubt my abilities, my actions, thus putting me in a corner from which I would be unable to escape, where I would be at her mercy, become her victim, so she would be free to do whatever she wanted, just like she'd been kept in purdah by an ayatollah!" Ayatollah, that was what she always called him. Did she even know what that word meant? It was an insult as far as he was concerned.

Defeat begins the moment that your enemy gets you to doubt yourself to the point that you start feeling guilty and you're ready to submit to her will and bend to her demands.

One of his friends had confessed to him that his wife used to scratch him during their arguments. "We're constantly at war," he'd told the painter, "and sooner or later I'll lay down my arms. Look, all our childhood friends have abdicated to their wives, they've been brought to heel and now they can enjoy peaceful lives. But I'm not at that point just yet. I'll keep fighting until she sends me to my grave!"

A writer friend of his seemed to live an exceptionally peaceful life. Not only did his wife not vex him, but she actually supported him, fawned on him, and took it upon herself so that nothing or nobody ever bothered him. The painter had asked him for his secret. After a deep sigh, the writer had told him: "I don't have secrets to share, I simply gave up. She controls everything. I don't even know my bank account number. I never travel without her and I never see anyone outside our close circle of friends. She's got access to my phone, my e-mails, and my post . . . she answers them for me. Journalists are afraid of her and so I've rid myself of all the bother of having to deal with them. I don't even remember the last time I saw a naked woman. So from time to time I watch some pornos while she sleeps. I leave our bedroom on the tips of my toes to feast my eyes and occasionally jack off. There's my secret. If you want peace, now you know the price you have to pay for it!"

Give up? One may as well disappear! What good would it do to become so small that people wouldn't even notice you anymore? Was married life impossible unless one of the two transformed into a shadow? The painter reread a book that his friend had written. Dedicated to his wife, the novel told the story of an official who worked at the Ministry of the Interior in a country ruled by a dictator who spent his days torturing political activists but became a perfect husband and father the minute he returned home each night. He would drop off his kids at school in the morning, kiss them, button up their shirt collars so they wouldn't catch a cold, and fifteen minutes later he would be taking off his jacket and rolling up his sleeves so he could start torturing his detainees in the basement of his office building. He had a clear conscience.

The allusions to the writer's personal life were unmistakable. The painter hadn't mentioned any of this to the writer. But as far as the painter was concerned, living like this would be unthinkable.

XV

Casablanca

August 28, 2000

If a recipe for conjugal happiness did exist, then all human beings would instantly stop getting married.

—SACHA GUITRY, *Give Me Your Eyes*

Tired of mulling over his dark thoughts on what was a hot midsummer afternoon, the painter closed his eyes and decided to reminisce about the women he'd known in his life. As though in a dream, the vision at first blended in with the horizon, then took on the colors of the sunset.

They suddenly flashed past his eyes simultaneously. He could see them without being seen himself. Some were dressed in black, others in white, but all were in mourning. But he wasn't dead yet. Could they have misinterpreted that mysterious invitation for a ceremony of goodbyes?

Only Criss was dressed in a variety of colors. She had almond-

119

shaped eyes and a vivacious face, and her arms were burdened with presents. She was looking for him but hadn't managed to find him. When she turned around, she saw the other women walking toward the horizon without speaking to one another. She thought it wasn't a dream, but it wasn't hers, it belonged to the man whom she loved, although she'd never lived with him.

It had been a story like no other. They had suddenly fallen in love, and then just as brutally fallen out of it. She'd fulfilled a fantasy, or even a wish, because she'd loved the artist before she'd even met the man behind that artist. Their love had been strong, then she'd gotten up one morning and said, "It's over!" He'd looked at her, made a gesture to indicate this was against his wishes. But she'd been serious, her face had changed, and even her way of moving. She'd become unrecognizable and, over the course of a single night, had transformed into a woman who was too busy for him. She'd confessed that she was afraid of men and that he'd confirmed those fears, thanking him as though he'd been a plumber or an electrician who'd just repaired something in her house.

Before shutting the door behind him, she'd said: "I'll always be your friend, we just won't be having sex anymore. I love solitude, and sometimes I betray that solitude by spending time with men who are much like you, artists who are famous, but not too tall. Then I go back to my solitary life and my work, which I'm very passionate about and which gives me a great deal of satisfaction. When I get horny, I pleasure myself and occasionally use a vibrator to orgasm. There we have it, darling. Know that we had something very beautiful and very intense. Goodbye!"

He'd lingered there a moment, rooted in his spot. Seeing someone change from one kind of person to another in the space of a single season had left a big impression on him. Criss hadn't had a sense of humor and had been immature when it came to her dealings with men. Maybe she preferred women but didn't want to admit it? Nevertheless, she'd said that she'd loved sleeping with him. He didn't argue: he'd torn up the photos they'd taken on a few trips they'd taken together and he'd decided to turn over a new leaf.

Then it was Zina's turn. She was the first woman he'd ever fallen in love with. He'd nursed the memory of her throughout his life without ever having laid eyes on her again. He'd never stopped looking for her in other people's faces: a brunette with dark skin and a body sculpted by desire and sensuality. Their affair had come to a dramatic end and it had been responsible for the greatest frustration he'd endured in his sentimental life. He'd never actually made love to Zina, or at least not fully, since they'd decided to wait for the wedding night that never took place for a series of complicated reasons. It was a time when virginity wasn't something that a woman could compromise, and when they'd been happy just to touch each other, their bodies rubbing against one another until they orgasmed, wiping up the mess with handkerchiefs that she washed in her sink after she got back home. They'd flirted with one other in the dark alleys of the city, or in cemeteries, right up until the day when they were chased out by the groundskeeper who threw stones at them. She'd been struck on the head by one of them, which had left a little gash on her temple. She'd had to cover herself with a veil until the scar had faded. They used to meet at the house of a friend whose parents had left to make the pilgrimage to Mecca. They'd loved that time of their life, when they'd felt safe and away from prying eyes, but they still hadn't had sex. That time of clandestine rendezvous had left a deep impression on him. Then one day he'd seen her walking down the street hand in hand with an older man. It had all come to an end, and it had been worse than a disappointment, it had been a disaster. Looking back on it, the painter smiled because the jealousy had made him do ridiculous things.

And there she was again thirty years later, walking through the white space while the painter took stock of his love life. She was wearing a veil and fingering a string of prayer beads. She'd become a believer and was said to frequent the circles of Sufi mystics.

All of a sudden, he saw Angelika gracefully break away from the group and come toward him. She was a Greek acrobat, incredibly beautiful, but also terribly fickle. She would affect naïveté, but actually always had her head screwed on right. Angelika had merely been interested in him. She'd never loved the painter, but had let him love her. She'd suggested taking him for a tour of her country's most remote regions in the depths of winter. Utterly in love, he had spent the little money he'd had to travel to where she was. Her beauty was an enigma, her body graceful, and she was prone to mood swings, but her voice had always been suffused with sensuality. He'd walked out on her the day another man had come knocking on her door, looking for his girlfriend. The painter had felt betrayed, used, and cheated by an actress who'd merely pretended to love. He still felt bitter about it to this day, even though he'd managed to erase all memories of her. He hadn't invited her, but she'd shown up anyway, looking like someone who'd stumbled onto the scene by accident. Angelika had always had a certain flair.

The only blonde he'd ever loved in his life came forward at this point, looking as radiant as on the day he'd met her. He'd been seduced by her deep-blue eyes, her sense of humor, and her laughter. He'd invited her to come stay with him in Morocco at a time when he'd still been single, and when he hadn't been looking for the "ideal woman," but for someone who made him want to be with her. He still remembered the moment when she'd arrived on the boat, beaming amidst the crowds of weary travelers. He loved those rendezvous at train stations or ports. It was the romantic in him. They'd spent the next few days fooling around. Then they'd left for Corsica, and their relationship had come to a brutal end without any explanations or acknowledgements. She'd simply not shown up. He'd waited for her in a Moroccan restaurant whose décor he still remembered. He also remembered the expression on the face of the young waiter who usually served him and who'd understood that the painter had been stood up. To console him, the waiter had said: "I get it, a woman did that to me, and I gave her a good smack!" The painter had lifted his gaze and replied: "No, I don't have it in me, and that's not my style. You can only keep women by being sweet to them, not hitting them. The way we do things here in Morocco is behind the times in most other countries!"

While she walked in front of him without noticing him, the beautiful blonde was thronged by memories of the lover she'd had for a few weeks and whom she'd called her "precious friend," whom she'd left so suddenly so as to have only good memories of him.

A hand abruptly pulled the painter out of the sweet reverie he'd plunged himself into. It was a nurse who'd come to give him his injections. Still stunned by his dreams, he thought she belonged to the group of women he'd loved. But she was a stern, efficient woman who dressed like a man. She worked in silence and barely even asked him where he preferred to have his injections.

When the nurse left, the painter felt overwhelmed by a great anxiety. After nightfall, the light in his studio had taken on a sad air. Against all odds, one of his former loves had made him feel nostalgic, a feeling he'd wanted to avoid at all costs—as he himself had always said: "Memories are boring!" Then his exhaustion made him numb again. He looked around himself and refused to believe that his life had come to an end, that his work would be left unfinished. He wanted to move but realized he could barely do so and with great difficulty at that. He hated himself and wanted to scream. He thought that if he could destroy everything around him it would at least be a means to answer the call of death, which had shamelessly settled within him. "Death is the disease!" he'd repeated.

Suddenly he'd heard a voice say: "Don't let it get you down, stay strong, it's just a bad moment and it'll pass. Come on, life calls out to you, and it's magnificent, believe me!" The painter tried to figure out where it was coming from, and turned around as best he could. It was his favorite nephew, an architect who was passionate about music and football, and who had come to pay him a visit. He'd brought him an iPod filled with songs from the 1960s. He didn't stay long, but before leaving he'd placed the iPod's earphones in his ears and had left him alone with Bob Dylan.

The painter shut his eyelids, listened to the music, and waited for the parade of the women he'd loved to start flashing past his eyes again just as though he were sitting in a cinema and the film could miraculously start exactly where it had been paused. All of a sudden, the journalist whom he'd used to make giggle all the time because he used to poke fun at her buttocks and bosom—which he used to say were as hard as a wax mannequin's—appeared just a few feet in front of him. Another oddball who at the time had been torn between her best friend and her boyfriend. She'd readily admitted to him that she loved experimenting with pleasure and that she was ambitious. As it happens, she went on to have a very successful career. The painter remembered having spotted her sitting cross-legged in one of the lounges of the Élysée Palace one evening while interviewing the French president along with another journalist. He'd amused himself by imaging her naked while striking all those risqué poses that she loved to make. At which point everything the president said became very funny.

She was walking elegantly in front of him, but didn't seem to notice him. He wondered why she'd accepted his invitation. Perhaps she was concealing a camera so she could get a scoop on the funeral of a painter whose canvases were growing pricier by the day.

•

Then came the turn of the woman whom he thought resembled Faye Dunaway in Elia Kazan's *The Arrangement*. She was a friend with whom love had come easily and with whom life had passed without any arguments. She'd come to see him because she'd been writing a thesis on contemporary Moroccan painting and its influences. She was hardworking and tall; she had a sense of humor and a penchant for lightness, which pleased him a great deal. The product of a mixed marriage—her father was Tunisian, her mother French—she was grounded in both cultures and loved to speak Arabic, albeit in a heavily accented way. They'd laughed a lot and often made love wherever they happened to be. She would drag him to a place he didn't know and passionately give herself to him. Whenever she came to his place wearing a skirt he knew she wasn't wearing any underwear. He would slip his hand between her thighs and she would let out a cry of joy. He adored her skirts, even the ones she wore in the winter. Whenever she arrived wearing trousers, he knew that she'd either had her period or wasn't in the mood.

Their relationship came to an end the day she went back to her country to get married. She too belonged to the time before he'd been married. He occasionally regretted not having gotten in touch with her again to resume their sexual encounters. She had a great character, a kind disposition, and plenty of charm.

Around the same time, the painter had been seeing a Moroccan student with exceptional skin. She had left to continue her studies in Canada and had met a brutal death at the age of twenty-four. Memories of her had haunted the painter and her death had wounded him enormously even though he hadn't known her that well. She'd given herself to him enthusiastically and had hoped for something more than quick get-togethers between classes. He looked for her silhouette in vain.

•

That same year, the painter had had another affair with a Moroccan woman, someone who'd borne her beauty as though it were a burden, or a tragedy waiting to happen. She had big gray eyes but it was as though something were gnawing away at her. She had a hard time being happy, cried often, and her body tensed up each time he touched her. It was the first time he'd been with a frigid woman. She would weep, cling to him, beg for long, sweet cuddles that helped her to calm down and fall asleep on his shoulder. He knew that she'd suffered some kind of trauma, but it wasn't his role to psychoanalyze her. Her father must have abused her, and she carried the secret of that wound as though she'd murdered someone. She'd allowed him to understand without spelling it out, then buried her face in a pillow and cried for a long time. She'd gotten married and her parents had thrown her a huge party, but her husband, a kind, charmless man, hadn't known how to deal with her. He would only return home late at night and neglect her. One evening, she'd called a friend of hers for help, but that friend had been unable to come over because he'd been suffering from angina. He'd spoken to her and had promised he would come see her as soon as he was better. He didn't want to infect her, he'd said. He'd tried to make her laugh, but the distant voice on the other end of the line had been that of a woman adrift on a vast ocean. "Wait for me, I'm coming!" he'd said. By the time he arrived, there was nobody there. She'd driven to a beach house, swallowed a huge quantity of pills, and gone to sleep. Her suicide had shocked everyone because all the boys of her generation had been driven crazy by her beauty and all the girl were jealous of her charm and elegance.

Next came the turn of those who called themselves the students, who'd come to see him because they'd been writing a dissertation or essay on painting and Morocco. They'd all accommodated his schedule and had welcomed his tactful advances. Some had come back for a few months, others instead had vanished. He'd regretted their disappearance, but then had quickly forgotten them. And now there they were, walking through his dreams, happy to revisit a shared past. He couldn't remember their names anymore, but he still recalled the perfumes they used to wear or the way they moved. There was a pretty Asian girl among them who, after working her way through not a few men, had taken holy orders and never returned. He remembered how fiery she'd been when they'd made love. When he found out she'd become religious, he hadn't been surprised in the slightest.

There was the one who wrote poems in Arabic and who'd dreamed of writing a book illustrated with his paintings. She'd thought of herself as intelligent and professional; she'd sent him a few of her books along with a portrait of her by the Greek painter Alekos Fassianos. A beautiful woman and a beautiful painting. The painter had known something would happen between them the moment she'd set foot in his studio. It was a matter of intuition, as well as the way she'd looked at him. She wasn't very tall but she had splendid black hair and gray-green eyes. They talked a lot about politics. She came from a part of the world that had been ravaged by war. She didn't say a word about her project. On her way out, she'd asked him for a favor: to let her take him to dinner.

"Or rather, why don't you let me take you out sometime next week?"

"That's out of the question," she'd replied, "I insist, and besides I'll be in Greece next week."

They'd had dinner the following night at a small restaurant. She was the one who'd asked: "Are you free later tonight?"

He, on the other hand, had responded evasively, "I usually sleep at night, or at least I try to."

Then she'd taken hold of his arm and whispered: "I don't want to sleep with my partner tonight, I want to sleep with you. I'll leave you alone after we've made love."

Their sporadic affair had lasted for two years. They rarely saw one another in Paris, but made time whenever they were traveling. One day, her partner had given her an ultimatum: "It's either me or him!" She'd opted for safety and security, and she'd married her partner a few months later.

Curiously enough, she'd appeared before him alongside her husband, who was older than her and a little bulky. He must have had hidden qualities.

There was the one whom he'd called the Angel of Brasilia, a young art history student who'd been sent to his studio by her professor, who was married to a Moroccan woman who happened to be the painter's cousin. Her beauty had reminded him of certain Egyptian actresses: buxom. She'd fainted when he'd grabbed her hand. It was the first time he'd seen a woman faint. He'd revived her as best he could, then after she'd regained consciousness, she'd apologized and confessed: "I always faint when I'm touched by a man I admire!" He'd smiled and promised he wouldn't touch her again. Laughing, she'd retorted: "But that's a punishment!" She became his mistress during his time in Paris, then they met again in Buenos Aires. It was like a party each time they met. She would let herself go and talk to him in Arabic, using phrases she'd learned by heart. Their love became a kind of friendship, a tenderness that they jealously guarded in their hearts. She told him she'd never loved anyone like him, but he'd stayed silent. He liked her, but pretending to be in love was be-yond him.

The painter opened his eyes, scanned his surroundings, and then called the Twins by pressing the bell, indicating he wanted to be taken out for a little stroll. He told himself that this procession was like looking at a catalog. He hated himself and refused to content himself with the images that flashed past his mind the moment he shut his eyes.

He drank some coffee that evening, hoping to put an end to it, but his imagination placed him on a balcony from which he could admire those women as they moved past him elegantly.

There was Caroline, the woman with perfect legs whom he'd met while she was in the midst of battling breast cancer. An exceptionally intelligent, tender, and sensual being. He'd been happy to see her, to clasp her in his arms, to confide in her. Their friendship had led to a cautious love. She'd found it difficult to be naked in front of him, having recently undergone a mastectomy. Making love to someone who was disabled was difficult. How could she tell him, or warn him? She'd blushed and then she'd told him: "They removed that unlucky breast but I'm waiting for my reconstruction surgery before the summer arrives so I can go to the beach with my children!" She'd asked him to close his eyes while she'd undressed and to switch off the light. Her chest had been wrapped in bandages. He'd touched her softly and delicately. He'd licked the tears from her cheeks and pressed her against him without hurting her. They'd taken a little time to get used to things and humor had been the best medicine. They'd laughed and swapped jokes, talked about how she'd get a new breast and would be able to show it off at a nice beach. That missing breast had haunted him for a long time. He would think about her and grow angry over how such a kindhearted, beautiful soul had been struck by such an injustice.

She never managed to make it to the beach. That woman really suffered a great deal. She'd had a lot of courage and hope. In lieu of seeing one another, they'd exchanged letters. Her last had read:

I'm writing to you from a waiting room, which is terrible, just like hospital waiting rooms usually are. I'm wearing pajamas and I've got a scarf around my head, which is completely bald. I feel ugly, abandoned by life, but I've got faith. The doctor's a friend of mine. He's an older gentleman who continues to prac-

tice despite the stupidity of French laws. He helps me to remain optimistic and he knows just how to talk to me and the right things to say. Here I am, I think about you, but then I'm here, watching gaunt elderly people whom death has shunted into a corner, I think of you and beg you to keep fighting so that nobody can compromise your integrity as an artist and as a man; nobody has the right to trample on you, or to steal what's most precious to you, your work, your art, your gift. I say this to you because I know how often selfish people have taken advantage of your sensitivity. Be strong, be well, and continue to amaze us, giving us the best that you have to offer.

I'm here, I'm waiting and I know that I want to live, I want to scream so that God—if indeed He does exist—can hear me and give me a little more time, so I can love again, have sex, eat a plate of lentils, drink some fine wine, and smoke a cigar with you. I long for that time, and I'll find it wherever it's hiding, I won't let anyone take it away from me.

There's a woman next to me and she's looking at me while I write. She leaned over and said: "How lucky you are, you've got someone to write to, someone you love, I suppose? I don't have anyone to write to. My children have forsaken me, my husband is dead, and my friends are all in the hospice, having completely lost their memories. Well, say something nice to that man. Tell him that Gisèle sends him a kiss. So he knows that there's an eighty-four-year-old woman out there whom he doesn't know but who's sent him a kiss. Thank you."

There we have it, my love, my tree, my music, my greatest folly. It's my turn to see the doctor now. Don't forget, don't allow anyone to compromise your integrity.

The painter had carried the memory of that woman's unspeakable grief for a long time, without ever being able to share it with anyone.

He could have lived with her because she'd given him an ensuring sense of serenity. She'd soothed him and loved him. Every moment he'd spent with her had been sheer bliss. They'd met when they'd attended a retrospective of Billy Wilder's films. The painter loved films from Hollywood's golden age, especially Ernst Lubitsch's and Frank Capra's. They'd spent entire evenings talking about the various cuts of Orson Welles's *Touch of Evil.* If her illness hadn't ended her life when she'd been so young, beautiful, and energetic, he might have spent the rest of his days with her. He told himself that in order to keep her memory alive. When he learned that her ashes had been scattered in Africa, where she'd grown up as a child, he'd been thrown into a state of panic and confusion. How could the body that he'd pressed against his own have disintegrated into ashes and been lost in the sands of a distant land? The idea of it tormented him. He put it out of his mind and focused on the image of her when she'd been most alive. He could still hear her sweet voice and peals of laughter. One day, her daughter had called him and said: "I dreamed of mama, she was so happy and she told me to call you, to tell you to take care of yourself and that she loves you!" He'd been taken aback, had lain down his brush and reread the letter she'd sent him that he kept hidden in a locked drawer.

She'd given him pride of place in her dreams, but wouldn't be coming to see him. He struggled to remember her and was gradually forgetting her features, as usually happened to him whenever he experienced strong emotions.

Instead, it was Ava's face that superimposed itself on hers in his mind. First with her bright gray-green eyes, her lioness-like hair, her impressive height, her naturally sensual voice, and that slender body of hers that always made his head spin, leading her to bust out in fits of giggles. Ava had entered his life a few months into his secret period of mourning, entering it like a storm or a burst of summer rain that made him marvel and kneel before her. An encounter right out of the pages of Nabokov or Pushkin, or even *Gone With the Wind* or *Pandora and the Flying Dutchman*, where his Ava could be played by Ava Gardner, except that his Ava wasn't a femme fatale who sowed misery and destruction in people's lives. His Ava stood for love, sweet madness, and adventure. She had an air of mystery about her and a solemnity in her eyes, but also a joie de vivre. He'd known they would have an intense affair the moment he'd met her. He'd completely changed the moment she'd sent him a note where she'd reproduced a drawing by Matisse by way of introduction. She'd written her phone number on the back of the note and had signed her name in the shape of a shooting star. When he'd called her, she'd answered with a burst of laughter, as if they'd known each other forever and had a shared past. She'd told him: "Your paintings break my heart! Life's already left too many scars on me, and you don't have the right to add any more!" Then she'd added: "Nonsense, nonsense . . ."

Ava understood that she'd entered the painter's life at a time when nothing had been going right with his wife. He was afflicted, miserable, tired of fighting against headwinds and still hopeful he could put an end to it all and free himself. He'd told his wife as much and she'd answered him: "That's not my problem! You've put children into this world and now you have to endure the responsibilities!" He'd tried to explain to her that there was a way in which they could separate without hurting the children, that one couldn't force destiny, and that all their attempts to reconcile had failed, but she'd refused to hear a word of it, and he'd been left utterly dismayed by her determined obstinacy. He was fighting all on his own. His words simply vanished into thin air, like dust. She refused to listen to him and she would push him away before he'd even had the chance to reach out to her. She only gave in a little when presented with facts, and even then she would suspect the influence of some sorcerer or evil female mastermind hellbent on wrecking her home. She would become ill and shut herself away in her room, letting the house fall apart and telling the children that she was suffering because their father was a monster, crying, losing weight, and making the atmosphere unbreathable. The doctor had taken him aside and told him: "She's using depression as blackmail, but she must take care lest she actually becomes depressed—that is, unless it's already happened!" She would take her medications, but would refuse to see a psychiatrist.

This was around the time that his work had met with great success at the Venice Biennale. Several galleries in Europe and the United States wanted his work. He needed to produce more paintings, but he was preoccupied by the breakdown of his marriage. His wife had found out about Ava's existence, but hadn't managed to learn more than that. She didn't know her name or where she worked. She'd begged him to tell her who she was, but he'd held steady and refused to say a word, minimizing the affair since he didn't have the courage to come clean at the risk of provoking another huge upset. In her irrationality, his wife was highly capable of causing a lot of damage. She would throw everything she could get her hands on at him, calling him names so as to make him feel guilty. The children witnessed all those theatrics and would ask themselves what their father was guilty for. He would refuse to involve them, but his wife would do so in his stead and upset them. She felt betrayed, and was doing everything she could to avenge herself, wanting to inflict five times the harm that had been done to her. He would remain silent and then run away, abandoning her to her distress. He didn't talk about it with Ava; they could only enjoy a few moments together, and he was keen to live them to the fullest. He felt a strong desire to leave his wife, but his weakness—or rather what his wife called his "cowardice"—prevented him from making such a decision.

The mystery of the night was compounded by bouts of insomnia, a cruel kind of suffering that left his body and mind feeling battered. He also had high blood pressure and tried to look after it without managing to keep it entirely under control. He experienced peaks that rose to worrying levels and then returned to normal. The night scared him, as did the risk of apnea. He dreaded the coming of night and the moment when he would have to go to sleep. He slept in his studio, but tremors ran up and down his limbs, enervating him. He would get up, pace around the meticulously tidy space where he stored his canvases, his equipment, his collection of art books, and his documents. He would drink some water, take a second sleeping pill, go back to bed, and wait. Nothing would happen. He could follow the progress of the clouds through the sky of Paris through the skylight on his roof. Exhaustion would assail him toward dawn and he would then finally be able to sleep for an hour or two.

He'd acquired the habit of calling Ava every morning at the same hour, just before she left to go to work. He would wish her a wonderful day and spend the rest of his time waiting for her.

Sneaking around made their encounters more pleasurable. They would say: "We're like thieves! Our happiness is our secret and our love is how we survive! We refuse to be thwarted! We live this love and know that we'll one day be inconsolable creatures!" Then came the break. It was brutal, definitive, and cruel. She finally left him because she knew he would never leave his wife to go live with her. She'd guessed right. He was afraid of how his wife would retaliate. It was an insurmountable fear. He was stuck, unable to move, unable to turn his back on a miserable life and go somewhere else with the woman he loved. That was when he'd accepted a suggestion that a friend of his who was well versed in stories of witchcraft had made him. The friend had said: "Leave it to me and please let me know what happens. Give me leave to go consult an old man who lives in the mountains far from the cities, a man who is blessed with extraordinary powers and knows what happens between people, he has a gift for that. He's a holy man who only uses the Qur'an—he doesn't use any gris-gris or black magic. He just reads the Qur'an and uses numbers!"

He let his friend go ahead. After all, what did he have to lose?

The old man's assessment of the situation had been impressive!

"This man has been manipulated by his wife for a long time, she's trying to obstruct his path and tighten her grip on him so that she can control him. He is surrounded by many kinds of talismans; he is an artist, someone who is successful; she is jealous of that and is being advised by people from her bled. He must leave. We are not usually in favor of separating a man from his wife, but in this case he's at risk. I don't know what exactly, but she'll never give him peace. Here, take this talisman, tell him to wear it and to read a page of the Qur'an every night before going to bed. This will help soothe him since he is so restless. If he wants to stay with his wife and children, then he will have to submit, otherwise his life will become a living hell because she is in cahoots with men who will impede him from achieving any- thing. Every time he meets a woman, they will make all the necessary efforts to ensure that this relationship fails. He will always find it diffi- cult to sleep. A curse hangs around this man. May God fill our hearts with His kindness! She'll never give him peace!"

The painter had been left speechless and openmouthed and he'd started to look around his studio for any gris-gris his wife might have planted there. He found a few hidden under the couch where he oc- casionally slept, while he found others in the bathroom, the kitchen, and even at the bottom of his bag. He was surrounded by them. Even though he'd never believed in these things, he changed his mind and became suspicious. He realized that the spells they'd cast on Ava had worked. He told himself: "Now that I know what's going on, I'll do everything I can to get back together with the woman I love!" He made several attempts, but they were all in vain. Ava had moved, changed her telephone number, and he'd been unable to find any trace of her. He spent the following couple of years without any news of her, continuing to live with his wife while hoping to make the neces- sary preparations to leave her for good. But he never had the time to do so. His stroke happened right after their terrible fight.

XVI

Casablanca

September 12, 2000

You're a selfish old man. You're utterly ruthless and never
listen to anyone but yourself. But you hide it all behind your
old-world manners and charm. Beneath your benevolent
exterior, you're as hard as nails.

> —the daughter-in-law to her father-in-law
> INGMAR BERGMAN, *Wild Strawberries*

Sometimes he would remember seemingly insignificant episodes from
his childhood right in the middle of the day. They would dance before his eyes, like puppets at a funfair. It surprised him each time it
happened. That was how he'd been able to once again see the wooden
bucket his father used to take to the hammam with him. It was an
old bucket, nothing special about it, it used to be brown before it
had blackened with age. Before leaving for the hammam, his father
would fill it with a bar of soap, a towel, and a pumice stone to scrape

away dead skin. Why had that bucket appeared in his mind half a century later? On another day, he'd suddenly seen the old straw mat that his parents used to perform their daily prayers on just as clearly as he'd seen the bucket. There was nothing unique about the mat either. Still, there it was, right next to the bucket. A beggar woman whom he'd once given a piece of bread, and received a cube of sugar in exchange, also appeared before him in the same manner, complete with her wrinkly face, her toothless smile, and that star-shaped cube of sugar that she'd held in the palm of her hand.

A few days after that, he'd seen the legless cripple who used to sing out of tune in front of his school, then that sick dog who used to limp around the old alleyways of Fez that the children used to chase and throw stones at. That poor animal used to find it very difficult to walk around. The painter asked himself: "Why am I suddenly thinking about this dog?"

He could have asked himself the same question about those knickers that he'd torn at the knee after he'd fallen off a swing. That memory dated from when he'd been six years old and had gone on a swing for the first time. His older brother had given him a push and the ropes had snapped while he'd been in mid-flight, at which point he'd found himself on the ground with his face all bloodied up. Strangely enough, the torn trousers had left a deeper impression than his bruised face.

Then an old cardboard suitcase, which his father had used to store old issues of *Life* magazine from the days of the war, appeared before him without any warning. As a child, he'd often pulled out an issue and thumbed through it. Why could he still recall that young American soldier's face as he cried in front of his dead friend's body? His name was Solomon. It was a bizarre picture: Solomon on his knees, with his hands covering a face drenched in tears. What had become of that young man? He pictured him on his return home, a car salesman married to a redhead.

On another occasion, he was haunted by a moth-eaten scarf.

Red, worn so thin it had become useless, just like those burned-out lightbulbs his father used to store in a drawer, hoping that they would somehow fix themselves. He also saw a paper bag filled with nails of all sizes that was kept in a corner of the kitchen, and the dirty tie that his Arabic teacher used to wear, which was covered in grease stains. And his primary school teacher, a newlywed girl who used to spread her legs a little whenever she sat down on her chair, who also came to pay him a visit. He'd also inexplicably recalled the license plate number of his uncle's Chevrolet: 236MA2. His uncle had been the only person in the family to have a car at the time.

One day, he remembered the first time he'd ever ejaculated, which had happened while he'd been playing with his cousin. Like a pleasant electrical shock had just jolted his penis. He'd gotten up and covered the stain on his trousers with his hand. He'd been ashamed, especially since his cousin, who must have been a year older than him, had invited him into her parents' bedroom while they'd been away on holiday. That powerful strange smell that had wafted up from his groin and the burning desire he'd felt on seeing his cousin waiting for him on the bed came rushing back to him, as intact as the day they had happened. He could see her again all too clearly, surrendering her rosy buttocks to him and saying, "Do it! Put your thingy in my bottom!"

The painter told himself that this barrage of memories had in all likelihood been caused by the paralysis that had affected his arms and legs. One day, the telephone had rung loudly when he'd been right in the middle of one of those visions. One of his assistants who'd been nearby had handed him the phone. It was his agent calling to see how he was doing. He must have been worried about losing his commissions! But the painter reassured him: he was getting better. He had to be patient, very patient.

XVII

Casablanca

October 5, 2000

Lower-class people are simply less sensitive. They look at a
wounded bull and their faces are completely emotionless!
—a middle-class lady to her friends before the play
LUIS BUÑUEL, *The Exterminating Angel*

That barrage of insignificant memories was followed by long rever-
ies and terrifying nightmares. The doctor had warned him that this
would happen, but the painter hadn't expected such frenetic cere-
bral activity. The first dream had allowed him to see his wife back
when he'd still been in love with her, as though she'd been standing
right in front of him. He'd been very attentive toward her and she'd
been gentle and considerate. She never annoyed him or disagreed
with him, to the point that he'd feared she lacked self-confidence or
was too submissive. He'd thanked the heavens each day that such a
woman unlike any other he'd known before had fallen into his lap.

After having been a bachelor for a long time, and never sticking with the women he used to meet, he'd been very moved by that young woman's eyes. She'd made him want to become serious. Toying with her youth and innocence had been out of the question. They were almost fifteen years apart in age, but he hadn't thought it would be a problem. Then the dream had taken him through the first two years of marriage, which had been happy. No fights, no arguments, and not a single cloud in the sky. They'd traveled, had fun, laughed, and made plans for the future. It had been marvelous. Too good to last. She'd been irresistible to him with her long brown hair and her impressive height.

But he also experienced some horrifying nightmares. In particular one in which a short, squat man had snared him in a trap and extorted a large sum of money from him, as well as a few paintings. He'd introduced himself as an art dealer, but had actually turned out to be a failed painter who'd reinvented himself as a businessman or rather a swindler who worked in cahoots with a brother of his who was a gigolo in the villas of the Côte d'Azur. Before his stroke, the painter had managed to forget him and contemptuously consign the memory of him to the trashcan of oblivion. He'd preferred to ignore what had happened instead of spending years stuck in the corridors of the law courts, especially since the only proof he had was a handful of phony receipts with made-up addresses, signed with a stolen signature stamp. But now that little man had come back again to mock him, just as he'd become physically infirm. The painter watched him as he walked around his canvases with a torch that had been soaked in alcohol and was ready to be ignited. The painter had shut his eyes, but the devil himself had appeared and burst out in hysterical laughter. The painter began to think of the ways in which he wanted to butcher him. He pictured him being crushed in a cement mixer and his bowels being spit out onto the mud, choking in the face of death after long agonizing hours.

Then he chased those thoughts of revenge from his mind and

asked God to one day mete out His justice, at which point the stocky scam artist suddenly disappeared, this time for good.

At night, the Twins helped him into the car to go to the studio. Yet since his wife was away on a trip, he asked them to take him back to the house instead and told them to call Imane so that she could come over as soon as possible to recommence his physical therapy sessions. He settled into the room, which he'd long since vacated. It smelled like his wife's perfume, it was littered with her things, and her clothes had been scattered willy-nilly. There were countless beauty products in the bathroom. He asked the maid to change the sheets and tidy the house.

Over the years, the painter had grown indifferent to how jealous others were of him. He'd come to terms with it and turned his indifference into a philosophical outlook. The most jealous people he'd had to deal with had been the women he'd loved and fellow painters who neither understood nor acknowledged his success. He'd put himself through much self-examination and had reached the conclusion that it was better to be envied than ignored and talentless. Nevertheless, his wife's jealousy still got to him and he wasn't able to be indifferent to it. She had to be stronger than he was and more determined than the others, steamrolling ahead without looking back to see just how much damage her repeated bouts of jealousy—which bordered on madness—had caused. There are many different kinds of madness, and his wife's wasn't extreme, but it was just enough to make his life a living hell. There was nothing he could do apart from suffer through it or flee, slip away or face more violence and cruelty. He chose to suffer through it, though under protest.

One day he'd told her: "Jealousy is a symptom of one's weakness of character and a lack of empowerment!" He'd tried to reason with her that men and women had to allow one another enough space and privacy; otherwise, everything would fall apart or blow up. But she'd refused to listen to him and had instead followed the advice her char-latans gave her to the letter.

Privacy. A notion she knew nothing about. As far as she was con-cerned, a wife and husband weren't supposed to have secrets between them. To her, a couple was a union where one plus one equaled one. It reminded him of a Moroccan television show where a journalist had interviewed four women from different age groups and varying back-grounds, all of whom were unmarried. The interviewer had wanted to figure out the causes behind this "anomaly." One of the women said she'd simply never had the chance to get married, because her boyfriend had been an alcoholic; another said she'd wanted to focus on her career rather than find a husband who would either exploit her or prevent her from working; the third said that she'd decided never to get married after seeing her parents go through a divorce; while the fourth said she was looking for a man with whom she could share everything to the point that their two personalities could merge into one. None of them mentioned the existence of a perfect place where two individuals could work on their relationship while still respecting each other's differences, not to mention their right to disagree.

He dozed off while watching a film. His mind felt fuzzy and lethargic. He thought he could detect the shadow of a man in the distance, maybe his father coming toward him in a white djellaba, with his trimmed beard, and a bright, smiling face. His father looked younger than he did. He looked at him and recognized him, but he couldn't hear any sounds, just like in a silent film. His father drew close to him, bent over, picked up his right hand, and kissed it. The painter told himself that the world had been turned upside down in this vi-sion. After all, he was usually the one who kissed his mother's and father's hands. Kissing someone's cheek had only been introduced to Morocco at the time when the country had become independent, in 1956.

After that kiss on his hand, the painter had woken up in a good mood. He'd paused the film and asked for some tea. They'd told him: "Imane is making some right now!" "Let's hope this isn't another vision!" the painter had muttered in reply.

XVIII

Casablanca

November 4, 2000

Coincidence is only extraordinary because it's so natural.
—MAX OPHÜLS, *The Earrings of Madame de . . .*

That night he had a dream that morphed into a nightmare and he'd woken up with a crushing migraine. He'd had to visit a head of state. It was summer, and he'd had to wear a white linen shirt and matching trousers. It was explicitly specified on the invitation card. On the way to the palace, a bird had shit on him, leaving a mustard-yellow stain on his beautiful shirt. He needed to change it, but he didn't have time. He asked one of his friends to lend him a fresh shirt. But that friend only had colored shirts. He wasn't happy about that. Time was running out and he had to make it to the reception. He chose a gray one, and when he left his friend's house, he was stopped by some plainclothes policemen: "You have to come with us, you've been convicted and we must take you to prison right away!" He'd tried to ask them what he'd been charged with, and they'd told him: "Don't make this harder on yourself, you know exactly what you've been charged with!" They'd confiscated his cell phone and said: "You won't be doing any painting in prison and you won't have any pencils or notebooks either. These are our orders!" He'd screamed, but no sounds had come out of his mouth. His wife had looked at the scene from the threshold, alongside his best friend. But they hadn't done anything to help him. He'd wanted to call his lawyer, but his mind had suddenly drawn a blank and he couldn't remember his telephone number or his name. He had a headache. Then he woke up. He would have loved to stand up and open the window. It was three o'clock in the morning. Everyone was asleep. He managed to sit up in bed and kept his eyes open so he wouldn't return to that nightmare.

By the morning, tiredness had made him fall asleep. He hadn't woken up when the Twins brought him his breakfast. They had left the plate on his bedside table and gone.

A new bout of pain interrupted his sleep. A cramp in his left leg. He yelled out, then shut his eyes, waiting for the cramp to loosen. "The day's gotten off to a bad start!" he told himself. It would be best not to go to work in his studio. Instead, he needed some comfort and some massages.

When Imane arrived, he'd been in the bathroom while his assistants groomed him. He always found those moments particularly painful and humiliating. Grooming was when he felt that the weight of his disability was truly unbearable. Having one man wipe you while another washed you and barely being able to stand while they scrubbed your intimate parts always made him angry, although he kept quiet about it. He thought, "This should be my wife's job, at least in theory, but nothing in the world would make me want her to do that. I just want her to leave me alone and allow me to recover my ability to move."

But once he'd been washed, shaved, and clothed, he felt a little better and he managed to forget those unbearable moments. He smiled as soon as he saw Imane and detected her scent, Ambre Précieux. "Today," she told him, "we're going to spend the whole day together. It's my day off and I'm going to massage you, give you your injections, and feed you a few little things I cooked. Afterwards I'll tell you the rest of my story, unless you want to do something else or you would prefer I went home . . ."

He was excited. Imane was so sensitive that she restored his hopes and helped to speed up his recovery. "How can I possibly thank you?" he asked her.

After a moment's pause, and while she was massaging his leg, she said, without lifting her gaze:

"You know, you're old enough to be my father, and yet that's not the way I look at you. We're almost thirty years apart in age, but I find that your art and your temperament express a kind of humanity that is sorely absent in today's youth, especially here in Morocco where everyone wants to become a success as quickly as possible and make a lot of money, and where appearances are considered more important than substance. I love spending time with you and trying to help you find some relief, having my hands try to massage the pain out of you and throw it far away from you, that's why you see me shake my fingers at the end of each session after I've removed the suffering inside you. It's as if I'd soaked my hands in black water and then needed to shake them to get rid of it. An Indian guru taught us this technique during a training session in Rabat."

Following the session, she suggested that he lean on her while he tried to walk a few steps. He told her: "But that's what my assistants are here for, I'm too heavy for your delicate shoulders." She helped him get out of bed and handed him a cane, and they started to walk slowly around the room. He stopped and asked the Twins to help him into his going-out clothes. He wanted to look elegant while leaning on that beautiful woman's arm. When Imane came back, she was surprised by how different he looked. The artist was a handsome man. She took his arm in hers. He felt her body against his and was embarrassed to see he'd gotten hard. The doctor had told him: "Erections are controlled by the medulla oblongata and impulses are channeled by the spinal cord." His left arm hugged her waist while they walked and their bodies grew closer and closer together. He wanted to hug her, to kiss her and bury his face in her hair, but he restrained himself. Besides, in his condition he couldn't even stand in front of her without being assisted. He wondered whether she'd noticed his erection. She was talking to him, but he wasn't paying attention to what she was saying, his mind was preoccupied, and so he asked her to help him sit in his armchair so he could stretch his legs. She sat down on the floor next to him and propped her head against his left leg. Then she suddenly stood up, made some tentative dance steps, and said: "It's time for lunch. Leave it to me. I know your cook is fantastic, but I've got some of my grandmother's recipes, which are really amazing!" He wasn't hungry but he forced himself to eat and swallowed what she fed him with her hands. In any other circumstance, he would have found these gestures fairly erotic, but in this case they were purely utilitarian. She was feeding him just like one would a baby or a senile old man. When she slid a straw into the bowl of soup, he told her: "No, thank you, I'm full." Even though he loved that kind of soup, the thought of drinking out of a straw in front of a beautiful woman depressed him even further.

The Twins took him to the studio and Imane followed them. They installed him in his wheelchair.

"Do you want to keep making me happy, Imane?"

"Of course, my captain!"

It was the first time she'd called him that, probably in reference to the sailor's cap that was hanging in one of the studio's corners. It had belonged to one of the painter's friends, with whom he'd fallen out of touch.

"I'm happy to hear you call me captain. The last person who did that was my eldest daughter, it used to amuse her a lot. Good, now grab that Pléiade edition of Baudelaire's works and open it in the spot marked by a yellow leaf, where he wrote about Eugène Delacroix, and read it out to me. I love that passage."

She drank a glass of water to clear her throat and began to read. The captain closed his eyes so he could better savor her words. Imane's voice had a severe tone to it. If she worked on it, it could become quite beautiful. When she stopped, having finished the passage, he told her:

"You see, when that artist spent a few months in Morocco in 1832 he was able to capture something of the country's soul. He produced many drawings and sketches, but he never painted anything here. I regret the fact he never left any of his works in this country, by way of offering his gratitude and recognition. When he was in Algeria, he painted the women of Algiers in their apartments, which are truly wonderful canvases. There, I'm going to lend you a big book on this painter, my dear Imane. Look through it and you'll see how that genius reinterpreted this country. And if one day you get a chance to read his *Journal*, you'll be surprised by what he said about our ancestors. He didn't have any nice things to say! But those sorts of ideas were quite common at the time."

XIX

Casablanca

November 6, 2000

I hate having to repay people's kindness!
—CHRISTIAN-JAQUE, *A Lover's Return*

The time came when everything in the painter's life seemed like it was starting to get bent out of shape and was taking a different direction. The walls were closing in around him, the ceiling threatened to collapse, his voice trailed off, his body grew stiff, and his head was dizzy from spinning. Sometimes the painter's body trembled all over, even when he wasn't cold. Even though his assistants were never far away, he felt terribly alone. He felt as though he were living inside a dark tube and that he had to run in order to save his skin. Sometimes he felt he was being pursued by a shadow, others by a noise, others even by a wave of heat emanating from a ball of fire. It was like being in a film where his body was exactly like it had been before his stroke, but his mind was that of an invalid. Two overlapping states of consciousness: one where his body had seized up, been crippled, and was now under repair, while the other featured a young and lively body. He was hounded by misfortunes. His wife would surely have claimed this was due to the evil eye, or had been caused by a spell cast by a neighbor. But inside that dark tube, the painter never stopped running, then falling down, then getting up again, and then falling down again, getting swallowed up by a big black hole. The fall had left his entire body shaking and in distress, but his mind was as sharp as ever.

It's often said that depression is the quintessence of solitude at its most cruel. During his worst nightmares, the painter would find himself inside a cave where the neighborhood rats used to gather. He'd always been horrified by those pests, in fact he had such an irrational fear of them that he couldn't even bear to see them in a picture book. It probably dated back to his childhood when he used squat toilets. A rat had bitten his ankle once. He'd been saved by a young doctor who'd given him an injection on the spot. In his nightmare, the painter was forced to live with those rats and put up with the horror they inspired in him. His body wouldn't obey him while he was in their midst. Who could have put him in such a dark, macabre place filled solely by the sounds of those pests, who were capable of exterminating a whole city with the plague? Among those rats, his young supple body had disappeared and been replaced by a cumbersome and diseased one. The rats would climb up his legs and blithely run along the length of his body, squabbling next to his head, biting him here and there and dragging him wherever they liked. All of a sudden, a big black rat drew close to him, lunged at his genitals, and bit them with all its might. The pain made him scream, but it was useless to call for help because his voice had been extinguished in his nightmare and nobody could hear him. By the time he'd resigned himself to a slow death, an even more ferocious bite took him by surprise and he abruptly woke up. He was drenched in sweat, and tears were streaming down his cheeks in an endless flow. He'd had enough: he was fed up with his condition, fed up with that house, and fed up with all the people around him. He couldn't take it anymore, but he suffered in silence.

The moments when the painter was attacked by something but couldn't fight back were the ones he feared the most. He tried to resist falling asleep as best as he could, doing everything he could to stay awake, but unfortunately his medications and his boredom would finally overwhelm him and he would fall asleep. Never one to give up, whenever this happened he would press the bell and call for coffee, "Yes, coffee! Even if the doctor forbade me to drink it, I want to be wide awake!"

The painter loved coffee, especially good Italian espresso. He always started his day with a *ristretto* and then followed it up with a *lungo*. He always felt better after that. At which point he could look behind him, where just a moment earlier he'd seen the dark tube and the trap that harassed him. He knew he was being stalked by the specter of depression, and that any moment now, the same thing that had happened to his friend Antonio Tabucchi could happen to him. He too could fall into a depression that could last three years. One day, Antonio had been reading his newspaper as usual just before getting up to go to work in the next room, but when he'd tried to get up, nothing had happened. His wife later found him in the same armchair she'd left him in that morning. But nothing obvious had happened to trigger that depression. He and his wife were happily married—they had stuck together and knew how to make common cause. The doctor had told the painter: "Depression is a real illness, it's not a mere question of gloominess or melancholy or a passing cloud. It's a serious condition and one must be cautious. Insomnia is a serious indicator."

His recurring nightmares worried him to the point that he decided to redouble his efforts when it came to his physical therapy. He went out into the city every morning. The Twins took him to the seashore, where he walked while leaning on them and breathed in the salt air, insisting on doing all his exercises. At first he hadn't wanted to show his face in public to avoid noticing people looking at him or even running into certain individuals who would take pity on him. One day, he bumped into Larbi, his frame-maker, a talented guy who'd been trained in Spain and whom he liked a great deal. He'd always liked speaking to him because this man, who was twenty years older than he was, had decided to keep working instead of slipping into lethargy like all his other colleagues. He had a keen intellect and loved to tell funny stories. The painter had asked him to come visit him in his studio so they could chat, just like in the old days.

The following day, Larbi came to see him and brought some *kif* and a couple of pipes. They smoked it and drank some tea. Larbi would hold the pipe for him and then help him to drink. Just two old friends who used to party together back in their foolhardy days. Larbi asked him if the "boss" was "still in business." The painter nodded to say yes, while raising his eyes to the ceiling to indicate that all his women had distanced themselves from him.

"You need to do something about it. If the Boss stops working then he might never wake up!"

"I know."

At that moment, Imane entered the room wearing a djellaba and a matching headscarf. It was the first time that the painter had seen her covering her head. She told him that she did it in order to avoid being harassed by men in the street. She then pulled her scarf and djellaba off, revealing tight jeans and a pretty blouse, loosened her long hair, and brought the oils she used to massage him. In awe of her beauty, Larbi excused himself and made to leave, reminding the painter on his way out that he needed to look after the "boss."

"So, captain, must I call you 'boss' now?" Imane asked.

He smiled.

"Captain suits me just fine," he said.

He remembered how his wife would go out in the evening when he used to suffer from his yearly bout of angina—despite having been vaccinated, he would spent two to three weeks floored by a flu that would eventually develop into angina—and how he would stupidly wait for her to come home. He'd get all worked up and be unable to fall asleep until she'd returned, or he would call her and only get her voicemail. He would look at his watch: 2:10 a.m., 3 a.m., 4:05 a.m., and then he would hear the gates of the villa open to let her car through. He would close his eyes, he didn't want to talk to her or find out where she'd been. Besides, she would simply tell him: "I was with the girls, and we talked and talked and I didn't notice how time flew by!" She would reek of alcohol. He hated that smell on her breath. He would curl up in bed and try to get some sleep, while she would doze off the moment she laid her head on the pillow. While that young woman was busy taking care of him, he would measure the differences between her and his wife. Needless to say, Imane was his employee and he paid her a salary, but there was something else to her, she exhibited a kindness and charm that had nothing to do with work.

He had feelings for her—but he kept them in check. He missed her whenever she wasn't there. And whenever she came back, he suddenly sprang back to life. He didn't want to label his feelings, but it was a discreet kind of joy.

Once, a magazine had asked him how he defined happiness. Without even thinking about it, he'd replied: "Lunching with friends under a tree on a summer day in Tuscany." Despite a few betrayals, he loved friendship; he also loved Italy, and felt happy while sitting in the shade of a huge tree, as though it protected him or blessed him, recalling his parents, or his devotion to spirituality.

XX

Casablanca

November 2, 2002

Katarina thinks I'm a spineless lump of jelly.
> —Peter, to his friends Johan and Marianne
> INGMAR BERGMAN, *Scenes from a Marriage*

It had been nearly three years since his stroke. Thanks to his doctors'
and Imane's talents, the painter had recovered the use of his hand.
He could now hold a brush and paint on small formats without his
hand trembling. His leg still hurt him, but he could get around by
himself in a wheelchair. He had recovered his power of speech, and
he could talk fairly normally and sustain a conversation. An exhibition of his new works had been planned. His preparations for it
were meticulous because it had assumed a special significance: it
marked his triumph over his illness. In addition, his style had also
gone through yet another transformation. His canvases had acquired
a spareness and simplicity, exuding a feeling of profound serenity.

The experts dedicated to his work had been quite struck by this new development.

His wife had grown closer to him. Although they hadn't seen much of each other in two years, she'd started to visit him in his studio; at first she only did so from time to time, but then her visits had become more regular when they'd started being able to talk to one another again. She was the first person to congratulate and encourage him when he went back to work and put the finishing touches on his first new painting. She even organized a little party to mark the occasion. They were able to resume some semblance of married life in both the house and the studio. The painter would use his wheelchair to go see his wife after he'd finished working his studio in the afternoons. He took his meals with his wife and children and spent his evenings with them. Yet even though his body was recuperating, he quickly realized that his marriage would never heal. Soon enough, arguments began to creep back into their daily lives, to the point that he started to yearn for those months when he'd been paralyzed and confined to his bed and his wheelchair, but at least far removed from her.

"The older you get, the more you start to look like your father."

This was not a compliment, at least not from his wife's lips.

"What do you mean by that?"

"That you're getting increasingly bitter, nasty, two-faced, and hypocritical."

She'd burst into his studio unannounced while he'd been in the midst of preparing a complex mixture of pigments for his latest canvas. He pretended that he hadn't heard her. She then renewed her assault.

"You see? You don't even try to deny it . . ."

The painter continued to focus on his work, while she disappeared and then returned carrying an Arabic magazine where he had been photographed in the company of a young Lebanese actress. She threw the magazine at him, causing the palette to slip out of his hand and hit the canvas. The painter turned around and calmly told her:

"Please leave me alone, I'm in the middle of painting and I can't talk to you right now. I have to think about the painting, and nothing else. Leave me be."

"You're nothing but a coward."

She left. The painter locked himself inside his studio, but as soon as he'd done so he realized he'd lost all desire to paint, so he sank into his armchair and felt like he wanted to cry. He thought about his father, to whom his wife had just compared him. What a faulty comparison that was, he was so different from him! His father had certainly had a bad temper, but he'd been anything other than mean. His father had never been very attentive toward his wife, but that had been the way things were done in those days, and their way of life was completely removed from the painter's own, which always required him to travel since he was so highly sought after. All in all, the painter's parents had loved each other, even though they'd never been effusive or conspicuous about it, but something bound them together, whether it was habit or tradition, or perhaps more simply just affection or a kind of mutual respect. Their arguments had never approached the levels of violence that characterized the ones between the painter and his wife.

To cheer himself up, the painter had called his friend and confidante Adil—a wise old man and a longtime devotee of yoga and tai chi—and told him about his wife's latest outburst. Adil told him: "Your physical and psychological health must come first. Don't go through life wearing horse blinders, or stick around to watch the ship sink. You have to take the bull by the horns. Keep your spirits high and make an effort to stay calm. I know, separating from your wife will lead to heartbreak, but you must be certain that it's the right decision for you. Your children will thank you for it later. Death also causes heartbreak, but it helps to put matters into perspective. Life ends in the blink of an eye, it's a spark that flickers and fades. Time is an illusion. We live and learn to coexist with that illusion. By the time we die, all the little aches and pains life inflicts on us stop mattering. Be brave!"

Imane arrived late the following morning. She was in a bad mood and kept apologizing while she got on with her work. The captain was now nothing but an ordinary sailor. The painter was taken aback by the sudden change in her, but left her alone. While she was busy massaging him, he turned his mind to the painting he would work on after his session. Imane's hands came to a stop on his left calf, and she looked up at him, her eyes full of tears.

"Those tears are going to fall if I start talking, won't they?"

"Yes, I'm very unhappy."

"Would you like to tell me what's making you so sad?"

"No, captain."

She picked up her bag as soon as she'd finished her work.

"This will be my last session, you must find someone else. I can help you with that, give you some addresses . . ."

She started crying again.

"No, don't go. Let's brew some tea and talk about it."

The painter understood that his wife must be behind all this.

"So she came to see you . . ."

"Yes, she offered to pay if I would agree to give up working for you. She was kind, she wasn't violent and she didn't threaten me, but she was determined. She told me: 'He's my husband and I want to re-pair our marriage and keep him. Nobody's going to stand in my way.' I refused to take her money, but I promised her that I would leave."

"Let me talk to her. I'm the sick one, not her, so please keep do-ing your job and don't worry about her meddling."

"All right, but I've already given her my word."

"Your word, that's exactly right. I love the sound of your voice and I need to keep hearing it. I need you to keep doing your job and need to feel your presence."

"OK, but I need to speak to you about that. I would prefer to leave because I'm not sure I'm doing the right thing by looking after you and then spending extra time in your company."

"I know, I know, it's not just about how you take care of me . . . but what can I do about that? We're only human after all . . . in any case, keep in mind that thanks to you I've made such progress that the doctors were completely amazed. I can paint, I can walk, and I can talk. That's all thanks to you. Even though I had to put some effort into it myself, and go through all my exercises on my own when you weren't here. Meaning I just can't do without you. My own feelings aside, I'm perfectly aware that you can't have a future with me, you have the right to fall in love with a nice man of your own age and your own choosing, while I'm just an old shoe, and nothing more. I just wanted to tell you how much I was in your debt and you're free to do as you like."

Imane hung her head, raised the captain's hand to her lips, and kissed it, as though to thank him. Avoiding his gaze, she told him:

"I think about you all the time, I don't know what to do. My boyfriend came back from Brussels two weeks ago so we can get our marriage license, and the nearer the time draws, the less I want to marry that man. He emigrated to Belgium and drives a bus there. He's big, young and strong. He's even kind, too. But I don't want to be a bus driver's wife, I have other dreams. I've got nothing against him, but I don't have good things to say either. I want to read, go to museums, mingle with artists . . . a bus driver won't be able to give me all those extravagances. Besides, he's already warned me that I'll be living with his mother, and that's making me sick to my stomach. Do you realize what that's going to be like for me? She'll keep her eyes pinned on me and spy on me all the time. Oh no! I have a friend who was forced into living with her husband's mother, and it all ended badly, fighting, police, divorce . . . I'm sure he'll make a good husband, he's muscular, we flirted once or twice, and we didn't have anywhere to go so we could be alone so we went to the movies. We kissed. He's fiery, after all, and, well, none of that really matters—you're the one I want."

He looked at her tenderly.

"But, my poor Imane, I'm neither young nor muscular, I've always been horrified by the thought of sports and working out. What would you have me do at my age? I've got nothing to offer you and besides, I've taken an intense dislike to anything resembling marriage. Do you know what Chekhov used to say about marriage? 'If you're afraid of loneliness, don't marry.' I would be more of a burden to you than a companion. You'd quickly tire of me and my habits, because—I'll be honest with you—I'm obsessive-compulsive, a pain in the ass. I want things to be in their proper place; I don't like clutter; I don't like people who aren't punctual, who act in bad faith, or are hypocritical—and I especially love being alone, it seems unbelievable I know, but that's the way it is, I love being left alone without anyone to bother me. I sleep alone out of respect for my wife since I believe that my bouts of insomnia shouldn't annoy the person who shares my bed. My wife always thought I was trying to avoid her, whereas the truth is that I was worried about disrupting her sleep and calm. Our entire life has been a long series of misunderstandings. If I arranged them end-to-end, our fights would look like the longest train in the world. I'm starting to lose my thread here but I promise you that we'll talk about this again the next time you come over. But I meant what I said, I don't want a different nurse and physical therapist. That's out of the question. Don't worry. I know what to say to my wife."

Imane broke into a smile and looked even more beautiful than the first time he'd seen her. She remained silent and then said: "Until tomorrow, then."

XXI

Casablanca

November 20, 2002

We are God's police. People suppose that when they die all their difficulties are solved for them. It is not as simple as that.

> —the angels in black suits to Liliom,
> when they come to take him to heaven
> FRITZ LANG, *Liliom*

On that morning, the Twins had helped him into a bathtub filled with warm water and left him alone with his thoughts. Speaking in Arabic, he told them: "Leave me alone for just an hour, I want to take advantage of the heat and the silence to listen to my bones." Whenever he used to come back home from school he would find his mother lying on a couch in the living room and she would tell him: "I took advantage of your absence to listen to my bones!" That expression always made him laugh. How can you even do that? Where would you put your ear to listen to them? And what would they have to say? What if those bones started to fidget, play hide and seek, or exchange courtesies? They would simply go back to their rightful place. The warm water was helping to relax those bones, even though it was his muscles that were the true beneficiaries of that.

He loved those peaceful moments where nothing disturbed him. On that day, he started thinking about Ava again, beautiful Ava, the woman who'd left an indelible impression on his forty-year-old self. They'd managed to slip away for a few days to a magnificent hotel in Ravello. They swam, spent hours talking about books and films, ate simple dishes, drank good wine, made love several times a day, and shouted their happiness from the rooftops like children who'd been freed from all constraints. In the evenings, they would take a warm bath together and she would massage him with some restorative oils, light some candles, and tell him: "I love you, and I've never loved anyone like this before." He would reply that he couldn't find the right words to express how he felt. Instead, he used colors, or stars whose names and histories he knew, told her about films she'd never seen or operas she'd missed. Sometimes they'd been so happy that they'd started to cry, because they knew it couldn't last, that reality would eventually catch up to them, especially in his case, since he was cheating on his wife but didn't feel the slightest bit guilty about it. Whenever he spent time with a woman who was simply his friend, he never thought about cheating on his wife; this was the first time in his life that he'd been so passionately in love with someone, and he no longer belonged to the woman he loved. He'd given himself over to Ava wholly and utterly, and he was happy about it.

This love affair had completely revolutionized his style of painting. It had left him brimming with ideas and he'd wanted to put them all into practice as quickly as possible. He'd made some sketches, scribbling the names of the colors in pencil, but most of all he felt that this happiness, this love, this passion, which he'd long looked for, would nourish his creativity and help to illustrate it.

On his return to Paris, the painter had locked himself away in his studio and spent weeks working in a feverish state of excitement. Ava had come to visit him, look at him, admire him, kiss him, and bring him fruit and wine. They hid away, living in fear of being discovered and their love being shattered. She had wanted a child but he had put off that notion without directly telling her no. She was thirty years old and wanted to become a mother with or without him. This fueled their first dispute. She realized that he was incapable of leaving his wife, that he was afraid of her carrying out the reprisals she'd threatened, and that he wanted to try to reconcile the opposing forces in his life. Ava was more self-assured and braver. That applied to his wife too. He wanted to keep the two women in his life at arm's length from one another. It was his most detestable character trait: the desire to please everyone, to be friends with everyone, avoid all conflicts, be a mediator, and he always struggled to avoid making choices, so that he'd never have to cut anyone off. Apparently, he preferred to endure a faint but lasting ache over an intense pang of pain, even though the latter would be short-lived. He hated fighting. He'd never understood the concept of power or those who fought to the death trying to attain it. It just didn't interest him. He'd never left a woman, it was always women who got angry with him and left him. He always tried to remain friends with them, and unfortunately for him he usually succeeded. He would be happy to see them again and occasionally resumed his former relationship with them. He was pleased with the ambiguity of these situations and how flexible they were, even though deep down he knew he couldn't keep that artificial and unhealthy balancing act going forever.

The painter had kept Ava's love letters locked in a safe to which he alone possessed the combination. He would occasionally pull them out and read them, just like a teenager. He told himself that they gave him the strength he needed to paint.

The road of regrets is strewn with promises and reflections. A love lost in the embrace of the night, a love drenched by rains concealed within the clouds, a love that becomes a most exalted pain, a faint star that digs its grave besides those of lovers who were ruined by the long wait.

I went to the Centre Pompidou this morning and spent a long time looking at the only painting of yours exhibited among other contemporary artists. I was very proud. It was the painting you were finishing around the time we first met. I remember how you told me: "It's a strange piece, a harbinger of happiness to come, even though the colors aren't happy!" This painting exudes a kind of energy that borders on dread. Do you remember how you told me that you thought dread exercised a tremendous hold on your body and mind? I quoted Kongoli to you by way of reply: "She was just like me, incapable of committing suicide, and so she tasted death throughout her life."

This may seem strange to you, but that sentence truly summed me up before I met you. Today I'm going to go out and enjoy my life, you are a part of my life and my life is a part of love. Love and its flowers: desire, laughter, sweetness, abandon, the act of sharing; there are also thoughts, the gold button/ buttercup.

You're my love, my everything, my joy.

He'd kept everything, including the last letter she'd sent him after they had broken up.

I'm happy to know you're busy painting. I have faith in your high standards of dedication, which you must see as urgent and all-encompassing. I miss you. I know how much you loved me, I never doubted that, just like I can never forget that you didn't know how to choose us. I'm all yours, a tender memory, sweet and smiling. I continue to share the great emotion that will bind us beyond the reckoning of time.

The emptiness of my night sometimes overwhelms me. I'm growing up, but I'm trying not to become too old. I snuggle up inside words. I wait for the flower to bloom, I become acquainted with my pain. Sadness has settled at the bottom of my soul. I've withdrawn, unable to step further into the light, afraid of the shadow that will come to block it out. I remember your shut eyelids. I stroke your face, slowly, lengthily.

He'd also sent her letters, as well as poems, cheerful drawings, caricatures, and occasionally even painstaking, meticulously detailed drawings of flowers. She'd kept them all and guarded them jealously. She scolded him whenever he was late in answering one of her letters. "So, we're being lazy this morning?"

She was a romantic and her life had been neither easy nor carefree. A girl who'd been wounded at every turn in life and who kicked her feet in deep waters whenever she was about to hit the bottom. Then she would resurface, fighting with all her might, propelled by her need to love, thirsty for life and happiness.

The painter had forbidden himself to feel any regrets because it would serve no purpose. He would tell himself: "Regrets and nostalgia are merely the trappings of our weakness and helplessness. They are lies that we camouflage with words to soothe us and help us to sleep. They make our defeat seem less cruel."

He hadn't known how to choose her. He'd had his reasons, but what good could possibly come of revisiting that happy period of his life? Sometimes he tried to picture what his life might have been like if he'd divorced his wife and stayed with Ava. The scenarios he conjured were worthy of a horror film. He pictured Ava as a disloyal, malicious, and insatiable wife . . . no, he stopped watching that film. It was impossible. Ava could not have had such an evil doppelgänger.

The painter knew he'd thrown away the opportunity to have a

real life, he'd missed out on the woman who had meant the most to him. For a long time, Ava's ghost governed his days and nights, guiding and advising him. He needed her intuition, her intelligence, and her romanticism, even though it sometimes made him laugh. Ava had been the love of his life, and she'd just passed him by, leaving him stuck on the docks, weighted down with guilt and chained by his conjugal bonds, frozen in fear. The only thing he hadn't messed up in his life was his art. When he'd told his psychiatrist that even though his marriage had been a failure, his career had been a success, the latter had retorted: "You can't think of this as a system of communicating vessels; each phase of your life has had its fair share of failures and successes. One does not make up for the other, or vice versa. Otherwise life would be too easy!"

XXII

Casablanca

December 1, 2002

I find you utterly repulsive. In a physical sense, I mean. I could buy a lay from anyone just to wash you out of my genitals.

> —Katarina to Peter, her husband
> INGMAR BERGMAN, *Scenes from a Marriage*

The painter, who was obsessed with labyrinths, and had spent much time mulling over the subject after reading Jorge Luis Borges's stories, now found himself right in the middle of one, except that instead of opening up to let him through, the walls were increasingly closing in on him, so much so that he felt he was suffocating. His condition still got on his nerves, but it didn't bother him as it once had. His mind was perfectly lucid, in fact more remarkably so than ever before. He could now clearly grasp his situation without embellishing it. One thing was certain: he had to free himself from his wife's controlling influence and her destructiveness. He would have to toughen up in order to achieve that. He often recalled Nicolas Chamfort's final words: "the heart must either break or turn to brass." But how can a heart turn to brass? Or be replaced with a rock? Some people are born with a piece of metal inserted where their heart should have been, while others are born normal. People who belong to the latter category are more numerous, but they often become victims.

His wife had a good heart, and often ran to the rescue of anyone in need, especially if they belonged to her tribe. She was generous, always warmly welcomed her friends and never went to a dinner party empty-handed, calling her hosts the next morning to thank them. She had a good heart indeed, but whenever she felt wounded, every fiber of her being mobilized to avenge herself. The other woman inside her took over. She turned into a savage, became completely irrational, and was ready to do anything in order to sate her desire for retribution. Hers wasn't an act, she would loudly proclaim her intentions and then carry them out. He remembered an incident where a poor seamstress had ruined one of his wife's caftans and yet had refused to refund the payment or admit she'd made a mistake. His wife had subsequently ruined that woman's reputation in the space of a week and had succeeded in destroying her business.

He'd understood he would never be able to escape from her now. She had forgiven too many of his mistakes and absences. Sick or not, he would have to suffer through this until the bitter end.

Why should anyone pay so dearly for having fallen out of love? A Spanish member of parliament had introduced legislation to criminalize breakups. Meaning that when a man or a woman fell out of love with their spouse, they would be liable to pay a fine, and, why not, perhaps even spend a few years in prison. Exactly how many years would one spend in jail, and how much would the fine be? This was exactly the sort of punishment his wife would have liked to exact, who, feeling betrayed and humiliated, would have loved for a judge to make an example of her husband, a man who'd had the audacity to stop loving his wife and to go around spending his children's money on other women. When she'd stumbled across proof of his affairs, he'd refused to apologize. Besides, he'd just about done everything to ensure he'd left a trail she could follow. After all, why should he apologize when this could contribute to his being freed from a situation that he could no longer put up with, a life built on lies, hypocrisy, tantrums, and outbursts of uncontrollable anger?

He could hear Caroline's voice telling him: "Why should anyone suffer? Is there a law that says one must suffer at someone else's hand? Don't forget that you are your own capital, there is no other!" Which was pretty much what his psychiatrist told him. Nothing can justify you being trampled on. As for his mother, she'd told him: "Nobody has the right to wash their feet over you!"

His nihilistic Swiss friend had given him the usual speech: "In the end you're an artist, and you're entitled to some respect despite all your screwups and bullshit: after all, who doesn't eventually screw up? Just run away, and remember, we live alone and we die alone. From time to time we manage to break through that solitude to enjoy moments of pleasure, but make no mistake, these moments are fleeting, my friend, fleeting! Do as I do, go live in a hotel, spend your money, go for a dip in the best swimming pools of the world, and as for your children, they'll go on with their lives, work, and don't ever think they'll come to sit by your bedside when you're dying in a hospice like poor Francis, the great luminary of French culture, who'd been so disfigured by illness that when he was sat drooling in a chair he couldn't even recognize the people who'd come to visit him. One must always visit friends who've been ravaged by illness. It's a good lesson to keep in mind. Once you've taken all of this into account, it's certainly wise to stake your future on lightness!"

•

He could notice the progress he was making with each passing day and saw that he was in a better shape. The prospect of seeing Imane made him rejoice. One day she arrived with a bouquet of roses.

"Today we're going to walk for an hour, it's nice outside. You're recovering your reflexes in your left leg and arm. You can stand up on your own by leaning on a crutch."

The walk did him a lot of good. Imane met her mother on the promenade. She introduced her to the painter. She was still young. She thanked him for all that he'd done for Imane. Once she'd left, the painter stopped and told Imane:

"What did she mean by all the good I've done for you? You're the one who's done a lot for me, you're so patient and your hands have healing powers . . ."

"My mother was referring to something else, which I haven't told you about. I lied to her and told her you'd agreed. You're wondering what I'm talking about? Well, it's about my brother, whose dream is to leave this country and go to Europe to look for work. My mother thought that your fame and connections might be useful to him. I didn't dare bring it up with you, you know what Moroccan families are like."

"Oh, I'm well aware, there's nothing wrong with helping some-one out, let's talk about it some other time."

Then, after a brief silence, he said:

"This idea of leaving Morocco at all costs is very new. This coun-try has missed out on every opportunity it's ever had, and this is the result, all its young people are leaving! I'll try to find your brother a job, but I'll look for it here, close to you, which will be easier for me, and besides, Europe is not the land of milk and honey that people think it is."

While they talked, the painter tried to think of ways to keep Imane close to him. He wondered whether she might make a good as-sistant for him, but on the other hand he worried about being unable to keep his work and personal feelings separate.

•

Once they'd returned to the house, Imane massaged his legs and then sat by his feet as she so often liked to do and began telling him a story:

Once upon a time there lived a little girl who wanted to grow up faster than time would allow, mistaking herself for the south wind, which was strong and forceful. She would arrive somewhere like a storm and sweep away all in her path. They called her "Fitna," which in Arabic means "internal turmoil" and by extension "panic."

But by and by as she grew up, the little girl calmed down and transformed into an "evening breeze," so people started calling her "the murmur of the moon." In the evenings, she would stay up and walk the streets along the riverbanks, collecting the stories that were handed down from generation to generation and placing those stories inside cups of wine, which poets, especially the cheeky ones, were fond of drinking.

Once she'd grown up, the girl left for the mountains and was never seen again. A legend was born amidst the stones and the wild weeds. The young girl had become the goddess of solitude, reigning over a kingdom of the hardest rocks known to man, barring way to all illnesses that hailed from diseased, unloved countries.

It was also said that this woman had given birth to three sons after lying with the devil. Once they'd grown into adults, her sons caused a great deal of havoc and violence: stealing, killing, torturing, and always managing to evade the law. Quite the contrary, in fact; they prospered and managed to mingle with the city's most distinguished notables. One night, their mother came down from the mountain and ate them. In the early hours of that morning, the bloated corpse of a mare was discovered lying in front of the city's gate, and when they sliced it open, they discovered the bodies of the three men, whose skin had turned green and whose eyes had gone missing . . .

On seeing the captain's astonished expression, Imane stopped and said:

"Don't worry, I just made that up, don't be scared!"

"Are you sure you don't have a nicer story to tell me before you leave?"

"Yes, I love you."

"Now that's a nice story."

XXIII

Casablanca

December 19, 2002

I know why Katarina and Peter go through hell. They don't
speak the same language. They have to translate everything
into a common language. Sometimes it's like listening to
preprogrammed tape recorders. Sometimes all you get is the
vast silence of outer space.

—INGMAR BERGMAN, *Scenes from a Marriage*

On his psychiatrist's request, the painter used a tape recorder to list all
the reasons why he'd fallen out of love with his wife. He used several
tapes. He wanted to be specific, and tell the whole truth in so far as
he saw it. He might have made some mistakes, but in any case this
was meant to be an outlet for him, and not an indictment against his
wife.

He pressed "record" and launched into a preface of sorts:

Here is the list of reasons that led me to the conclusion that my wife and I haven't loved one another in a long time. I may be wrong, and needless to say, these reasons are subjective, and they aren't exhaustive either. Well, here we go:

My wife always does what she pleases.

My wife is a flash flood, a flood of words, a storm.

My wife is a diamond that nobody polished.

My wife believes in things she can't see: she believes in ghosts, in haunted houses, in the evil eye, in bad energies and destructive vibes.

My wife is in love with love and the idea of a Prince Charming.

My wife likes cars that are big and beautiful. She can't stand being driven around. She always drives on the left side of the road and thinks that all the other drivers are always wrong.

My wife never admits to any of her mistakes and doesn't know how to compromise.

My wife doesn't know how to keep track of time, but she does however have a keen sense of direction. She's also good with numbers and sums . . .

My wife always thinks she's sincere. She tells the truth when she lies.

My wife is a wild woman who is still haunted by hunger and an inclement land.

My wife turns into a fury when she's upset, an animal whose wound becomes her weapon.

My wife displays a kind of logic that no mathematicians could have ever predicted. She's the only one who knows how it works and the only one who uses it.

My wife is capable of destroying herself so long as it proves the other person is guilty.

My wife has convinced herself that she's oppressed and that my family's always been out to get her.

My wife is a happy and crazy drunk. Yet she claims she's never abused alcohol or been drunk.

My wife believes a married couple cannot have any secrets between them. She thinks they should live in sweet harmony and that partners should be blindly complicit and assimilate into a single, uncomplicated person.

My wife's memory is very selective, and she's possessed of great charm and intelligence, is fiercely determined, and displays a kind of calculated madness that is just shy of crazy enough to make it seem like she's not mad.

My wife doesn't like analyzing things, or questioning them, hates doubts and the possibility that she might be wrong.

My wife isn't a witch, but she trusts all the sorceresses she comes across and would more readily believe a magician than a scientist.

My wife is like a house that was built without foundations.

My wife is sweet to everyone except her husband.

My wife thinks her parents are actually her children.

My wife calls every drama a tragedy.

My wife wants to cut me down to size so I'll be at her mercy.

My wife doesn't have a sense of justice, but she sees herself as a paladin of justice anyway.

My wife is fiercely jealous.

My wife has never thanked me.

My wife has never told me she loved me.

My wife is only tender toward her children, brothers, sisters, and parents.

My wife thinks other couples don't have any problems.

My wife annoys me at least once a day.

My wife acts in bad faith with certainty and triumphalism.

My wife confuses "true" with "good" and "false" with "bad."

My wife has never sought my advice before making a decision.

My wife pretends that she's never had a lover. Which I very much doubt is true. But I pretend to believe her when we're face to face. It's a bad idea to offend a woman who's cheated on you.

My wife thought that she loved me—and so did I. I don't love her anymore and that's fine by me . . .

A few days after finishing his list, he listened to the tape before heading out for his appointment at the psychiatrist's. The painter felt he'd missed the big picture. So he hit "record" again and said: "I'm solely responsible for this failure. There were many more differences between us than simply our social standing or ages. No, the real difference between us was a lot worse than that. We've never shared a life throughout the entirety of our marriage and we never even realized it."

XXIV

Casablanca

January 4, 2003

Dying is easy. Living's the hard part.

> —Mrs. Menoux to Julie
> FRITZ LANG, *Liliom*

He'd never taken the initiative to leave a woman. His wife would be the first. His decision was final. He'd taken a long time to reach that decision, but the stroke had finally helped to sway him more convincingly than any of his friends or his psychiatrist. He'd waited for Christmas to pass, had prepared a speech, had completed the paintings he'd been working on, had rested, then had chosen a day when she'd seemed calmer than usual and had asked her to come see him in his studio late that afternoon.

When he'd announced his decision to leave her, and told her that he didn't love her anymore, she pretended that she hadn't heard him and instead asked him where he wanted to dine that evening. He didn't answer her. A long silence ensued. All of a sudden, she went on the offensive: "But what will become of me? Everything you have you owe to me: your career, your success, your money. You're nothing without me, just a wreck stuck in a wheelchair. It was thanks to me and my intelligence and the energy of my youth that you became famous and celebrated, and that your paintings are now worth hundreds of thousands of dollars. All of that will fall apart when I'm gone. Not to mention that I'll make you pay dearly for this! You have no idea what I'm capable of. You wanted to have children with me, to start a family, and so you'll have to assume your responsibilities. I won't lift a finger to help you and one morning you'll wake up and find yourself face to face with cruelty in the shape of a woman. I'm the one who made you, and I know how to destroy you!" On that note, she left, slamming the door behind her. The painter wasn't shaken. He was going to hold steady.

When his wife realized a few days later that he wasn't kidding, and that he wasn't making idle threats and was serious about wanting to leave her, she took the initiative and handed him a letter written by a lawyer asking the painter for his opinion. The lawyer suggested an uncontested divorce. Knowing his wife and having heard all the threats she'd made, the painter was initially surprised. He read and reread the letter, then told himself: "After all, it's better this way, this will make things easier and quicker."

He grew disillusioned in the weeks that followed. His wife had absolutely no intention of agreeing to a compromise. She was going to be ruthless, sick or not, disabled or not, she'd made up her mind: that man would have to pay for the audacity of wanting to leave her. The painter couldn't find any rest. War had been declared and nothing would be able to stop it. "Uncontested divorce!" The idiot who'd come up with that term—one of those formulaic sentences of which there were so many in the world—couldn't have imagined that the word "uncontested" didn't mean anything to his wife.

Some of his friends volunteered to talk to her, to try and bring her to her senses since she was being so unreasonable. They wanted to help them reach a solution that would be mutually beneficial, without any more damage being caused and without involving the kids. Poor friends! They spent hours talking to her, which was a complete waste of their time. She listened to them, smiled, thanked them for their friendship and their concern. But it was like she had a thingamajig, a blender situated between her ears that pulverized their words into nothingness. Sometimes she swore that she would call her lawyer and withdraw from the divorce proceedings, then she would return home and ask their children to act as witnesses: "Your father wants a divorce, he wants to leave us, he's found a girl who's got her clutches on him and who wants to steal our money. I will have to ask the girls to lend me some money."

When one of the children told her that it was the driver who always went out to do the shopping and run errands, and that their father still gave him money for that, she dodged the question and said: "I know, but he doesn't want to anymore . . . Regardless, I wonder what kind of woman could possibly want him, considering the state that he's in. He's just a wreck, a vegetable, he's good for nothing, he can't paint anymore and his agent told me that he's very worried because the price of his paintings have dipped lately!"

She was ready to do anything so long as it accomplished her aims.

One morning, after a sleepless night, the painter finally managed to doze off and had an erotic dream, something that hadn't happened to him in a long time. He found himself at a party, where he met a young, sexy woman, with laughter in her eyes, and a slender, well-proportioned body, who was married with two children. She had come to the party without her husband. She worked as an official at the Ministry of Sports, and was away from home for work. As he'd been about to leave the party, she'd caught up to him and said: "Are you driving home? No? In a taxi or on foot? I have a car, why don't you let me give you a lift?" To thank her, he'd placed his fedora on her head. It suited her really well. "Keep it!" In the elevator, she unbuttoned her blouse and pounced on him. When they got to the ground floor, she dragged him to a dark corner and pulled her skirt down. She wasn't wearing any panties. Their excitement had reached its zenith, and they made love right there on the spot, standing up, the fedora fell off her head and tumbled onto the floor, then a rat passed by below. On seeing the rat, the painter had screamed and woken up with a start. "Damned rat!" he'd exclaimed.

Who was that young woman, where had he seen her? Where do the faces we see in our dreams come from? She resembled a French actress whose name he'd forgotten. Perhaps he'd watched one of her films on television or somewhere else. The painter smiled, but it turned into a grimace when he saw the lawyer's crumpled-up letter in regards to the uncontested divorce lying on the bedside table amidst a jumble of medicine bottles. Without wasting a moment, he called his lawyer to check in with him and ask him to speed up the proceedings.

When the painter was ready and had washed and dressed, he called the Twins so he could start his physical therapy session. It now consisted of a series of gymnastics exercises and little walks. His assistants took him to a gym and helped him with his exercises. As he wanted to chat a little, he asked one of them:

"Are you married?"

"I am, sir."

"Are you happy?"

"Let's say it's fine."

Then he turned to the other.

"What about you, are you married?"

"No, sir."

"And why not?"

"Have you seen what Moroccan women are like these days? Freedom, equality, they're the ones in charge now. I see how much my poor brothers suffer . . ."

"But a lot of Moroccan women aren't liberated, besides, that's a good thing, they work, they can contribute to the family budget . . ."

"One day, my mother got tired of my father never talking to her and so she asked him if they could have a conversation—she was bored. Without taking his eyes off the television, my father told her, 'Tomorrow, tomorrow I'll talk to you.' The next day, my mother was very happy and impatient to have that conversation with him. But my father remained silent. 'What are you thinking about?' she asked him. After a long silence, my father told her: 'This is what I'm thinking about: if I'd killed you eighteen years ago, I'd only have two years left of my jail sentence right now!'"

"But that's horrible."

The painter had always been horrified by crimes of passion. He simply couldn't understand why killing one's partner could ever be seen as a solution. He'd never entertained such notions. He worried every time his wife was late in coming home, or when she was out driving. He couldn't bear to see her ill and would look after her and counsel her. Truth be told, even though he didn't love her anymore, he still felt somewhat devoted to her, a kind of affection he couldn't explain. One day, she'd broken her arm when she'd slipped on some snow. They'd been in Switzerland at the time. He'd run around like a madman to look for help, and needless to say he'd taken her to the hospital and had slept on a cot in the same room as her. However, the next morning they'd had another argument and she'd nearly thrown a cup of steaming coffee in his face. No, he'd never wanted to harm her, or prevent her from fulfilling herself and accomplishing whatever she wanted. He'd helped her put on a showcase of musicians from her village, even though he hated that kind of music. He'd also found her a producer and a venue. His wife had then spent a year promoting a troupe of Berber musicians in France, Belgium, and Switzerland. He'd made all his contacts available to her and had called on his friends to help and ensure that her project was a success. When she'd been busy working, she'd left him alone. So he'd told himself: "She must always have something to keep her busy!" After her musical project had come to an end, he'd suggested she put on an exhibition of handicrafts from her region. This new project hadn't gone as well as her previous effort. Once again, she'd heaped endless reproaches on him. So he redoubled his efforts and put together a charity auction, asking his friends to donate paintings. It took some effort because he would have had to set up a foundation, but someone else hosted the event under the aegis of their foundation instead. Thanks to that auction, his wife raised enough money to brighten up the village, build a school, and above all improve the inhabitants' living conditions.

Her chief virtue was that she was willful and direct; her worst trait was that she never saw what she started through to its end. So he got tired of helping her and gave up. Perhaps it was a mistake. One day he'd told her: "You see, darling, if you'd married a boy from your village, someone who spoke your language and understood your silences, then you would have been a lot happier."

He was profoundly certain that this was the case. As a result of his experiences, he'd stopped praising the concept of multiculturalism; he stopped believing that the confluence of cultures was enriching, and without being seduced by the stupid notion of endogamy, he'd reached the conclusion that leaving one's tribe was no guarantee of success.

As he so often said, there was no such thing as a clash of civilizations, only a clash of ignorances. He'd admittedly ignored every aspect of his wife's Berber heritage. It had just never interested him. His wife knew nothing about the Morocco that lay beyond her ancestral village. Thus, it was no surprise that the resulting clash turned out to be violent, and that it inflicted a lot of damage on both their married life and their families. But he'd fallen in love with her—and love, whether blind or levelheaded, couldn't be held accountable for people's actions.

The painter thought about Imane and was looking for a way to keep her close to him for good, despite her having admitted she was fond of him. Her presence always dispelled the fog that occasionally brooded in his mind. He looked at her as though she were a painting, or at a push a model who didn't want to leave his studio. This had actually happened to him once, at a time when he'd still devoted himself to portraits. The woman in question had been a young student who posed in order to pay her way through school. She was graceful, professional, and knew how to sit still and didn't talk. One evening, after she'd finished sitting for him, she'd asked him for a glass of wine. He'd offered her a choice of red or white. Once she'd drained her glass, she'd drawn close to him and kissed him. He'd gently pushed her away. He had a rule about never sleeping with his models. But the young woman insisted. He rejected her a second time, explaining that the painting wasn't finished yet and that it would ruin everything if they slept together, that it was a matter of principle. She'd then left and slammed the door behind her. He'd never seen her again. A year later, he'd run into her at the market on Rue Daguerre in the company of an older man: her husband. He'd told her, "You should come by the studio, you never picked up your check, and besides it would be a good opportunity to finish the painting."

"It would be my pleasure, but I'll call ahead."

She came by the next day.

"I'm not your model anymore."

"Yes, you are, because we never finished the painting, so let's try to complete it, and if we do, we'll celebrate."

The painter eventually finished that piece and the model became his mistress. Their affair lasted for a season. She didn't talk much and didn't ask him any questions. They quickly, and very naturally, established a ritual. She would come by once a week in the afternoon, kiss him, and undress. Sometimes he would be completely focused on his work, and so she would wait for him in bed, and if he took too long, she would say: "I'm going to start on my own." He would join her as soon as he'd finished, and they would spend a very gratifying hour together that was unmarked by any sentimentality or conversation, just pleasure for pleasure's sake. She would never wash at his place, she would simply hurriedly put her clothes on again, give him a little kiss behind his ear, and leave. He, on the other hand, would linger there, exhausted but satisfied. The sun would have already set. He then took a shower and went home. Nobody could have suspected anything. So long as he still made love to his wife, she didn't have any doubts, or at least never showed it.

One day, the painter received a visitor: the man whom his model had introduced as her husband when they'd met at the market. A weary-looking man who'd aged before his time. He apologized for arriving unannounced, lowered his sad gaze to the floor, and said:

"She's left us. I know she used to come see you, she told me all about your little naps. I was jealous, but I tried not to let it show. There were thirty years between us. That's a lot. She left us for an Italian actress, an ugly woman, thin as a stick, completely charmless and humorless. Well, that's what I came here to tell you, hoping I could share a little of my misery with you."

The painter offered him a drink and told him he shouldn't beat himself up about it.

"She's a free spirit and only does what she feels like, let's hope she's happy with that woman!"

XXV

Casablanca

January 25, 2003

In marriage, where one is wise, two are happy.
—Paquita, Celia's chambermaid
FRITZ LANG, *Secret Beyond the Door*

He'd always been afraid of what people referred to as "hell." He'd heard others refer to their married life as hell, that divorce was a catastrophe, that falling out of love with someone was a violent act perpetrated on that person . . .

Over the course of a dinner, he'd learned by chance that one of his friends who lived in the south of France, and whom he rarely saw as he didn't like leaving his farm—he was a musician—had gotten divorced. The painter called him to find out more about what had happened.

"Yes, I got divorced, I lost everything, I gave her everything, I'm completely penniless, but in return I've gained something priceless: my freedom. I'm broke, but I can breathe. Besides, I've asked some friends of mine to help me find a studio in Paris. I'll make some money eventually. I've got a few concerts lined up for next year, but I lost my house, my boat, and my car. She even asked for something on top of alimony, which I didn't know existed, I had to pay her a sum to compensate her for her loss of standing, for the damage done to her reputation after I left her. What about me? What about my standing?

"But it's finally over, I see my kid every other weekend and I can start a new life. As for hell, I can talk to you about that for hours, it's better to lose everything and to be able to leave that hell behind instead of clinging on and keeping fighting. I've been defeated. But nobody takes me seriously. I've been beaten up both physically and psychologically but I don't even have the right to complain. There we have it, my friend, since you're a painter, why don't you paint a fresco that depicts battered men, that would be original! Well, come to think of it, I've never seen a film about battered men. It wouldn't be a bad idea to give people a window onto a reality that nobody talks about. What about you, how are things going with that beautiful rebel of yours?"

He told his friend he'd decided to leave his wife. They were going to get divorced too, but their lawyers hadn't yet reached an agreement. As he told his friend his story, the painter was suddenly overcome with a panic attack and felt an intense tightness in the middle of his chest. After hanging up the phone, he swallowed a Valium, then called his lawyer. The latter reassured him and asked him to be patient. He said that the situation was under control.

Nevertheless, a few days later some bailiffs burst into his studio completely unannounced.

"We've come to do an inventory of your work. We have to appraise and catalogue all the paintings you have here in your studio and elsewhere. We've been commissioned by your wife. Though you should know that we admire you a great deal, you do us proud. Please forgive us, we're only doing our job."

He let them carry on with their work. Most of the paintings in his studio were incomplete or had been left unfinished. He led them to the basement where he kept some paintings that friends of his had given him. They took note of everything and said they would come back in case . . .

Later that evening, he tried to talk to his wife about their visit. As he was in a hurry to finish some work for an exhibition scheduled to open at his gallery in Monaco, he contented himself with pretending to be offended and asked his wife to calm down. He couldn't bear the idea of having another fight with her.

"I don't trust you, and so I must take precautionary measures. If you run off with someone else tomorrow, then I'll be left completely destitute and out on the street. I won't let that happen. The other day I saw you drooling after that peroxide blonde who's married to one of your dear friends even though she's almost half a century younger than him! Anything's possible, so I'm taking the initiative . . ."

"Don't worry, just let me paint. I just need some peace and quiet so I can finish a big commission. I'm working a lot at the moment."

"You'll never have peace and quiet!"

The painter and his wife lived as though they were enemies spying on each other. The moment he left the house, his wife would rifle through all his things and make photocopies of any and all documents she could get her hands on. Which she would then send to her lawyer. Over the course of those weeks, the painter's work took a new direction and acquired a certain depth and cruelty. It was like a condemned man's last days on earth. His art thrived in the midst of that adversity. He knew that, and thought he should take a holiday once all this was over, he could go somewhere with Imane, maybe to an island. He'd never fantasized about deserted islands, but thought that once he got far enough away, he would be able to breathe a little and reflect on his work. But did he really have to go to the other side of the world in order to do that?

XXVI

Casablanca

February 3, 2003

I don't think there is such a thing as the truth. No matter
what we say or do, it will hurt.

—INGMAR BERGMAN, *Scenes from a Marriage*

Imane arrived in the afternoon wrapped in a blue djellaba. She'd just
left the hammam. She put her things down, gave him his injection
and a long massage. She smelled wonderful, but it wasn't a new perfume, it was just her body's natural fragrance after it had spent a few
hours in those baths, where people's tongues loosened and wagged.

"I'm going to tell you a love story," she told him, while packing
away her equipment. "I didn't make this one up, in fact I just heard it at
my neighborhood hammam earlier today. Even though women talk a
lot of nonsense in those places, where the heat and the steam free their
minds and imaginations, I still think the story I'm going to tell has
a kernel of truth to it. So lend me your ears and judge for yourself."

This is the story of Habiba, a woman who ate her husband.

The day after her wedding, Habiba decided to eat her husband so she could always keep him close to her. First she sniffed him, just like a cat does when it's encircling its prey, then she started to nibble on him, then began eating him, taking care not to arouse anyone's suspicions.

On the first day, she focused on the parts of him that were easiest to swallow. On the second day, she helped send him off to sleep by stroking him for a long time, and licking his armpits and genitals. Despite the sedatives that she'd put in a glass of almond milk, her husband would wake up from time to time. He let her carry on, and with his eyes half-shut he smiled, his penis fully erect. Habiba was so excited that she hummed to herself, pleased. She enjoyed being able to do whatever she wanted to her man, and couldn't believe her own prowess.

Her friends had filled her with horror stories from their own wedding nights, and she'd been afraid of the violence of the sexual act, and she'd been especially terrified by the notion of those bloodied sheets. Especially since she used to touch herself as a little girl, and had found out after a doctor's visit that she'd broken her hymen. As she'd never slept with a man, she'd refused to have her hymen restitched.

On her wedding night, she'd offered herself up to her man, just like a traditional woman should, acting submissively and shy, keeping her gaze lowered, and letting him be in charge. Whereas in fact she had a plan: she would lure him into a sense of false security so she could prepare him for the following day. Her husband had ripped her satin sarouels off, spread her legs, and penetrated her unceremoniously. In pain, she'd pulled him closer to her and kept his member inside her for a moment, preventing him from moving. He quickly ejaculated and pulled out, proud of himself. They didn't exchange a single word. Which was not the done thing in those cases. When she'd gotten up to go to the bathroom, he'd seen her in all her splendor and had gotten hard again. Then he'd pounced on her, grabbing her by the arm, and tossed her onto the bed. Then, once more without stroking her or kissing her, he penetrated her and came, emitting a groan which she thought sounded like he was thanking God and his mother for having given him that woman. It was at that moment that she'd slipped the sedatives into the big glass of almond milk, which her husband had drunk in a single gulp. By the time she came back, he'd fallen into a deep slumber.

Thus on that second day, Habiba had observed her husband while he slept for a long time. The idea of eating him piece by piece excited her. Her desire for him grew and grew. She was sweating and shaking. She drew close to him, started stroking his arms and then moved onto his hands. She sucked his fingers, one by one, and gleefully munched on them. On the third day, she started eating his arms. On the fourth she ate his feet and most of his legs. On the fifth, she severed his head and placed it in a crystal jar, which was a gift from her uncle, who'd made his fortune working in the Gulf. Finally on the sixth she ate what was left of him, taking care not to damage his genitals, which she placed in a magic box. By the seventh day, there was nothing left of the man she'd married. Or rather, every part of him was still there, just inside her. Habiba hadn't even put on any weight. She felt happy and proud of herself.

Finally a successful marriage. Habiba and her husband had become a single person. Nobody noticed anything. The wedding party had been in full swing when Habiba had been busy eating her husband, taking to it rigorously and methodically, scrupulously following the advice that her mother had given her a long time earlier: "You must always hang on to your man, my daughter, you can't share your man with anyone else. And there's no better way to keep him all to yourself than by eating him! If you do that, you'll never need to talk to him, or threaten him that "I'll cut off your balls if I catch you cheating on me, or if I see you with someone else I'll slice both your throats" . . . *You must stay one step ahead of him, otherwise it'll be too late, men quickly get used to having us under their heels."*

Habiba had always told herself: "My man will be mine and I'll be his. There won't be any differences between us. We'll be so inseparable that you won't even be able to slide a thread of silk between us. We'll become one person and we'll stay like that forever. A perfect, total union, which nobody would ever destroy or surpass. That is love, crazy love. That's what mothers teach their daughters. Men are hard to find. So women have to do everything in their power in order to keep their husbands close and prevent them from being lured away by other women.

Just because Habiba ate her husband, this didn't mean that he vanished off the face of the earth. She would spit him out every day so that he could go about his business, go to work, make a living, and then return straight home without even looking left or right. As though he were being guided by remote control, he obeyed his wife's wishes, since she had the power to restore his human form whenever she chose. Whenever her husband came home, he would kiss her hand and offer her a bouquet of flowers, sometimes even some jewelry or some nice fabrics. He never came back empty-handed. He lowered his gaze whenever he spoke and never raised his voice. He would perform his prayers and wait for a sign from his wife, who would be ecstatic to see him. They would eat in silence, and he would give her all the tastiest morsels, doing so gracefully and politely. She would appreciate his silence and the kindness of those gestures. Toward the end of the meal, she would feel desire rising in her; it would only take a look to make her husband get up and precede her to the bedroom. He would sit there without asking any questions and wait for his sweetheart. He would also feel a strong desire rise within him. She wouldn't give herself to him right away. She loved to make him wait, walking around him, brushing her fingers against his penis, assessing how hard he got and making his cock into her plaything. Her man would obey her and kiss her hand, her mouth, and her sex. He was completely in the moment and hers alone. The entirety of his sexual energies were devoted to his lawful wife.

However, one evening he seemed a little distracted, and he ejaculated before making her climax. Habiba slapped him resoundingly across the face. Ever since that time, her husband made love to her even more attentively, devoting himself entirely to her pleasure. His mind, which was fully involved in the sexual act, would stimulate her and prepare her for the lovemaking. She would entice him with her perfume, and the scent of her flesh, the natural smell of her armpits, and the folds of her skin. He once imagined that he'd found her in a tent in the desert at night, her face draped in a veil. She crawled on the carpet on all fours, the veil slipped off her head, and she started sucking his testicles, sometimes swallowing them until she almost choked on them. On another occasion, he saw her while she'd been squatting and in the midst of cleaning her intimates, and had come up from behind her, taking her by surprise, and mounted her. She let him have his way with her, moaning like a woman in need. Sometimes the way they moved their limbs made them look like they were in perfect sync. While they made love, they spoke only a little, moving and loving and falling asleep in each other's arms. They had become one and the same. He never tried to dominate her. He knew she wouldn't tolerate it. Each time she spit him out again, she told him all about her desires and fantasies. The moment Habiba desired her husband, he would awake and fulfill her cravings. Sometimes after they made love, Habiba even told her husband to sleep in another room. He wouldn't object, knowing she had her reasons. Her man belonged only to her, and nobody could ever take him away from her.

Habiba and her husband were an exemplary couple. Her friends envied her so much that one day they asked her to reveal the secret behind their perfect relationship. Habiba told them: "He loves me, that's the secret, we're in love, that's all." But her friends weren't satisfied with her answer, they argued with their husbands all the time, were convinced they were cheating on them, gambling the family's money away in casinos or wasting it on liquor in bars and on prostitutes. They would go back to Habiba and ask her to give them more details. So she would tell them: "If you want to keep your husband close, then don't wait until he's already run away, you must take care of him on your very first night. A man who has left the house is already lost to his wife. You must never let him go, so that he belongs to you and you alone even when he's not in the house."

Lamia, one of Habiba's friends, suspected that she'd been consulting a sorcerer. "Not at all," Habiba protested. "Sorcerers are charlatans. No, there's no need to resort to such absurd and ridiculous tactics. My recipe is unbeatable. It's been put to the test. My mother gave it to me. My father was the most loving and submissive husband ever. He loved my mother and always did what she said. I followed her advice to the letter. No scruples, no hesitation, it's him or me, so it might as well be me, right, ladies? I'm rather proud of my achievement.

"I'm telling you, the first night is decisive. You mustn't wait until the following day. As soon as he'd climbed inside the dekhchoucha, *I saw that despite his enormous height and weight, he was just a little lamb deep down. I knew he would be mine. But he was the kind of man who was bound to resist. I stared him right in the eye and forced him to lower his gaze. The rest was a piece of cake. A man who lowers his gaze will be like putty in your hands. He's yours, and he'll stay that*

way forever. There's no need for any potions, incense, or magic scrolls. It's just a matter of willpower. This is what my mother taught me: you just need a little almond milk and a pinch of white powder . . ."

"What's the recipe for this powder then?" Fatima exclaimed. "You must take pity on our unhappiness, you can't be the only one to be able to leave this nightmare, while the rest of us are stuck here like wet rags waiting for our husbands to come home, hoping they don't return stinking of booze after having emptied their wallets and scrotums."

"I've told you once and I'll tell you again: there's nothing I can do for you, it's too late to remedy the situation. You have to cut off the snake's head on the very first night."

"What snake are you talking about? We married men, not snakes!"

"You're doomed . . . there's nothing I can do."

But her friends insisted and had her surrounded. "We won't let you leave until you reveal your secret."

"Fine, since you insist, I'm going to tell you what you should have done. You should have eaten your husband, that's right, you should have gobbled him up and kept him inside your body forever. It's what I did and it worked out for me. But it's already too late in your case, I've told you that. Your husbands have become too leathery, tough, and uneatable. You can't turn back time."

"You ate him, you really ate him?"

"I did, I ate him all up. He's right here inside me, and he only comes out when I want him to. I had no choice. It was either that, or I would have wound up being his dog, at his beck and call, so he could mercilessly exploit me or beat me up whenever he wanted. And I never would have had an orgasm either!"

"Are you planning to have children with him?"

"Not for the time being. I'll exploit him as much as I can

for now, and then we'll see. If we have children, there's a risk he'll escape. At which point I'll have to come up with another scheme to keep him completely submissive. I'll ask my mother, who will ask her mother, but I must be quick about seeing as how she's dying."

A few days later, Habiba went to see her grandmother. She was over ninety years old, tiny, frail and thin, but her eyes were still sharp and bright, and she didn't mince her words: "All men are bastards and cowards," she told her, "they'll make your life miserable if you don't keep them in check. Marriage is nothing but a declaration of war celebrated with music, good food, perfumes, incense, pretty clothes, promises, songs, and so forth. There's only one way to keep a man in check: you have to eat him." She visualized her words by bunching her fingers and pointing to her open mouth. "Sometime you can't do that, but you shouldn't give up, there are other options. Your grandfather, for example, was completely uneatable. He was hard as a rock, it was impossible to swallow any part of him. So I pretended to be his slave for many months. I did whatever he wanted me to, and crawled on all fours in front of him, never refused anything he asked of me, and did anything I thought would please him. After a few years of careful training, he could only find pleasure with me. Now that's what I call keeping a man. He never cheated on me. I'm sure of that because I hired a number of spies to keep me informed. He went from the shop to the house and from the house to the shop. He never once paid a visit to those disloyal women who cheat on their husbands. No, he was immune to that. When he was dying, he spent the whole night crying, saying he would be unhappy without me in heaven. I don't know if God sent him to heaven, but wherever he is, I know that he's waiting for me. I'm in no hurry to join him. I still have a few years left to live and places to see. God will surely have taught him to be patient.

"That's the way you make a marriage work, my daughter, that's the only way. And don't forget that your husband will take advantage of you the moment you lower your guard. Marriage is a small war that is won through subterfuge, because when the shouting starts and you've run out of arguments, then it's the beginning of the end. When I look around me, I see nothing but failures. Women cry and men triumph. It's not fair. If everyone followed my example, that kind of thing wouldn't happen anymore."

Habiba had listened closely to her grandmother and had kept her lessons closely in mind. After a year of married life, however, Habiba started to get bored. She was no longer attracted to her obedient husband. Habiba only had to make a gesture and he would start to please her right away. She even started to throw up. She wasn't pregnant, she was just fed up. A man who did whatever she wanted, was always at her mercy, and was only devoted to her was like a dish without any spices, completely devoid of surprises.

Habiba chose to act, and to make changes to the wonderful world of the women who'd eaten her husband. Her mother suggested throwing him up a little. She thought it was time for the next stage of the plan: to give him a little freedom, let him go somewhere on his own, perhaps go on some adventure, and to let him sleep with another woman to put the spark back into their relationship.

Habiba listened to her mother's advice and spent the entire day throwing up. She felt lighter that evening. After a few days, her man was standing right in front of her, completely free, but she couldn't bear to look at him. She wasn't interested in him anymore. She felt better whenever he wasn't around. She told him that he was free to leave and that she wouldn't try to keep him anymore.

Habiba decided to gobble up another man. She set her heart

on a man who had been married to one of her cousins, who was an invalid, thereby ensuring her new man would come out of a marriage that hadn't worked. Before her death, Habiba's cousin had told her: "I'm warning you, he's tough. Brutal. Don't try to swallow him on the first night, otherwise you'll get indigestion. That's how I got sick. Trust me, take care!"

But Habiba's legendary beauty triumphed over that young man and overcame his resistance. She ate him up, turned him into her plaything, and did whatever she liked with him. Other women followed her example and that's how the tribe of man-eaters was born. Ever since then, peace has prevailed in this country where the swallowed men no longer have a say.

After a moment's silence, Imane burst out laughing, as did the captain.

"Did you really hear that story at the hammam?" he asked her, "I actually think you made it up yourself. You should write it down, work on it and turn it into a novel. I'm sure it would be very successful."

Imane had wanted to be a writer ever since she'd been a little girl. She never dared to talk about her ambitions, but always told people her stories whenever she had a chance. When she couldn't sleep at night, she would let her imagination run free. She would look out of her window at the sky, count the stars, give the clouds names and think up characters and plots featuring them.

On her way out, she leaned down toward him and said:

"You're right, I didn't hear that story at the hammam, but I didn't make it up entirely. Isn't that what artists, what writers do? See you tomorrow, captain."

She left the trail of her perfume behind her, and since the painter was a daydreamer, he became melancholic.

His feelings for that young woman were unlike any he'd experienced before. He'd desired other women and had done all he could to be with them, and for a time, be it a few days or a few weeks, he'd fallen in love with them; but none of that had happened with Imane. He needed her, and not just so she could look after his health. He needed to see her, to hear her tell her stories, to confide in her. It was all he wanted.

XXVII

Casablanca

February 12, 2003

I believe we can save our marriage. We could make a fresh
start. You must give me a chance! Let us face this together.

—INGMAR BERGMAN, *Scenes from a Marriage*

By the time his lawyer came to see him, so they could take stock of
how the divorce proceedings were going, the painter was fully im-
mersed in his work. He was painting a crinkled linen tablecloth that
he'd reproduced in all its minutiae with a painstaking attention to
detail. It was impressive work.

"If you didn't replicate the pleats and folds with such accuracy,
nobody would know the difference. Besides, you're the one who rum-
pled it up, right?"

"That's right, I did, I realize that, but that's not the way I do
things, it would be like tricking people, and I wouldn't even need a
tablecloth in front of me to paint it. I can paint any kind of tablecloth,

but this painting depicts this particular tablecloth and you couldn't confuse it with any other tablecloth on earth. And once I've finished painting it, what you see in front of you won't be a tablecloth, it will have transcended it and become something else."

"I see. So you could call your painting 'This is not a tablecloth.'"

"That's not very original."

"Forgive my impertinence."

"Don't worry, you're not the first person to tell me that. Look at it this way, it would be as if you reused the same defense speech that got your client acquitted in one case in a completely different case, that wouldn't do, now, would it?"

"No, you're quite right."

"So, is there any news? I'm ready to hear the good and the bad."

"Well, truth be told I don't think your wife wants to get divorced."

"That's the last thing I needed!"

"Given what her lawyer has asked for, one would think she'd made such shocking demands in order to change your mind about the divorce. Going by the last letters I was sent, her requests are nothing short of exorbitant. She's asked for literally everything that you have, for the children's sake, in addition to a compensatory allowance of several million dirhams. If you accept her terms, you might as well buy yourself a little tent and find a little nook sheltered from the winds where you can spend your last days."

"Do you think I'll have enough left to buy that tent as well as a few things to keep me from dying of cold in the winter?"

"Well, I'll buy you one if you like! But jokes aside, you need to take action. I can see only one way out of this. If you trust me, we'll file a request for divorce here in Morocco, where you'll have the upper hand. We must act quickly since the way this will pan out will depend on the laws of the country where the request is first lodged. It's a matter of precedence. Ever since the new Moudawana came into effect, the rulings of Moroccan courts have gained international recognition, so you won't be running any risks from a legal point of view. Try not to worry too much. You know, I'm fully aware that you were planning to offer your wife—the mother of your children—a comfortable pension, as well as the house and even a hefty lump sum. The courts will recognize that your offer is more than reasonable."

"Let me have a little more time before I give you my decision. First I must finish this painting. If I have the strength to work all day tomorrow then I think I'll be able to complete it, then when my nurse Imane comes over she'll be the one to say whether I've pulled it off or not. In fact, my decision on this matter rests on this particular painting, which unlike my other paintings will have a name: *Break Up*."

The lawyer couldn't understand why such a famous painter would rely on a simple nurse's advice, but he didn't let on what his thoughts were. He lowered his voice and whispered:

"Please reassure me, nothing happened between you and this girl, right?"

"Nothing at all. She's good at her job and I trust her taste because she's neither an art critic nor a historian. She's just a simple girl, charming and efficient. I've been able to feel alive again ever since she started taking care of my therapy."

"Does your wife know?"

"Of course, she's already tried to fire her twice."

When he resumed work on his painting, he felt readier for a fight than ever before, especially since he'd found a title for his canvas. It had come to him out of the blue, just like that. It pleased him. Each wrinkle on the tablecloth represented one of the conflicts he'd suffered through. Each shadow stood for a moment of sadness or melancholy. Everything on the canvas represented something whose meaning was only known to him.

As usual, he took a little nap in the afternoon. He loved to doze off after reading a book or a magazine. All of a sudden, he could clearly hear the sound of someone whispering in his ear: "You've screwed up your marriage, at least make sure you get your divorce right." He woke up with a start and looked around, but there was nobody there. He called for his assistants. His left leg was hurting. He asked the Twins to lift him up and carry him to the chair situated in front of the large easel so that he could finish his painting.

When he finished painting that tablecloth late the following afternoon, he called Imane over so she could give him her opinion. Her eyes beamed so intensely the moment she'd looked at the canvas that he knew right away that he'd completed a masterpiece. He remembered that he owed his lawyer an answer. He called him around seven o'clock in the evening.

"Go ahead, I'm going to take your advice. Regardless of what happens I'll always be considered the guilty one and there's no way I'll be able to save face anyway."

After calling his lawyer, and once Imane had gone home, he suddenly felt the urge to write his wife a letter, a letter that he would never send her. He didn't know how he should start it. Should he begin with "Dear," just use her first name, or instead start with a simple hello? In the end he just cut to the chase.

I want you to know how sorry I am for everything that's happened with us. I want to apologize for leaving you and to tell you that it's neither your fault nor mine. We forced the hand of fate. We forced each other's hand and thus it was always fated to be. I believed in love, in fact I believed in it so much that I thought it could solve impossible problems. But for a long time now I've lacked courage and determination and now here we are, breaking up right in front of our stunned children's eyes.

I would have truly liked for us to reach an agreement without causing all this damage, without airing our dirty laundry in public or throwing lawyers into the mix.

I hope we'll at least be able to have a cordial relationship and act civilized toward one another since we'll certainly see each other again because of the children, and you know that they are all that matters to me, as is the case with you. Be reasonable, I beg you, and be at peace with the fact that we don't love each other anymore. Love isn't a decision or something that can be forced. It comes to us and then just as easily goes away again. There's nothing we can do about that . . .

XXVIII

Casablanca

February 18, 2003

—I want you to make love to me. Please? For old times' sake.
—The best thing would be to pack my things and leave.
—INGMAR BERGMAN, *Scenes from a Marriage*

The painter woke up early that morning. Imane usually arrived around eight o'clock, but she was running late that day. He tried not to be impatient and convinced himself that she must have gotten held up somewhere. When she finally arrived two hours later, he immediately noticed that she'd been crying. She quickly set to her work, in silence. After a moment, he tenderly asked her if she wanted to confide in him.

"We're friends, we can talk to one another and share our burdens. What's wrong, Imane?"

"I have to leave Morocco and go live with my fiancé."

"I thought that was all over."

"It was, but he redoubled his efforts, he also offered to get my brother a visa and find him a job in Belgium. That's very important to my family. Despite having a diploma, my brother's been unable to find himself a job, even though it's fair to say he hasn't been looking very hard, he's frustrated with the way things are done here, corruption is rampant, and you can't get anything done unless you bribe someone."

"Are you in love with this man?"

"I don't know, I barely know him. He showed up in a new car, a Mercedes, and you know that a car like a Mercedes is a door opener here and a status symbol. I don't want to cause my parents any grief and I especially want to help my little brother get out of here."

"But you're sacrificing yourself!"

She lowered her gaze to avoid breaking into tears again.

The painter knew that Imane's departure would affect him deeply. He'd grown attached to that woman, and he would miss her fervent imagination, her soothing charm, and those gifted, healing hands. He knew she'd be very unhappy in Belgium. That fiancé of hers who'd shown up in a flashy car was surely up to no good. He'd seen girls follow their husbands abroad only to discover that they had another family there. At which point they would run back to their parents in tears and wait for a man who truly loved them to show up. Some of them even wound up married to hashish smugglers who used their spouses as mules.

The painter asked Imane to promise that she'd never forget him, that she would come visit him soon and let him know how things were going. Moved, she fell into his arms and nestled her head into his shoulder, and he held her tightly against him. He didn't want that embrace to end, even though he would have preferred to keep his distance, since he had nothing to offer her. Yet his thoughts were quickly negated by a sudden erection. He was both delighted and disappointed. He didn't want to make love, especially not to Imane, so he restrained himself and tried to gently push her away, but she pressed herself even more tightly against him. He could feel her warm body, her little breasts pressed against his chest, and smell the scent of her hair. He wanted to speak, but then gave up on it. She was already on top of him, ready to mount him. They got up and she helped him to lie down on the bed, locked the door to his studio, pulled the curtains, switched off the lights, and drew close to him, taking off her robe. She was completely naked, warm and trembling with desire. He didn't resist. She stroked his belly and then worked her way down to his groin, grabbing his shaft and kissing it, then got on top of him, allowing him to penetrate her slowly, then began moving forward and backward, leaning over him and brushing his face with her long hair. He mostly managed to stay hard, but whenever he felt he was going limp, her lips would make him hard again. When he came, she cried out with pleasure because she'd also climaxed and had been waiting for that moment for a long time.

They lingered for a long time with their bodies pressed against one another. She caressed his face while he thought about the pleasure he'd just rediscovered. Nevertheless, he knew that they would never sleep together again and this was her parting gift. Without a word, Imane stood up, dressed, picked up her belongings, leaned down to him, and gave him a long kiss. He felt her tears stream down and mix with his, which he was trying to conceal.

"Another woman will come to take care of you tomorrow. She's a nice lady, very sweet and competent. I chose her. Goodbye. I'll write to you, if you prefer I'll call you from time to time."

She left without looking back. He swallowed a sleeping pill and went to bed without dinner. He tried to keep those heavenly perfumes in his lungs to help him persevere down the long road of recovery.

XXIX

Tangiers

September 23, 2003

—I gave you a good home.
    —Yes, but it smells of paint. I can't stand the smell of
paint, and your pictures cluttering up the hall, if you don't rid
of that trash I swear I'll give it to the junkman. I swear I will.
Go ahead and eat, and then do the dishes.

                —FRITZ LANG, *Scarlet Street*

Taking his doctor's advice, the painter left Casablanca behind and
headed to Tangiers with the Twins to spend a few restful days at his
friend Abdelsalam's house on the outskirts of Tangiers. It was the end
of September, and more than ten months had passed since he'd told
his wife he was leaving her.

    Whenever it rained in Tangiers, the Chergui winds would join
the fray, they would blow and make the hills of the Old Mountain
tremble. The winds would continue blowing even after the rains had

stopped, shaking even the tallest and sturdiest trees. It was said the winds helped sweep the city clean of diseases and its mosquitoes. Others insisted that it made people crazy, and that madmen needed those winds to get excited, sing, dance, and laugh.

His friend's villa held steady against the winds, even though its doors and window shutters shook, allowing the coldness of that untimely visitor to seep through the house. The Chergui would leave no stone unturned and stir everything in the city out of the lethargy into which its inhabitants had so happily slipped. Those who loved hot drinks would snuggle into their thick djellabas and sip glasses of mint tea. The fishermen didn't go out to sea, the fish market was closed, and the bars would fill with people while they waited for the winds to exhaust themselves. When they finally stopped, everything would be still for a while and one could hear the silence, and appreciate it. The storm left a sense of peace and sleepiness in its wake. The painter loved those moments of renewed calm, and he called that kind of silence Mozart-like.

The painter compared his wife to those forces of nature. One moment she would be violent, brutal, and menacing, and then miraculously become suddenly sweet, calm and kind. Imane's departure in February had plunged the painter into a strange sort of melancholy. "She was my last wife" he told himself, convinced that in his enfeebled state, he was unlikely to ever meet anyone else again. He hadn't felt good since then. From a physical point of view, he'd begun feeling heavy again, just like in the early days of his convalescence. His heart rate slowed. He'd entered a decline.

While looking out at the sea, the painter asked himself for the umpteenth time how he could free himself from his wife's clutches since she was refusing to allow the divorce to happen and had so far outwitted all of his lawyer's stratagems. He'd tried to come up with ways to force his wife to accept their separation, but he now realized that she would never give up. He would have to radically change his tactics, but he'd run out of ideas save to sink into an unbreakable silence. Whenever his friends came to see him in Casablanca, he would insist on seeing them by himself. Otherwise, if his wife were there, he wouldn't say a word; but when he was on his own, he would be able to speak again and explain to them that he was under house arrest. Nobody believed him. His friends would instead try to put his mind at ease. "Why would you think such a thing? Why don't you focus on the fact that you can have her beside you, she's so devoted to you. Look at how thin and tired she'd become. How will you manage on your own? You don't realize in what bad a shape you're in." Whereas he actually realized what shape he was in and merely dreamed of living on his own, surrounded by people who valued his company and who actually helped him. But he had neither the strength nor the desire to tell his friends about his conflicts with his wife, so he would hang his head and force a weak smile, as though he agreed with them.

His wife would eavesdrop on them behind the closed door. Whenever she'd decided the right moment had come, she would burst in with a tray of refreshments, keeping her gaze fixed on the floor as though to show how the situation weighed so heavily on her shoulders. Sometimes she would even mop a tear from her cheeks. Some of his friends would take pity on her, while others would rejoice at her presence and praise her, saying that she'd sacrificed her youth and spent all her time looking after an impotent husband, a moody invalid, an artist who was impossible to live with and a man who thought that the mere shadow of his presence would somehow suffice to keep his wife happy.

Ever since he'd filed for divorce, his wife had been both strong and frail, because she did honestly cry whenever she was alone in their room and far away from him. She knew that her life had been a failure, a waste. She lost weight, neglected herself, and almost never left the house. Only Lalla, her guru, would come visit her, encouraging her to resist her husband's efforts at all costs, persuading her to punish him for all the suffering he'd caused her over the years and for the fact he wanted to leave her. Lalla's eyes had a pernicious glimmer to them, as though she herself had been a victim. Lalla had told her about a new sorcerer who'd arrived from Senegal, a young man who used herbs that were unknown in Morocco. This sorcerer was so successful that one had to wait several days before having the chance to consult him.

Unfortunately, she would refuse to leave the painter alone, even if only for an hour. Lalla was ready to make the trip to Salé, where the sorcerer had set up shop, but she had refused. After all, she didn't need his help. Her husband was right there, and unable to go anywhere, and that was the best way of punishing him. She could now get whatever she wanted out of him. She didn't even need his signature to withdraw money from the bank. She'd discreetly managed to secure power of attorney, which put her in complete control.

She had triumphed over him, but the situation was less comfortable than she might have believed. Although he was at her mercy, he'd been able to find refuge in his illness. He maintained a glacial silence and barely looked at her. It was a catch-22: regardless of what she did, he would never belong to her in the way that she'd dreamed. The painter devoted himself to his art, to his friends, and to his family, but never to her. Her frustration upset him, but there was nothing left to salvage, nothing left to repair. It was the end, and what a miserable outcome it had been for both of them.

Lying on his side, his head turned to face the garden of his friend's house, the painter observed an unhappy-looking fig tree that had long since stopped bearing fruit. He started at that stumpy, bare-branched tree, a gray ghost of its former self that should have been cut down long ago, and experienced a profound melancholy at the thought that his destiny resembled the one in store for that useless old tree. "If I still had the strength to paint," he told himself, "I might paint that tree and call it a self-portrait." Tears streamed down his face and stained his pillow. He couldn't stop them from flowing. Those tears comforted him and gave him some relief, although he simultaneously detested the feel of that tear-drenched pillow against his cheek. It reminded him of how his father had started silently weeping the moment he'd realized he would die that day. The doctor's grimace had told him he was screwed and that there wasn't any hope left. That scene had left a deep mark on the painter. Seeing the father he so admired reduced to an old man waiting for a death foretold had filled him with an intense wrath. He'd leaned over and wiped the tears from his father's face as he prepared to die sobbing like a child.

The part that the actor Michel Simon had played in Jean Renoir's *La Chienne*, that of an old painter who'd been robbed of all his possessions and thrown out into the street, came to the painter's mind while he looked out at the sea from his friend Abdelsalam's house. He'd seen the film as a very young man and had found the plot entirely pathetic. He'd later watched Fritz Lang's American adaptation, *Scarlet Street*, where the role had been reprised by Edward G. Robinson, an actor whom he greatly liked, but he'd never taken an interest in the fate of that artist who'd fallen victim to his passion and naïveté. Nevertheless, the parallels to his own life were obvious. Sure, unlike the lead character, he'd never stooped so low as to paint Kitty's toenails, Kitty being the bitch who steals his money and fame. He hadn't had his work stolen from him, his wife had just gotten in the way of his pursuing his art. Also unlike the lead character, he hadn't turned into a homeless man who opened the door of a car whose owner had just purchased one of his paintings. But the painter was stuck with his wife and confined to his wheelchair, all wrapped up, as though he were a package waiting to be delivered. It would be impossible now to break through and get away, freeing his limbs so he could make his escape from the prison and run free like a wild stallion.

It had been months since he'd stopped speaking to his enemy. Henceforth he would stop even looking at her, he would ignore her and withdraw into himself by shutting his eyes whenever she approached him. If she asked him any questions, he would simply refuse to answer, he would remain still and refuse to make a single gesture, not even a grimace. He would live in his own world, wall himself off entirely, overcoming his desire to fight fire with fire. Unable to leave her as he'd wanted to, his victory would be complete on the day when he would be able to stop hating that woman. She would simply cease to exist.

A fly buzzed around him. The painter raised his right hand and moved it a little. The fly flew off. He rolled up a newspaper and waited for it to come back so he could permanently eliminate it.

PART TWO

My Version of Events

A response to

The Man Who Loved Women Too Much

Prologue

Obsessive, unsettling, amusing, diabolical. I am a fly. Restless and reso-
lute. Gluttonous and stubborn. A fly, just a worthless fly. To be uncere-
moniously hunted down, swatted, and crushed when caught. Something
to be despised, but also feared. There's nothing nice about flies. Nothing
to be proud of either. Unlike the queen bee. Black, gray, shameless, and
unscrupulous. Yet it's free, and it amuses itself with those who chase after
it. Doesn't care about anything. Doesn't have a house, or belong to any
country. Arrives on the back of an evil wind and just settles there without
asking anyone's permission. It's only discouraged by the rain or the cold. It
dares to do whatever it likes. It flies into fashionable salons, mosques, and
alcoves, sneaking its way into the most intimate and secret spaces: bath-
room cabinets, kitchens, laundry rooms, following its instincts wherever
they lead it. It disturbs the dead, and bites into their lifeless flesh, then
wanders off somewhere else. It bites into a baby's soft skin, causing it to
swell up. It goes wherever it likes and is unstoppable. Free and stubborn.
I'm going to be a fly this morning. It'll amuse me. I'll enjoy being fearless
and shameless. I'm going to become a fly in order to annoy my husband.

I'm very good at that. I'm happy whenever I can settle on his nose and watch him being unable to swat me away. I giggle and cling to him. I tickle him, make him itch, and make his life hellish. I like that. A small kind of revenge. Let's put it this way: a taste of what's in store for him.

It's crazy how men are so afraid of being alone. What a sin! I'm not afraid of being alone. I even go to the length of creating that solitude and allowing it to reign. It doesn't make me neurotic. I'm just like a fly, I'm independent-minded and don't like compromises. My man thought I was rigid. He's certainly right, but I don't like that word. It reminds me of death. As for solitude, I get along with it just fine. There's no need to whine about it to other people, people who are probably all too happy to despise you. I am solitude. Solitude is the fly that takes its time and refuses to budge. I am the solitude that crawls under my man's skin. I've stopped calling him that. He's never been "my" man, but has instead always belonged to other women, starting with his mother and those two sisters of his, both of whom are witches.

Today I'm a fly. We've lived in solitude for a long time, way before his accident happened. I'll admit I'm exaggerating a little, dramatizing this as much as I can. I'm left without a choice. I suck blood out of the tip of his large nose. I bother him, bump into him, insult him, spit on his skin, and there's nothing he can do about it, he can't even move his arms, hands, or fingers. He's been taken hostage by his illness and I try not to neglect any details.

I'm nothing but a fly, any old fly, stupid and stubborn. I'm obstinate. It's in my genes. The only way I know how to be. It's just the way things are. I know that's moronic, but that's how it is. There's nothing I can do about it. I am—and always have been—stronger than he ever was. Just like a fly. I have eyes on the back of my head and I'm suspicious of everyone, and I think this suits me very well. This is how it is and nothing's ever going to change my mind. I'm a fly, a dangerous fly.

My Version

Before giving you my version of events, I must warn you that I'm nasty. I wasn't born that way, but when people attack me, I defend myself by any and all means, and I give as good as I get. Truth be told, I don't give as good as I get, I inflict even worse damage. That's how it is, I'm not nice, and I hate nice guys, they're weak, vague, and they're all alike. I like my relationships with people to be direct, frank, free of compromise and hypocrisy. Yes, I'm inflexible. Flexibility is for snakes and diplomats. I'm not ashamed to say what I'm like because I'm an honest woman. I don't lie. I cut to the chase. I don't equivocate. I sprang out of rocks and prickly pears. I was born in an arid land, devoid of all water and shade. There were no trees or plants where I grew up. But there were animals and men. Wretched animals and women resigned to their fate. I rebelled against all that. I reacted to droughts by becoming hard. As far as I'm aware, animals don't bother with civilities. I'm tough because nice people always wind up dead, wondering why people treated them so badly.

I don't know the meaning of fear. I've never been afraid. I don't know the meaning of shame. Nobody's ever been able to shame me.

That's how it is. No shame, no fear. I'm not afraid of anybody. I'm ready to die, anywhere, any time. I forge ahead, and I don't look back.

I endured hunger, a great deal of hunger. I endured thirst. I endured the cold. Nobody ever came to my rescue. Very early in life I understood that life isn't an endless series of dinner parties where everybody loves everybody.

I'm right, and I keep my head high. I don't allow anyone to push me around or betray me. Betrayal is the worst thing someone can do as far as I'm concerned. I'm capable of killing anyone who betrays me. That's how it is. I don't hide my intentions; besides, I don't have any intentions to start with. I follow through with my decisions. I belong to the night, to a cruel, unforgiving world.

I wonder why I felt the need to warn you. It's not like me at all. I don't waste time on chatter. I act. But all I've done here is talk. At the risk of failing to act.

My name is Amina, and I am the woman mentioned in this story. I'm tall, five seven, and have brown hair, my natural color. I love life, I'm comfortable in my own skin, and I like to help people. I'm not formally educated, but I'm curious and I'm an autodidact, I read and look things up all the time. I'm telling you all this because I want you to know who I really am. My husband took a lot of liberties with the truth.

I come from a dry, rotten land where nothing grows, that's dotted only with rocks and prickly pears. It wasn't even a village, or a *douar*, but a cemetery inhabited by the living. Sometimes the dust was gray, sometimes it was ochre. It would depend on the day. The dust clung to the wild weeds, to the young girls' faces, and on the hungry dogs and cats. The rest of the world couldn't have cared less about my village. It was just a nameless place in the middle of nowhere. Some called it Bled el Fna, the village of nothingness. No saint or prophet ever stopped by there. What would have been the point? Why would they have bothered? For some miserable peasants and a few starved animals? Nothingness, that's right, the village of nothingness.

My father wanted me to be a shepherdess, and I obeyed him right up to the day when I discovered school. Instead of collecting firewood and looking after the cows, I followed my cousin to the school that lay an hour's walk from the village. I covered my head in a gray scarf and blended in with the other children. Since most kids hardly ever showed up, the teacher didn't notice me until I squabbled with a classmate who'd refused to lend me a pencil and a piece of paper. I'm violent, and if anyone refuses to give me something, I just take it. That's the way it is. I snatched her satchel away from her and started to use it. Then she screamed, and the teacher stepped in and made me spend the whole morning standing in the corner. My father was told about the incident. In any case, he'd never wanted his girl to mix with boys at the local school. "What's the point of learning how to read and write?" he'd told me. "It would be better if you learned how to birth a calf or an ewe." My mother didn't share his opinion and wanted me to study to help dispel the gloominess that sometimes took hold of me and made me very sad. But she had no say. My father was kind to her, but he said it was better for everyone to know their place and to resign themselves to it. He forbade me from going back to school and entrusted me into the care of his uncle Boualem, a grocer in Marrakech who treated me as though I were his maid. Boualem was a miser, a real miser. He spent all of his days in the shop counting tins of sardines, then moving them around and counting them all over again. He never washed very often and thought the ablutions before his prayers were enough—it was his way of being pious! His grooming was incredibly basic. His clothes stank of sweat. He was skinny as a rake, not an ounce of fat on his bones. It was said that skinny men lived for a long time. My aunt would scream at him. Once, he struck her ferociously. She cried. I cried. He forbade us to eat that evening. I was always hungry. On one occasion, I snuck into the grocery shop, which was connected to the house, and stole a jar of jam. I'd never tasted jam before. The next day, he slapped me so hard it almost knocked my head off my shoulders, without even asking me a question. "That's the price I had to pay for stealing a jar of jam," I told myself.

The day Boualem told me he was going to send me to live with strangers, I was frightened and yet relieved. He dropped me off in front of a house where the gate opened by itself. There was a sign that read: "Vicious dog." I advanced slowly, carrying all my belongings inside a plastic bag. I saw a lady who seemed to find it difficult to walk come toward me. "Come here, little one," she said, "I'm going to show you your room." At first, I didn't understand what I would have to do there; those people were very nice to me and bought me some new clothes (yes, that was the first time anyone had ever bought me any clothes, my mother would usually dress me in hand-me-downs), and they gave me plenty to eat and let me sit at the table with them. I didn't know how to behave, I found using a fork and knife difficult, so I ate with my fingers, which shocked them. I had to learn to cut my meat and bring it to my mouth gracefully with a fork. They told me about distant countries and the travels they'd been on. They said they were happy to be my new parents. I didn't understand everything they said, but Zanouba, their maid, translated them for me. I cried and I tore up my new blue dress. They bought me some more dresses and enrolled me in a private school that didn't have many pupils. They would drop me off there in their car and give me a snack they'd wrapped in a piece of very shiny white paper. I didn't say a single word at school. I made grimaces and gesticulated, pricked my ears wide and learned French. I remembered everything, I had a great memory. In the evening, I would tell them what I'd learned that day. I got words and things mixed up. Whenever I missed my parents a lot, I would go to Zanouba and cuddle up to her. She would whisper kind, reassuring words and console me. I was lucky, she told me. Yes, lucky to be torn away from my parents and siblings. I never missed the bled, but I couldn't forget my grandmother. My difficulties at school made things more difficult. The French couple hired a young man to tutor me. He was handsome. I think I fell in love with him. He was a high school student. I didn't dare look him in the eye. I must admit that he helped me a lot. He taught me how to read and write. My life changed completely from that moment on. One day, I bled all over my panties. I was ashamed. Fortunately, Zanouba explained it all to me and cleaned me up. I was in love then, and so I started paying attention to what I wore. I wanted to draw the young man's attention. But by the time the summer arrived, he left and I never saw him again.

I saw my parents twice over the course of three years. They came to bring me my share of oil and honey that my cousins had distributed amongst the villagers.

One day, my new parents told me that they had to return to France. We went to the bled. I felt weird, as though I were a stranger in that village that was devoid of water. There were children covered in flies playing with a dead cat. They had snotty noses and nobody was looking after them. My father came out to meet me, and I thought he was going to kiss me like my foreigner parents did, but instead I was the one who had to kiss the back of his large hand that smelled like dry earth. Without looking me in the eye, he told me: "We'll see one another again someday, my daughter." Then he spoke to me about a trip and papers that had to be signed. I saw bundles of banknotes being exchanged between the French couple and my father. I suddenly understood what had happened. My father had sold me! It was dreadful! I started to cry. The lady consoled me. She told me that my father would always be my father. They hadn't been able to adopt me, so they'd needed a letter from my father so that I could leave with them. That's how I got my first passport. It was green. The man from the *wilaya* told me in a menacing tone: "Be careful, this is valuable, if you lose it we won't give you another one, and you'll spend the rest of your life without a passport and you won't be able to go anywhere." When I was about to leave the office, the same man grabbed me and whispered in my ear: "You're lucky that these Frenchmen are looking after you, so make sure you don't embarrass us. Don't forget that this little green booklet means you are representing Morocco!" But he was wrong, I wasn't representing anyone, not even my mother, who'd stood motionless while she watched me leave. Maybe she cried too. I shut my eyes and decided I would never think about that unhappy village ever again.

A few weeks later, I left with the French couple in a ship bound for Marseilles. They didn't speak throughout the entire journey. They were in a bad mood. The woman cried in secret. She told me that she didn't want to leave that wonderful country but that her husband had to go back to look after his parents, who were old and ill. I told myself that he was a good son. But there was something else that was wrong with this couple who had never managed to have children. I could feel things even though I wasn't able to call them by their names. They would argue over trifles. The woman wanted to be in charge and her husband would resist her, while I would watch them and remember that my parents had never raised their voices.

We went to live in an apartment that wasn't very big. Our neighbors, who were Armenians, came to welcome us and brought us marzipan cakes. They had a daughter who was very beautiful, tall and with brown hair. She was seventeen years old even though she looked like she was in her twenties. She quickly became my friend. She often invited me over so she could show me photos that people had taken of her. She wanted to become an actress. "And what about your studies?" I asked her.

"You don't need to study to become an actress!" she replied, laughing. She already worked as a fashion model and had been fairly successful. As we were the same size, she told me: "You know, if your parents agree, maybe you should try your luck too. People are interested in girls like us now and it's our turn to become famous. Never cut your hair, instead let it grow and get it blown up, so you'll look like a lioness!"

I thought that was funny. I loved my hair and took good care of it, I used henna that gave it a nice red color with brown highlights. My friend then undressed herself, asked me to do the same, and started comparing our measurements: waist, chest, and hips. She said that if I wanted to, I could be a big hit in the fashion world.

I attended high school and took my studies seriously. My Moroccan parents had simply disappeared, whereas my French parents were often nostalgic for Morocco. Then a bunch of their time was sucked up by a complicated drama over their inheritance after my French father's parents died. For the most part, they gave me a lot of freedom and their absolute trust. I would take advantage of this and accompany my Armenian friend to her fashion shoots. That's how a guy with red hair asked me to walk in front of him as though I was carrying a jug full of water on my head. I tried to picture what that might look like and walked carefully. "Watch out," he shouted, "the jug's going to fall and shatter into a thousand pieces!" So I took a deep breath and walked normally. A woman took me by the hand, undressed me, and told me to put on a weird dress that was full of holes. In fact it was see-through. I didn't want to wear this dress that made me look like I was naked. So she gave me another dress that was more presentable and told me to walk around the room.

In the space of a few moments, I had become a model at the mere age of seventeen and a half! An exceptionally good job that meant I left each shoot with armloads of presents. My parents turned a blind eye to all of this. On one condition: that I wouldn't fail my final exams. I didn't listen to their advice and in June I was forced to take remedial classes. It was a slap in the face. I'd never thought of myself as a poor student. I hadn't realized how many significant gaps there were in my learning. I was so arrogant that I thought I'd be able to catch up in no time. After all, it wasn't my fault that I'd had such a chaotic and troubled education. I didn't even know who I was anymore! Was I Lahbib Wakrine's daughter, or did I belong to Mr. and Mrs. Lefranc? Was I Arab or Berber? French or Belgian? Mrs. Lefranc had Flemish roots . . .

I attended my remedial classes and managed to barely pass my exams. My French parents had nothing to say in that regard. I enrolled at the university, but never set foot there. I preferred to waste my time on far more futile endeavors and went to photo shoots. I was an adult by then and I didn't realize how time was slipping through my fingers.

Although I'm not exactly sure as to how it happened, my Armenian friend got herself sucked in by a producer and featured in some explicit scenes in movies that were never shown in Marseilles's bigger cinemas. She got into a big argument with her parents and disappeared. That drama made me snap out of my waking dream. I left that filthy scene behind and started taking my art history course seriously.

But all of a sudden, from one day to the next, I found myself on my own. My French parents wound up separating, and I barely noticed, since truth be told I'd been spending so little time at the house. They divided up all their possessions and I got caught in the middle. Mrs. Lefranc asked me if I wanted to go live with her or stay with her ex-husband. I was embarrassed. But as luck would have it, everything worked out: a court decree authorized my right to family reunification. My father, who'd set himself up in Clermont-Ferrand, sent for his wife and two of his other children. Forgetting all the sadness I'd suffered in the past and the pain I'd felt when I was abandoned, I suddenly felt the urge to join them. The botched adoption had merely been an interlude that had allowed me to have a fairly normal education. My parents were still my parents. My name was Amina Wakrine even though the Lefrancs called me Nathalie. As it happens, I never figured out why they'd chosen that name. At school, everyone had called me Natha. As for the guy with red hair, he wanted to call me Kika. And why not? My name seemed to change all the time, but I was still the same person, my parents' daughter.

Once I got to Clermont-Ferrand, I felt like I was having a panic attack. That city felt like a prison to me. It was ugly, gray, and stifling. I wanted so badly to leave it and never return. Seeing my distress, my father decided not to say anything and allowed me to leave for Paris so that I could continue the studies I'd begun in Marseilles. He opened a bank account for me and deposited some of the money that the French couple had given him. It was a considerable sum, especially since it had been supplemented by the money orders that Mrs. Lefranc had been sending me ever since she'd gotten divorced. Leaving for Paris was a turning point for me. I was finally independent and free of all the guilt I'd ever felt toward my parents. I was determined to make the best of it. I would never have dreamed at that time of the monumental failure that would await me with the painter many years later.

I must admit that it wasn't very long after I'd moved to Paris before I'd acquired a lot of boyfriends. But I remained a virgin, as I wanted to save myself for marriage. Go figure why a rebellious girl like me who'd known such a difficult life would care about keeping her hymen intact. Traditions and customs appeared to be stronger than I was.

My future husband never knew any of this. I never wanted to tell him and he hardly ever asked me any questions about that time in my life. Maybe he thought that everything that had happened before we met was ancient history—Jahiliyyah, the time of ignorance, as the Muslims call the centuries before the arrival of the Prophet Mohammed.

I only saw Mrs. Lefranc one last time after that, when she was in an old people's home. She wasn't even that old by then, but she had nobody to look after her or keep her company. She hugged me tight and I could feel her crying. When I left, she gave me a little suitcase. "You'll open it on the day you get married," she told me. But I couldn't resist the urge. I opened it as soon as I got home. I was impressed: it was filled with jewelry, photos, a notebook with addresses, some of which had been scrawled out, a Moroccan dress that she must have bought at the souk on Place de la Kissaria in Rabat, and lastly a letter addressed to Maître Antoine, Esq., 2 bis Rue Lamiral, etc. I didn't open it and I still have it somewhere in my files. One day I'll go visit this Maître Antoine . . .

The Secret Manuscript

You must be asking yourself: how did I come to learn of the existence of the manuscript you've just finished reading and which I'm now rebutting point by point? By stealing it. Yes, by stealing it. I knew that one of his best friends, an amateur who wrote in his spare time, was up to something. But I suspected that they would try to conceal the fruit of their labors. So I started spying on them, taking care that they didn't notice anything. Here's how they went about it. Over the space of six months, his friend would come visit him very early in the mornings. They would spend hours talking and then he would pull out his laptop and edit their conversation, polishing it up into a proper text. When he was satisfied with the results, he would immediately print out the pages of that strange kind of biography and locked them up in the studio's safe, to which I had neither the combination nor the key. A month ago, I took advantage of the fact that my husband would be spending the day at the hospital to run some tests and I called a locksmith to open the safe for me. After all, there was nothing strange about that, it was my own house and no locksmith would refuse to open up a safe, simply assuming I'd lost my key to it. I raided its contents and grabbed everything inside it. Before leaving, the locksmith asked me to think up a new combination code and so I'm now the only one who can access the safe. The manuscript was inside a folder marked "confidential." I had a blast reading it. I breezed through it and made notes on it in the space of a single night. I was beside myself with rage, but for the first time my desire for vengeance was well-founded. His friend never came back. I believe he fell gravely ill. My prayers bore their fruit.

When my husband realized what I'd done, he didn't do anything. I thought I heard him complaining to himself. I brought him an herbal infusion, but he gave me a look to signify he didn't want it and then made it clear that he wanted me to leave. On my way out, I deliberately knocked a pot of paint onto an unfinished canvas. I regretted having done something so petty. I ruined a painting that could have one day made me a lot of money. Now let's move on. We never act the way we should. My instincts often trump my ability to think rationally.

Foulane owned a collection of rare Arabic manuscripts. He was very proud of it, he would show it to his visitors and talk about it at length. I took advantage of him leaving the house to go for a medical checkup to steal them. I hid them at Lalla's, since she owned a large chest. I will use them as a bargaining chip one day or another. I made sure he noticed their disappearance, which sent him into a fury. He went all red in the face and his body started shaking as though he'd been having an epileptic seizure. I stood right in front of him, and savoring my victory over him, I said:

"Now you're going to pay. I'll never let you go and this is but a taste of what's to come. You'll never see your precious books again. When I decide to burn them, I'll wheel you out to see it so you can watch them burn! You'll be stuck in your chair and won't be able to do a thing about it!"

•

I'll start from the top, just like in a police report. No hesitations, emotions, or concessions. Reading that manuscript left me feeling unexpectedly invigorated. Being at war suits me just fine. I feel alive. I'm ready to kill and I'm always sharpening my blade. It's going to be a fight to the death. After all, after having read about all he's said and done, I have no qualms about speeding up his demise. I'm not well educated, I don't have any fancy degrees, and I'm not sophisticated; I'm straight up, direct, and sincere. I can't stand hypocrisies. I don't try to sugarcoat things. His family's always done plenty of that. Let's go straight to the facts.

I hope you noticed that he never referred to me by my name through-out the entirety of his manuscript. I was nothing to him, a gust of wind, a smudge of dew on the window, not even a ghost. Just like his father, who never called his wife by her name. He would just shout, "Woman," and she would come running. Very well, I'll do the same. From now on, I'll refer to my husband as Foulane, an Arabic word used to refer to "any old guy." I know, it's a little contemptuous, per-haps even a little pejorative. "Foulane" means someone who doesn't really matter, a man just like any other, without any distinctive char-acteristics. When people are talking quickly, they often drop the "ou" in "Foulane" and pronounce it "Flane," meaning someone whose ac-tual name and origins are unknown. Besides, it was precisely his ori-gins and roots that led to the failure of our marriage. He often spoke of how important his roots were to him and talked about them as though he were a philosopher: "Our roots follow us wherever we go, they reveal who we really are, they show our true colors and subvert our attempts to try to be something we're not." One day, I finally un-derstood that despite all his gobbledygook, he'd always looked down on my peasant origins: on the fact I was the daughter of poor, illiterate immigrants. He disliked the poor. He gave out alms, but always wore an expression of disdain. He would give his driver some money and tell him to distribute it among the beggars at the cemetery where his parents were buried. On Fridays, he would ask the cook to prepare large quantities of couscous for the needy, thus performing his duty as a good Muslim. After which his conscience would be clear and he would be able to devote himself to his paintings where he imitated photographs and gave them such shameless titles as "Shanty-town," "Shanty-town II," and so forth.

What exactly was he hoping to accomplish with this novel—what I read of it clearly indicates that it is a novel, especially since his friend the scribe called it such below that ridiculous title, *The Man Who Loved Women Too Much*? Did he want to publish it? Why? Who would bother to read such a pointless web of lies? There isn't an ounce of truth or originality in it, starting even with the title, which is a rip-off of François Truffaut's film, *The Man Who Loved Women*. Foulane simply added his two cents and tagged "too much" on the end of it to be a smart-ass. As for his friend, he was hardly a great writer. He self-published his books and nobody read them, so the copies just piled up in his garage. The book is just a series of falsehoods and allegations, each more intolerable than the last before it. Doesn't one get the distinct impression that I caused his stroke by the time one gets to the last page? It's a terrible insinuation. Isn't it criminal and irresponsible? I may have been nasty and devilish, but certainly never criminal, not even close!

He already suffered from migraines, high blood pressure, tachycardia, and a host of other nervous disorders by the time I met him. They were congenital and I had nothing to do with them. You'll have noticed that before describing the scene that caused his stroke—which I must stress was the sheer product of his artist's imagination, which was intoxicated with his own success—he devoted a number of beautiful pages to me, even going so far as to say that he loved me. Don't fall for any of it—he was utterly incapable of the slightest praise, he never had a kind word to say in the morning, no tenderness before going to bed, nothing, he lived in his own world, and I had to dwell in his shadow and cower in it. Oh, that ubiquitous shadow, it was bleak and heavy, followed me everywhere, harrying me and over-whelming me to the point that it immobilized me. It pushed me into a corner and kept me there. A shadow doesn't speak: it hovers over you menacingly and crushes you. I would wake up exhausted and empty in the mornings. The shadow had haunted me all night. I didn't have anyone to talk to, and besides, who would have believed me? Struck by a shadow! People would have thought I was crazy, which would have played into his hands. It must have taken a lot of effort for him to ever say anything sweet. So he avoided it and closed in on himself. He would reach his hand out and rub my knee whenever he wanted to make love. That was the sign, his way of asking me to welcome his advances, as though I should be constantly at his disposal, willing and available, all so Foulane could reassure himself that he could still get it up. He was always in a hurry to satisfy his needs. He would push himself inside me a little forcefully and fuck me in a robotic manner for a few minutes until he came, at which he'd puff out, like a toy whose batteries had gone dead.

For instance, he never once bought me some roses. Buying some-one flowers is easy, it makes them happy, it makes a statement. But he never bought me any. When he came back from his trips abroad, he would occasionally bring me a piece of jewelry, a necklace or a watch, as though to ask my forgiveness. But he always managed to find a way to tell me how much it had cost him. That's just how he was, petty and miserly. He lived in his own world, inside the bubble of a famous artist, except that he always forgot he only started getting successful after we met. He never admitted that his career prospered thanks to our marriage. I brought him stability, inspired him, and even had a hand in the development of his radical new style. Before we met, his paintings adhered to a bland, unimaginative realism. He just copied whatever he looked at. Simply improved on photographs. But, as you might have guessed, nobody could tell him that lest he fly into a fury. Yet once he was with me, he found the courage to develop his style and technique. His paintings became lively, surreal, flavorful, and human. He never had the honesty to admit that my presence and sensibility had enriched his work. I looked after everything when we lived in Paris, the house, the children, everything, while he would lock himself up in his studio, which was situated in a different neighborhood. Was it really a studio? Yes and no. I knew that he used it as a pad where he could meet with his other women, whores and those innocent young girls who swooned when they looked at his paintings. One day I asked him: "Why did you set up a bed in your studio?" "Why, it's obvious, so the artist can rest," he'd replied. But he never slept alone. His circle of acquaintances always included at least one or two women who would jump in a taxi whenever he called so that they could have a little "siesta" (as he put it). I knew all of this and yet made a superhuman effort not to burst in on them and make a scene, like any normal wife would have done in my stead. I was dimwitted and naïve. I was never scared of what I might find, I've never been afraid, instead it was an undefinable feeling. I just didn't want to bother him. Yes, that was my intention, I knew that he worked hard, and I didn't want to burst into his studio because I knew my wrath would be difficult to control. But one day when he was abroad on a trip, I noticed that he'd forgotten his keys to the studio in his satchel. I couldn't resist the temptation to visit the lair that he used to cheat on me all the time. I went in, I was ill at ease, shaking a little, steadying myself to be slapped in the face by a reality that I'd hitherto refused to see. The bed was unmade, there was a painting that he'd barely begun, and a half-empty bottle of wine on the bedside table with two glasses next to it, one of which was stained with lipstick. A banal and clichéd snapshot of adultery in all its splendor, and as a bonus I also found a bottle of my own perfume, which he must have sprayed on his women in order not to stray too far outside his comfort zone. As though guided by my instincts, I went over to the trash cans and found two condoms filled with sperm. Instead of flushing them down the toilet or putting them in a trash can outside his studio, the idiot had instead left irrefutable proof. I wanted to save a little of his sperm inside a bottle so I could give it to one of my sorcerers, but how could I do that? Some of his sperm would have been perfect for a potion that would make him impotent. I also went through his drawers. I found quasi-pornographic love letters, various photos, presents, dried flowers pressed between two leaves of paper that also bore the imprint of a kiss, and scented Chanel No. 5. I sat down in his armchair, lit a cigarette, opened one of his bottles of wine (far superior vintages than those he brought home), and began to reflect. I couldn't just pretend as though I'd never been in his studio or forget what I'd discovered. I wasn't going to forgive him or act oblivious, agreeing to share my life with a man who led his real life in that filthy shithole. I needed to react. Calmly. React so I could put an end to that abnormal situation. He was mocking me, and had been doing so since day one. I'd always known that, but seeing the undeniable proof made me want to throw up. I had to act as quickly as possible. I said to myself: "For once I'm going to plan things out and be rational about it. The wine is good, I'm calm, and I need to have a precise idea of what I'm going to do next. I can already picture him on his return, wearing that grin of his, with his potbelly, his raffish air and arrogance. I feel like putting out his eyes, or better yet cutting off his hands, just like they do to thieves in Saudi Arabia. A painter without any hands, now that would be a sight! No, it would be far better to slice off his prick, not that there would be much to slice off, but at least it would hurt. I should stop babbling since I'm not actually going to shed his blood. The best thing to do would be to keep quiet about what I've discovered so I can destroy him all the more when the time is right. I don't know whether I'll be able to keep my mouth shut. I'm hot-blooded. But one thing's for sure, he'll never touch me again! First I'm going to put the fear of God in him, and that fear will gnaw away at him, wreaking havoc in his life. I spent the first ten years of my life ridding myself of fear. It was a matter of life and death, so I know all about fear, one could say it's my specialty. I've endured droughts, thirst, hunger, I survived them during heat waves and glacial winters, and while fighting off snakes, scorpions, and hyenas . . . I had no other choice. I tamed my fears and now I know how to instill them in both men and animals."

I picked up all the proof that I'd found and went to see a lawyer to ask him if this was enough to ask for a divorce. I also called my mother, who suggested I travel to the south of Morocco to consult one of our ancestors who was endowed with extraordinary powers: "He'll know how to punish Foulane, loyalty matters before everything else in our family!" I told everybody. I had to avenge the insult and the shame. He had to pay. One of my brothers offered to slash all his paintings; another offered to send a couple of tough guys to teach him a lesson. I told them not to. If anyone was going to do anything it was going to be me, and only me.

After he'd returned from his trip, Foulane pretended to be tired, using the usual excuse that he had a migraine. I asked him where he'd been and he told me: "You know exactly where I've been, in Frankfurt, so I could talk to my gallerist about the coming exhibition. It was a difficult trip, the people were nice but I didn't like the city, so I tried to get everything done quickly so I could back home. So, what's for dinner tonight?"

Without hesitating I replied: "English condoms in rotten white sauce to be followed by angel hairs cooked in sweat and a few drops of Chanel No. 5."

He wasn't amused. He remained frozen in his chair. He picked a magazine up from the floor and began flipping through it. At which point I threw a large glass of water at his head, although I would have preferred vinegar, but that's what I had in my hand at the time. I hated him for not reacting to it. He just stood up, coolly wiped his face, and left the house. He came back five minutes later and just as coolly packed some changes of clothes, stuffed them in his suitcase, which he still hadn't unpacked, and left again. Later I called him at his studio and hurled a bunch of insults at him. I was in tears and threatened to sue him. In fact, I said whatever went through my head at the time. I was hurt, really hurt. Betrayal is a terrible thing, an unbearable humiliation. Just unacceptable. The children heard me shouting and crying. They slipped into my bed and slept beside me, murmuring: "We love you, mummy."

He spent the next three months living in his studio, or rather his brothel, to be more exact. During that time he received a letter from my lawyer, which was intended to scare him. Something else that he was careful to avoid mentioning in his manuscript. Then one day I cracked, went to his studio, and slipped inside his bed, because I was still in love with him, that's right, I admit it. I remember it all very well, he was watching television, and he didn't push me away, we made love without exchanging a word, and the next day he was mine again, he came home and our lives went back to the way they were. A grave error. My mother disapproved of my decision. She had to go seek out our illustrious ancestor in the southern reaches of Morocco to stop him in his tracks. If you're going to get back together with your husband, he might as well be in good shape, she told me.

I thought Foulane had understood, that he'd realized he would have to start behaving properly from then on. But he very quickly reverted to his old bachelor habits, without caring about how that might make me feel. He traveled, went out in the evenings for dinner—"work dinners"—only returning late at night and smelling of another woman's perfume. I kept my mouth shut and swallowed the bitter pill of humiliation. I would look at my children and weep in silence. When he slept with another woman, he would rush into the bathroom on his return and take a shower. Although he usually only showered in the morning just like everyone else. Whenever I tried to get close to him, he wouldn't even get hard. He'd used up all his energies on someone else. His balls were all floppy and his pecker was in a pitiful state. He was depleted, completely depleted. It was intolerable! I put up with it for years. I was incapable of doing anything else. My morals, ethics, and upbringing forbade me from cheating on him. In our culture, a woman who cheats on her husband no longer has any rights, everyone thinks badly of her, even if she was victimized by a lying, violent husband. Everyone in our village knew the story of Fatima, the only women in our village who ever dared to have a lover. She was banished and spent a few years begging on the streets of Marrakech, until one day she threw herself under the wheels of a bus not far from Jamaa el Fna. Poor Fatima! May God rest her soul and forgive her!

I would have liked to have flings of my own, and have scores of lovers, but at no point did my soul or my pride allow me to do that. My friends encouraged me to do so, urging me to get my revenge and return the insult fivefold, but I resisted. I wasn't even attracted to other men. I loved my husband and didn't want to give myself to another man. I was courted by handsome, interesting, freethinking, and generous men. But I rejected them all despite being flattered to be the object of such interest. "You're very seductive and beautiful and yet your husband neglects you; it's a crime against love that should be punished with love."

I loved him and yet didn't let him see it: it was a question of modesty. My parents had never kissed one another in front of us, and had never exchanged tender words. So where did this love come from? He was the first man I'd ever loved. The men I'd been with during my years in Marseilles didn't count because I hadn't been myself at the time. So I simply flirted a little with some friends, nothing more. He intimidated and dominated me. I needed to shift the power dynamic in our relationship and so I dared to defy him and knocked him from the public pedestal he'd set himself up on. What I admired most in him was his maturity, his experience, and his fame. I wanted him all to myself, there was nothing unusual about that, no woman ever wants to share her man, as far as I'm concerned any woman who sleeps with a married man is a whore and a slut. I can spot them a mile away and I hate them. I even started to hatch plans for how I would kill these kinds of women, plotting these crimes carefully, with a serial killer's rigorousness. Oh yes, I would take my time with them, make them fall into a trap and then disfigure them, one after the other. I loved to visualize those moments down to the smallest details, thinking about how I would approach them, gain their trust, and especially how I wouldn't leave any traces behind, the perfect crime. A female serial killer! I dreamed up plenty of scenarios, but never put any of them into practice of course.

You might not believe me, but I never cheated on Foulane. He was well aware of that, but yet he cast doubts on my loyalty in his manuscript. That he had the nerve to suspect me! It was certainly true that I spent a lot of time out with my girlfriends, and that since he traveled a lot I had plenty of opportunities to betray him. But I never crossed that line. However, I must confess that I regret that now. I was an idiot, constrained by principles that put me at a constant disadvantage. I thought about Fatima's story, but it's not like we were living in that village of virtue. We were living in Paris at the time, and we had a social life. He was in the public eye and I was the pretty little thing on his arm. Once, during a reception at the Élysée Palace, he turned his back to me just as he was talking to the president. Against all odds, François Mitterrand turned to address me and broke into a big smile. He asked me where I was from and what I was studying. When I told him I was married to the artist he'd just been speaking to, he said: "Oh, now I understand, you're his muse." He was right about that. I was his muse, his slave, his property, the trophy wife he could parade at receptions and soirées. This bothered me at first, but then I got used to it. Nobody was going to give me any complexes. I knew who I was and what I was worth. I didn't feel the need to pretend, or to be a hyp-ocrite like his sisters, who'd all had plastic surgery, felt uncomfortable in their own skin, and were all fat and charmless. I would watch them strut about at weddings, acting like peacocks, while I would remain isolated in my corner. I was the foreigner, the stranger, the bad apple that had to be avoided at all costs. I polluted the clean, limpid air of a society that was well-versed in all manner of hypocrisy and at keeping up appearances.

I suffered a long list of humiliations and I'm going to tell you all about them, I won't make anything up. After all, I'm not writing a novel. I'm going to get it all off my chest. He was always keen on smoothing things over, avoiding scenes, no scandals or noises, it was better to remain calm and stay flexible. "To turn a blind eye," as Fou-lane was fond of saying. But I've always kept my eyes wide open. I'm not flexible, and I never will be. What does being flexible really mean anyway? To always turn the other cheek and keep your head down? No, I'll never do that!

Our Wedding

Let's go back to the very beginning. Our wedding. What a disaster. Oh, I'll remember that Friday in April for the rest of my life. All brides look back on their wedding day with joy, but not me. That day will forever remain a black day, a sad day, a day when I cried a lot. Newlyweds usually cry because they are leaving one family to become a part of another, but I was crying because I was leaving my family to plunge into an unimaginable hell.

Allow me to set the scene for you.

My parents had leased a holiday home on the outskirts of Casablanca. It must have cost them a great deal of money. They had wanted to make a good impression on their future in-laws, whose urban origins intimidated them. People from Fez think of themselves as superior to all other Moroccans. They look down on the rest of Morocco as though their culture was the only one worth anything, behaving as though everyone else has to cook like them, dress like them, and speak like them. They have a natural propensity for intolerance and don't make any efforts to conceal their contempt. It's not that they're nasty, just cynical. My parents were set against my marriage for several reasons. My mother told me that my father, who rarely spoke, had told her: "We don't belong with them and they don't belong with us!" He'd also said: "I'm not sure our daughter will be happy in that family; that her husband is older than she is might not be such a big deal, but his family scares me. I never know how to welcome them or how to act, they belong to a different world and we're simply unpretentious folk. It makes me wonder whether we even believe in the same God! Well, there we have it. Tell her to do what she wants. Tell her I'm sad."

I remember that conversation with my mother and how I couldn't really disagree with her because I knew she had a point. But it was too late by then, I was in love. What did being in love mean to a girl who'd had to tackle so much misery so early on in her life? I thought of him as though I was living in a kind of modern fairy tale. I ignored all the defects I noticed. I thought he would live up to my expectations. But romantic love is in fact a fiction invented by novelists. I'd read several novels set in nineteenth-century Scotland. I would dream of those rainy landscapes, delicate characters, and those declarations of love that were imbued with poetry and promises. I thought of myself as one of the heroines of those novels and believed in all of it. The transition from fairy tale to reality proved difficult, very difficult indeed.

I remember how one day, before we'd gotten engaged, Foulane had waited for me in his apartment on Rue Lhomond. I had taken the train and on my arrival at the Saint-Lazare station I felt an incredible weight on my chest. For the first time in my life, I was frightened. I went into a café, ordered a cup of tea, and spent hours smoking and thinking, watching the film of my future life flash past my eyes. I had a certain knack for predicting how my future would turn out. Even though I was in love, I wasn't under any illusions. I knew that his family wouldn't miss an opportunity to remind me of my humble origins and how inadequate an addition I was to their family portrait. I knew that he wouldn't stick up for me and that he shared their ideas. I could clearly see that I was about to make a mistake, but I stupidly told myself that I was fated to marry him. I had read many French novels and identified with petty bourgeois characters from the provinces, and like them, I convinced myself that I had an intense inner life.

Foulane was waiting for me, but I didn't call him to say I would be running late. I didn't want to make that meeting, knowing that I would be lost if I crossed that threshold. When I'd smoked my pack of cigarettes, I got up, looked up the train schedules, and saw I couldn't get on one until 10:10, but that it was only 8:00 by then. So I started to walk, jumped on the 21 bus, got off at Boulevard Saint-Michel, and headed toward his apartment.

It was cold and I was only wearing a light jacket, so I was shivering. He took me in his arms, kissed me, warmed me up, cooked some delicious fish, and then we made love. It was the first time I'd given myself to him. I got up in the middle of the night and wanted to smoke, so he took the car to get me some cigarettes. He also bought some croissants for the following morning. I had a class that day and showed up late, so the professor of philosophy held me back after class. He made it clear that he wanted to take me out to dinner any time during the week except on Saturday or Sunday, which was when he saw his kids since he was divorced. Partly out of defiance and partly out of curiosity, I decided to take him up on his offer and agreed to see him on Friday. His intentions were clear: he wanted me to be his mistress. He was a handsome, intelligent man and was rather seductive. I refused his advances several times, then stood to leave, using the excuse that I had to catch a train. He grabbed my hand, kissed it, and said: "Don't worry, I'll drive you home." I tried to explain that it was over thirty miles outside of Paris, but he insisted, hoping he would thus have the time to convince me not to get married. Everyone knew that I was going to marry a famous painter. It had even been mentioned in a newspaper.

•

A month later, Foulane came to visit my parents in Clermont-Ferrand, accompanied by six of his closest friends, so that he could formally ask for my hand in marriage. It was a Saturday and my father was home from work. It went fairly well, certainly better than on the wedding day itself. His friends found out that I belonged to a family of immigrants and saw that we came from a humble background. This had never been a problem between Foulane and me. He knew where I came from, but I didn't know about his origins, or what his life had been like before we'd met.

The following week Foulane introduced me to his parents at a restaurant in Paris. He'd bought their airline tickets and called a friend of his who loved his paintings and worked at the French consulate in Casablanca to fast-track their visas. I heard his mother say behind my back: "This can't be the girl he was talking about, she's not . . . She's not even white." I pretended that I hadn't heard her. My skin was fairly dark because I tanned very easily. I smiled. His father was far more sympathetic. He immediately asked me a number of questions about my village, my father's property, and our traditions. He even asked me: "Is it really true what people say, that you people have magical powers?" I laughed and said, "I have no idea." But deep down he too disapproved of the match. You can't hide such things, I could see it in his face and in his eyes. I didn't know if he was talking about me, but I heard him say *"media mujer"* several times—which is Spanish for "tiny woman," an expression he often used to refer to his wife's small frame. I also heard him use the word *khanfoucha*, meaning "beetle" in Arabic; was he talking about me? I'd landed in the middle of a family of lunatics! They spoke in innuendos and metaphors. I wasn't used to those kinds of jokes. My parents never insulted anyone and never spoke ill of people. Some of the women who worked for my mother-in-law took me aside to warn me that my life would be difficult, that it was a matter of class complicity. One of them said: "You know, little one, Fassis don't like us much. There's nothing that can be done about it, they think they're better than us and they don't really respect other people! So watch out, your husband is a nice man but his sisters are absolutely terrible!"

I could have changed my mind, called everything off, and gone back to my parents' house. There was nothing stopping me. I can't quite understand what made me embark on that dangerous adventure. Love, of course. But I still ask myself whether I ever really loved him. I liked him and found him alluring and charming; besides, he was an artist, and I'd always wanted to rub shoulders with that wonderful magical world of musicians, writers, and painters. It was like a dream. So despite those worrisome signs, I pressed ahead and plunged headfirst into married life.

At the time, Foulane was all sweetness and light, always very attentive, cheerful, and loving. He always wanted to please me, and he'd rush to the other side of the town just to buy me a present. He'd put an end to his former days as a bachelor and ladies' man. But there were still traces of that former life in his apartment. A bra, a nightgown, designer shoes. I threw them in the neighbor's trash the first chance I got. Foulane didn't even realize that they'd gone missing. Or if he did he never mentioned it.

I found hundreds of photos in one of his drawers. Some were related to his work, but others depicted him in the arms of other women: blondes, redheads, brunettes, tall, short, Arab girls, Scandinavian girls . . . "What kind of a hole have I gotten myself into?" I asked myself. "Why me? What do I have that they don't? Oh, I get it now, the guy's pushing forty and so he's decided to listen to his mother and have kids, so I'm going to be his surrogate mother. Until he eventually trades me in for a younger woman."

My parents were very traditional. The marriage took place in the village hall. Once they'd arrived—late, of course—Foulane's family was completely shocked, especially the women. How could their son—the famous artist—possibly get married in a rented room just like immigrants did when they returned home? They exchanged knowing glances of the kind I would have to endure for years, then pulled some grimaces and went to greet my mother and my aunts. The men assembled on the other side of the room, where the *adel* was going to preside over the signing of the marriage contract. Foulane was wearing a white djellaba with slippers that kept falling off his feet; he was embarrassed and ill at ease. He felt that the union of those worlds was a losing combination. He was sorry about it, sorry about the fact his relatives were racists, sorry that my relatives weren't well educated, sorry that I belonged to a tribe that didn't know the kind of good manners that the people of Fez were accustomed to, because in their eyes our good manners weren't all that good.

I must admit that the dresses his female relatives wore—his mother, his aunts, his sisters—were incredibly beautiful and expensive. Our own dresses were no match for theirs. We were of humble stock, yes, but we were also proud. What did we have to be ashamed of? Of being who we were? Never. I don't think Foulane ever understood this character trait that was shared by all members of our tribe. We were incredibly proud. We had our dignity and our honor. All their pomp didn't make our heads spin.

The time came for the signing of the marriage contract. I had to say "yes" and then sign it. We were kept in different rooms. A door stood between us. I clenched my mother's arm until it hurt her, and I cried like a little girl whose doll had been stolen from her. I saw Foulane's father grimace as though to indicate his disapproval. One of his friends kept tugging at his sleeve to remind him not to make a scene. I would have really liked him to. It would have saved me, and frankly it would have also saved his son.

I wiped my nose, dried my tears, and whispered, "Yes." I had to say it again, then I covered my head and signed the certificate of my slavery, confinement, and humiliation.

The men prayed for the groom and the bride to be blessed by God and His Prophet, to keep them on the right path, to retain their faith, and for their souls to be cleansed of all impurities, and for them to be worthy of the happiness that God had in store for them!

Then they raised their hands to the heavens and began to recite verses from the Qur'an, then exchanged greetings amongst one another, with each family wishing the other a happy and prosperous life.

Our village orchestra played a selection of songs that belonged to our heritage. My relatives started to sing and dance, while his remained trapped inside their fine clothes. One of his aunts motioned me to come over to her and said: "Why have they been playing the same song over and over again?" How could I explain that the musicians had played at least twenty different songs? She then ordered me to sit beside her and said: "Do you know whom you've had the privilege to marry? Do you know what kind of family you've become a part of? Why can't you speak Arabic properly and what's up with that accent? Are you Moroccan or half French? Very well, you must come stay with us in Fez so that I can teach you how to cook, how to comport yourself, and how to address people when they speak to you."

I was stupefied. I burst into laughter, nervous laughter. I laughed until I started to cry, not knowing whether they were tears of happiness or sadness. Repressed anger. Subdued wrath. I didn't answer her but kept my gaze fixed on the floor, like a mad, distraught woman.

Dinner was served late. The women didn't like our cooking. The plates had been barely touched by the time they were sent back to the kitchen. The men ate as normal. My father, who hadn't had the time to change, was exhausted. My mother, poor thing, was very unhappy. My aunts stared at me as if to say, "Serves you right!" I observed my husband from afar and noticed how unhappy he looked. He wasn't smiling and wasn't eating. Maybe he wanted to run away. He would have done us a great service if he had. He came to take me away at around four o'clock in the morning, as per our custom. His friend dropped us off at our hotel. The room was a mess. There weren't any flowers, no chocolates and no greeting card. This time it wasn't Foulane's fault, but rather that of the hotel, which didn't deserve its five stars. Our wedding night had begun with bad omens. There were even cigarette butts floating in the toilet bowl. But who could we talk to at that hour? Foulane sent the hotel manager a fuming letter the following day. The party was over. In fact, there had never been a party in the first place, just a ceremony that we had to fulfill out of a sense of duty.

A photographer friend had spent the entire evening taking shots of us. My husband had some of them enlarged. We hung them up in the living room of our first apartment in Paris. The people who came to visit us would look at them transfixed: "Oh, it's like *One Thousand and One Nights*! How pretty the bride looks! How young! You look ravishing, darling, why didn't you invite us? What a shame! A big Moroccan wedding! What a party it must have been! And how happy you look!"

Nobody knows how to really read a photograph. How badly I'd wanted to tell those people: "But you're completely wrong! It wasn't a party, just a chore where everyone was uncomfortable, unhappy, and outside their comfort zone, which was celebrated to the sounds of Berber drums and flutes, which it turns out was a mistake, a monstrous mistake. What you can see in our eyes is a profound sadness, deep regret, and a crushing sense of fatality."

We always gave people the impression we were a happy couple. Those who didn't know us well held us up as an example of a model couple. I suffered under the weight of this impression, which bore no relation to reality. My husband acquired the habit of shutting me up whenever we had guests over. He behaved toward me in a way that he would never allowed himself to do with anyone else. One day, when he'd been entertaining his nieces and their husbands, he'd had the insolence to translate my words into "proper French," adding that he always had to provide subtitles for whatever I said! At which point his guests had laughed, amused by the way he treated me, and I just let him to do it, like the fool I was.

On another occasion, he told an English painter who was represented by the same gallery that he never took me abroad because he loved to travel free and without any luggage, that he didn't want to be encumbered by a wife who would doubtless have caused him a thousand problems. The painter had been confused by why Foulane would feel the need to talk about me like that, but since Foulane had given his words a comedic inflection, he'd limited himself to a polite laugh. Then there had been the time when a musician friend of his had come to see us to tell us he'd gotten married, at which point Foulane had cracked a few stupid jokes about marriage and quoted Schopenhauer's gloomy aphorisms on the subject.

He didn't just disrespect me in public, he also never stuck up for me in front of his family. He sometimes even joined the choir, fueling their rejection of me, not to mention their hatred.

And so our marriage began badly, continued badly, and ended badly.

Money

This is a painful, complicated topic. Foulane got angry whenever I talked about money. A typical reaction for a cheapskate.

Thanks to time and experience, I can safely say that this artist who made a lot of money was in fact a miser. At first I had thought he was thrifty. But now I know he was cheap. I spent my entire life tightening my belt, looking for bargains, and waiting until the sales so I could buy clothes for the children. Although we had a joint account, he hardly ever put any money in it. I was always short of cash. He would love to brandish the letters from the bank saying the account was overdrawn. "You see? Your reckless spending is going to ruin us!" What reckless spending? It was barely enough to cover the basics, I didn't spend it on anything superfluous or extravagant. My friends would buy designer clothes at full retail prices whereas I got by thanks to clearance sales. I never wore designer clothes or expensive jewelry.

Each time he went abroad Foulane would give me a small sum of money and tell me to "be careful with it" as though I were one of his children. He never paid for anything while he was abroad because he was always somebody's guest. But whenever we traveled together, he would forbid me from using the minibar because he didn't want to pay for the additional charges. He was completely miserly. When we would leave the hotel, he would pull his usual scene and complain about all the luggage I'd brought with me. Even though I would try to explain that it was full of the children's clothes, he would say: "Oh, stop it, will you, I'm perfectly aware that those suitcases are full of presents for your family, I've had it up to here!"

Foulane wasn't generous. You're not going to believe me because the impression he gave you was the complete opposite. He kept track of every single penny. He never spent a dime unthinkingly. He had a calculator in his heart. Nothing eluded him. He accused me of being an obsessive consumerist, someone who couldn't tell the difference between different kinds of banknotes and who thought a credit card was a bottomless well of money, and that since I'd never worked much, I didn't even know the value of money, and that I'd never even learned how to count properly. He also believed that I would have been far happier and more satisfied if I'd married a man who was as poor as I was. But what did he know about that?

I've lost track of how many times he went abroad without leaving us any money. I even had to turn to one of our friends so that I could borrow enough money to run some errands and feed the children.

He had bank accounts in just about every country. He'd made arrangements to ensure that the proceeds from the sales of his paintings would be deposited in accounts that I couldn't access. One day I accidentally discovered he had an account in Gibraltar because he'd left the receipt of a transfer lying around. I photocopied it and kept it in my files, alongside a bunch of other account statements, receipts, and various other records. I also kept photocopies of all the documents concerning his assets in France, Morocco, Italy, and Spain. I had my suspicions that he'd even bought a property in New York, but I was never able to prove it. My legal counsel asked me to assemble everything into a file in case anything fishy ever came up. All I would need to do was alert the Moroccan tax authorities and Foulane would be arrested in a heartbeat. I also discovered another safe whose combination I didn't know. I asked the locksmith to come back and told him that I'd forgotten the combination code to that one too. It took him half an hour to open it. I found countless things he'd been hiding in there: money, jewelry, invoices, receipts, packets of condoms, and even packets of Viagra. I was astounded. I emptied the safe of all its contents and stashed them away. How could I share my life with a man who kept so many secrets? How could I put up with the fact that he'd been leading a double life? Or even a triple life? That he'd been cheating on me I'd known for a long time, but now I'd uncovered his financial secrets too. Never having been able to trust him, I started putting money aside in a savings account. I knew he was capable of divorcing me and leaving me penniless. So I started making up house repairs that needed to be done, things that the children needed to buy, and would siphon off some of that money into the savings account. On one occasion, he refused to buy me a piece of jewelry that I really wanted, and that same evening he gave his eldest sister a large sum of money so she could get a boob job. I also learned that he'd ensured that a large part of his estate would go to his younger brother, who was married to a witch who hated me and had tried to do me harm by any and all means, including casting the evil eye on me. My *taleb* confirmed this. Years later, Foulane helped his brothers and sisters again when he bought them a splendid apartment on the Mediterranean coast.

Foulane was only avaricious when it came to me or my family. I must admit he wasn't stingy when it came to the children; still, one day our youngest daughter told him: "Papa, we're rich, why do you deny yourself things? Look at my classmates, their fathers are a lot poorer than you and they always have the latest video games!" In theory I actually agreed with him when it came to not wanting our children to be enslaved to technology, but this wasn't a matter of principles . . .

Money lay at the root of our biggest fights. On one occasion, I wanted to steal one of his paintings so that I could sell it, but unfortunately he hadn't finished any new ones around that time. I suspected him of being purposefully slow when it came to finishing them and only signing them at the last possible minute. He always took precautions. I compared myself to the other wives in our circle of friends, in particular the wife of a Spanish musician who always handed everything over to her when it came to money, including contracts, sales, and royalties. As the musician put it to us one day: "I play the gigs, and she rakes in the cash!" Another of our friends, a rich, celebrated writer, also let his wife handle their finances. He never had any money on him. His wife always took care of the bills.

At first I hadn't wanted to handle his finances, I just didn't want to be at the bottom of his list of priorities, an afterthought, as if I was nothing, as if I didn't mean anything to him. But he always trusted his agent more than he did his wife, even though his agent actually stole from him. I'd also started to notice that our children's inheritance was quickly going up in smoke. I had to act and stop that hemorrhage. His family, friends, and agent almost lived off our backs. As far as I was concerned, that was simply unacceptable. It was because Foulane was weak and naïve, and always got screwed over by the first person who came along. I've lost track of how many times I warned him against some of his so-called friends who seduced him with their words and flattery to further their secret, shameful agendas, which he never seemed to see through. That's how people had not only been able to steal paintings from him, but in one case also a lot of money— the little man whom Foulane wrote in his manuscript that he'd seen during one of his hallucinations, and who turned out to be an international con artist, a nasty, bright-eyed, and bushy-tailed man who laughed hysterically and whose eyes often reddened with jealousy. All because he had artistic pretensions and yet nobody bought his paintings. So he opened a gallery in Casablanca, exhibited Foulane's work, and sold out the show. He then quickly filed for bankruptcy and Foulane realized he'd been swindled and had no legal recourse. This story even found its way into the press, but by then the crook had switched trades and had opened a travel agency devoted to pilgrims wanting to go on the Hajj or the Umrah. He would sell those poor devils package tours and once the pilgrims arrived in Saudi Arabia they realized they'd been cheated and that everything they'd been promised was a lie. On their return home, they would also discover that they couldn't file any claims because the travel agency had in the meanwhile been replaced by a butcher's or a grocer's. Foulane had been friends with this con artist and hadn't even noticed how he'd been planning to make his move throughout the course of their relationship. To think that my husband had even loaned him some money to open his gallery. I'd always distrusted that guy, but Foulane had never listened to me, telling me: "You're just jealous of my friends and you're trying to come between us!" and so forth.

That's why money lay behind so many of our fights. One day I told him: "You've got serious problems when it comes to money, you should get some help."

I never forgot his reply, which made me cry for a long time: "I'd rather see my money go into my friends' pockets than in your family's."

As if my family ever needed his moolah. What a disgrace! It was then that I understood that he was out of his mind and that his family—meaning me and the kids—would always come after his friends, his sisters, his nephews, his nieces, and his cousins.

When I filed for divorce, I did in fact try to get my revenge and get my hands on as much of his money as I could to prevent the next woman who fell into his lap from taking it all. He was simply incapable of managing the family's finances, which was why I had to take charge once and for all.

Oh, I forgot to mention an important detail. Whenever he gave me a present, it was almost certain that he hadn't paid for it. He didn't buy me the traditional golden belt that Moroccan husbands usually gave to their wives; instead, his mother gave me hers. I had wanted one in a more modern style that would go with my figure and my dresses. But no, instead he asked his mother to give me hers because she'd gotten ill by then and never attended any parties or celebrations anymore. I never wore it. He also never took me on a honeymoon. Always because of money. He said that since we always got invited to go abroad, it was like being on a permanent honeymoon. He would even buy himself a business-class ticket so that his butt would be nice and cozy while forcing the children and me to fly economy because he didn't want to pay for an upgrade. He said that it didn't matter because we were all on the same plane and heading to the same destination. "You're all young, but I'm not young anymore." He would never admit he was old. He liked to pamper himself and was incredibly superstitious.

When my uncle and his wife spent some time at one of our old houses, which we didn't use and which was all boarded up, he insisted on charging them rent. How embarrassing! How disrespectful! That he would ask my poor uncle for money when he was making millions. Whereas my uncle was actually doing us a favor by living in a house and thus helping to keep it up, since empty houses depreciate in value, not to mention the fact my uncle was a migrant worker who barely made more than the minimum wage.

Whenever we ate out at restaurants, he would forbid me from drinking wine, under the pretext that this would fuel my burgeoning alcoholism. Whereas the truth was that he didn't want to spend any money. Besides, all Moroccan men consider themselves superior to their wives, and he couldn't stand to see me drink, thinking it was a sign of how disobedient and liberated I was. So I would drink to excess purely to make him uncomfortable and force him to reveal himself for who he really was: an ayatollah in Western clothes.

He was always very generous with our staff and paid them a lot more than the going rate, even going so far as to buy our watchman a sheep for Eid al-Adha. But when it came to me, he counted all the pennies. None of my friends ever had money problems with their husbands. I guess I was unlucky. It was my destiny. I always had to ask him for anything I needed; in fact, he made sure it worked out like that so I would have to rely on him and his generosity, as though I were a stranger or one of his children. He made a note of all the expenses in a ledger and every time he gave me some money he would say: "You spent a lot last month, it's too much . . . especially since you don't lack for anything!" One day I tore the ledger out of his hands, ripped it up, and threw it in the trash. He stared at me with an appalled expression on his face, as though I'd just ripped up some banknotes.

I never wanted to make things easy for him and went out of my way to upset him, waiting for the most inopportune moments, like when he was busy working, at which point I would burst into his studio and ask him for money. He would write me a check just to shut me up. One day he forgot to fill in the sum. So I rushed to the bank and asked the teller if the account was in the black. She said I could withdraw a hundred thousand dirhams and so I left with my purse stuffed full of banknotes. I felt light and carefree because my purse was full of moolah, his moolah! I paid for my parents' pilgrimage to Mecca, bought myself a nice watch and a few other trinkets.

I also purchased some very expensive cloths and asked the upholsterer to send my husband the bill. He was a gifted upholsterer but he charged wild prices. Which was why my husband hated him, even though he settled the bill in the end.

Despite his being suspicious of any kinds of merchants, one of Foulane's cousins managed to swindle him. He claimed to have found a Mexican collector who wanted to buy one of Foulane's finest paintings. The Mexican had even offered to pay an advance as collateral. The cousin delivered the painting to the Mexican, got his money, and Foulane never saw him again! A clever trick! Foulane didn't trust my family, but got conned by his own . . . And that's the truth.

Sex

Did you notice how Foulane almost never mentioned our sex life? If you asked him why, he'd tell you that it was out of modesty. Not that he ever concerned himself with modesty when it came to painting naked women in compromising poses. But whenever the subject of our sex life entered the equation, he fell strangely silent. He listed all his conquests in his manuscript and described those women down to the slightest detail, portraying himself as a Casanova or provincial Don Juan, then suddenly started to complain that old age robbed him of his libido, a situation he attributed to me and his stroke.

He preferred to remain silent about what had happened—or rather didn't happen—between us. We rarely made love, he was always so rough and in a hurry to finish, coming without even asking if I'd climaxed too. I must admit that I didn't really lust after him either. We would fall asleep, tell each other goodnight, and he would watch a film, getting up several times in the middle of the night to eat some fruit or yogurt, switching on the lamp, grumbling because he was finding it difficult to sleep, shift around in bed, then, as if that wasn't enough, he'd switch on the radio. I would go to sleep with the children and leave him alone with his insomnia. He would wake up in a bad mood in the morning, drink his coffee in silence, without so much as a smile, jump into his car, and head to his studio, where he could finally be in peace, as he put it.

I knew that he was never peaceful on his own, and that he took advantage of my being far away and busy looking after the children to fuck girls he picked up on the streets. He would come back home in the evening looking exhausted. My intuition told me he'd been having sex, even though he was completely impotent when it came to me. But no, he was actually reserving his sexual energies and desires for other women, some of whom were single, others married, but all of whom always hoped he'd leave me for them.

At least one of those affairs ended quite badly, a Moroccan girl who was studying at the École des Beaux-Arts in Paris. She'd come to ask him for some advice and was distantly related to him, a second cousin twice removed. Barely twenty years old and still a virgin. She got pregnant a couple of months after they met. To save face, she immediately had an abortion, and in order to conceal the fact that anything had ever happened, she got her hymen restitched at a specialist clinic. Foulane told me all about it, but was careful to omit the fact he was the father.

"I have to help her," he'd told me, looking all innocent, "her parents are very conservative, they'll be very upset and her boyfriend is penniless, and in any case he ran away!"

Foulane paid for everything, but as soon as she'd had the abortion, she completely vanished. I waited a month, then called her and went to see her, taking a bottle of wine with me since I knew she loved red wine. We drank, and once her inhibitions had broken down, she spilled her guts and told me the whole story down to the smallest detail, how he would fuck her and put her in positions that helped him come, how she sucked him off, and how he licked her feet, and probably her ass too. She even told me how they'd had a threesome with an Italian journalist who'd been in town to write about the Contemporary Art Fair.

When it was time to leave, I thanked her and asked her to do me a favor: "Give me a heads up when you go see him again."

But alas there wasn't a next time. Foulane broke it off with her and refused to pick up her phone calls. I had wanted to surprise him and catch him red-handed. Yet did I really need more proof?

What kind of woman would put up with these things? With her husband pretending he had a migraine when it came to her, then having threesomes with other women?

It's true that one day I sent him a text where I said: "*You don't satisfy me either sexually or financially!*" He never replied to that.

My friends would often tell me about their evenings with their husbands and I would remain silent, not daring to tell them the truth. I would suppress my frustrations and be ashamed of it. My friend Hafsa told me about how her husband used to shave her, which was apparently quite exciting. Maria's husband would spend a long time kissing her all over her body. Khadijia would wear sexy lingerie and she and her husband would do some role-playing where she played the foreigner. Most of them made love a few times a week. But I always had to wait until he felt like it. If only he'd taken his time and looked after my needs too!

I was lucky to meet Lalla, my neighbor, whom Foulane hated and tried to distance from me. Lalla saved me. She opened my eyes, gave me the means to defend myself. She's an exceptional woman: selfless, beautiful, wholesome, generous, and with the soul of an artist, who refused to make compromises, unlike Foulane.

Lalla talked to me about sexuality and explained that a woman my age needed to be satisfied at least once a day. I wouldn't have hoped for so much, but she was right, I had to leave that selfish, perverted monster who'd managed to make me lose my mind. I know that Foulane didn't like Lalla. She helped me to discover what he was up to: he was trying to drive me crazy so he could leave me, start a new life, and still keep everything.

I owe Lalla a debt for helping me to start achieving my freedom. He was jealous of her, very jealous. He would shout and scream, supposedly because he loved me. What a hypocrite! He'd spent his life being interested in just one thing—his ego—and when someone opened my eyes to that, he couldn't bear it. He thought that he'd married a quiet little shepherdess who wouldn't look him in the eye and would swallow all of his bullshit! Oh no! He was fooling himself, he had no idea what that little country girl had in store for him.

As for my sexuality, I'm still young, and people tell me I'm beautiful and alluring, so I hope that one day I'll finally meet a man who'll make up for all the frustrations, humiliations, and constant disrespect that Foulane put me through.

Jealousy

I admit it, I was jealous, incredibly jealous. I was never jealous of my friends, only of Foulane. He had a vicious knack for bringing out the worst in me, those awful—yet legitimate—feelings that drive couples crazy. Of course, his perversity only ever manifested itself in stealthy ways. He would compliment women with hideous hairdos and hideous dresses when we had guests over just to get on my nerves. He would take an interest in their lives, their children, asked them about what they liked to read or what they did to amuse themselves. Always employing that honeyed tone of his, which I loathed. On one occasion, we were invited to a party hosted by people in show business. A young starlet had been there wearing a dress with a scandalous neckline. Foulane's eyes never drifted from her bosom and he spent the whole night talking to her. I even caught him entering her number in his phone. I didn't do anything about it, but later that night I stole his phone and deleted all the numbers with women's names, starting with the young starlet, who called herself Marilin—"with an 'i,'" as she put it. He pulled a scene the following morning, talked about respecting boundaries and privacy, giving me one of his lectures about morals that made me want to puke. In fact, my jealousy wasn't fueled by my frustrated affections for him or by a desire to win him back. It was simply a reaction to his attempts to belittle me in public.

This other time, his Russian mistress—or was she Polish?—who was either a musicians or a painter, I don't remember which except that she had artistic pretensions, actually called at the house: "I would like to zee my old loover again, you zee I've knoon him for a loong time . . ." The nerve! I hung up on her. Later that evening, Foulane laconically said: "Oh don't mind her, she's a lunatic." That's the way he treated the women he claims to have loved!

One day, he asked me to help him pick out a necklace he wanted to buy for his gallerist's wife. He wanted to do something nice for her because they never came empty-handed whenever they visited us. We bought her a stunning Berber necklace made of coral and silver. I wrapped it up in gift paper. But a few months later I spotted it around the neck of a Spanish gallerist who must have certainly been his mistress. When I asked him why, he started stammering like a liar who'd been caught red-handed. Women called at the house from time to time, and I would give them his number so they could call him at his studio. Surprised, they would ask me: "But aren't you his assistant? Or his secretary?" "I'm his wife!" I would shout back. Then they would hang up on me and he would never offer any explanations. He always used the same excuse: "I'm not responsible for the letters or calls I receive." Then he'd add: "If you want to feed your pathological jealousy, you might as well focus on things that actually matter, and not these trifles that have got nothing to do with me!" What were these things that "actually mattered"? Marriage, love, a harmonious relationship? He would confess without revealing anything of import. Now that's what I call insincerity, which is something I loathe.

Foulane had mastered the art of wounding my pride, and he would poke at the deep wounds that had their roots in my childhood, and he would twist the knife just to hurt me. He hurt me a lot. He scoffed at my experiences as a model, saying that having the right proportions wasn't the same as being talented. He would use what I'd told him in confidence to grieve me and remind me that my parents were illiterate immigrants. To think he'd painted a mural in honor of immigrants! What a show-off! What a fascist! He painted the mural for the city of Saint-Denis, and a few months later the mayor bought a couple of his paintings, one of which he hung in his office, while the other was hung in the entrance lobby of city hall.

I was jealous of some of his friends. He was always at their disposal. Always kind and always available. There were these two exiled Chilean politicians who were truly inseparable. Their wives never said anything, they just accepted the situation: friends always came first, and their wives and children last. At first I suspected they might have been gay, but that wasn't true, they were just friends, and their friendship didn't leave any room for anything else. One evening, when they'd been invited to dine at our place, one of them had the audacity to tell me: "Take care of our friend Foulane. He's a great artist. You must be kind with him, we're very fond of him, and we're in awe of his immense talents!" I couldn't restrain myself, my wild streak took over and I slapped him. I left him speechless and gaping and the dinner came to an abrupt end. I never saw them again. Foulane obviously berated me, hurling a bunch of abuse at me, and the ensuing fight reached unprecedented heights. Voilà, my jealousy was nothing other than anger and extreme aggravation. Nothing more. But nowadays Foulane is weak and stuck in his wheelchair, so he can't do anything to me. He needs me whenever he needs to sit, eat, stand up, or even shit. He's at my mercy. My jealousy has become pointless.

The Mistake

I remember the night I didn't come home—which Foulane mentioned in his manuscript—as clearly as he does. Some girlfriends I'd met up with that afternoon told me that I looked awful and unhappy. So they decided to take me out that night. We had dinner at a good restaurant and we wound up at a fashionable nightclub. I danced like a madwomen, flirted with some blond guy, and later that morning I picked up some croissants and went home. Foulane was there waiting for me, car keys in hand, and he asked me where I'd been. So I told him: "At a nightclub!" He slammed the door behind him, rushed down the stairs, and left. It wasn't until later that I learned that he'd showed up at my parents' house to complain like people do in conservative families. Where the daughter, despite being married, is always seen as a little girl, and her parents, who always side with the husband, even have the right to punish her, beat her up and lock her away. But my parents didn't trust him as much as they trusted me. They didn't believe him, muttered a few stock sentences, and then discreetly called me to inform me of his sudden visit. They didn't like him. They found him arrogant and spiteful. They knew that he didn't make me happy, but we don't divorce in our culture, it's part of our tradition. Instead, my mother recommended I go see Hajja Saadia, who was capable of casting good and evil spells alike. I refused. Not that. Not yet. How many times had I slipped a potion into his coffee to make him devoid of willpower? A potion that apparently consisted of powdered hyena brains along with other African and even Brazilian ingredients . . .

I shouldn't have gone back to the house that day, it's true, but our son was six months old and I couldn't just leave him. After that episode, I felt like leaving him often, but whenever the thought occurred to me, I would quickly change my mind and tell myself: "He's going to change, he's an old bachelor who doesn't know how to share his life with someone and be responsible, but he'll wake up eventually and assume his responsibilities, he's going to understand that this isn't just about him, that he's got a family and has to act like it." So I would give him some time and the chance to give up his old solitary habits.

Not long afterward, he was awarded a prestigious international prize for his painting, which was followed by a number of trips and exhibitions. He took me everywhere with him: Egypt, Brazil, Italy, the U.S., Mexico, Russia, and so forth. I loved those trips, the fancy hotels, the great food, and the chance to discover the beautiful cloths and jewelry of the Far East. Whenever we traveled, we got along a lot better, even from a sexual point of view. But when we came back home, he would go into a sulk and lock himself up in his studio, where he found it difficult to get any work done because all the traveling had interfered with his painting.

By this time the 1980s had drawn to a close and he began to be hospitalized for various ailments, which would gradually lead to his stroke. I would worry about him because he looked so agitated, pale and stressed. I wasn't sweet toward him, because I thought that it would be better for me to remain strong and deal with the pain, especially because his prognoses weren't that alarming. He spent whole nights without sleeping, preventing me from getting any, blaming me for the parasite he'd contracted in China, a country he'd wanted to visit without me. It served him right! While he was in the hospital, I prepared his food, took care of his correspondence and canceled all his engagements. His American agent came to see him: not because he was worried about his client; quite the contrary, he came to weigh up the situation! If Foulane suddenly died, the price of his paintings would go through the roof. Armed with a box of chocolates he bought at the airport, he went to the sick man's bedside. Once he'd inquired after his health, he jumped back on the plane and went back to calmly inform the gallerists he worked with.

Foulane was overjoyed that his agent had come all the way from New York just to see him. When I expressed some doubts as to the real reasons behind his visit, Foulane flew into a fury, despite the fact he was wearing an oxygen mask. Three days after he was discharged from the hospital, Foulane lost one of his closest friends—who'd been among those who'd accompanied him when he asked my parents for my hand in marriage—to a rare disease. This loss affected him deeply, especially since he'd just had a close brush with death. Foulane was surprised to see I didn't share his grief. But I'm not the sort of woman who laid it on thick, or said or did sweet things. That's just the way I am. My father didn't kiss me after the age of three or four. Throughout those months, I had to put up with a hypochondriac who roamed around the house like an old man, never going out in the evenings, and who spent all his time drawing in his sketchbooks. He stopped painting. His gallerist called him and sent him an advance for his next exhibition. Since he loved money, he got back to work. No more illnesses, no more laziness. He would get up very early in the morning and go to his studio, and in the evenings he would tell me what he'd done that day. Now I'm going to have to see even more money slip through our fingers, I told myself. I knew he wanted to help a relative of his whose business had gone under. So I called his American gallerist and asked him to wire the royalty payments directly to me. His reply was curt: "We've had express orders from Foulane not to do so as long as he's alive."

I was dumbfounded. I mumbled an apology and started to cry.

My mistake was to think people can change. None of us change, not least of which a man who's already lived out most of his life. I entered his life at a time when he'd decided to stop having fun and settle down, because the anxiety of his encroaching death had begun to creep over him. I was the little flower who was going to take the reins, except that Foulane was the one who took my youth and innocence.

We were not made to be together. That was my mistake, our mistake.

The In-Laws

Foulane's indifference and the war his family waged against me were calculated to drive me crazy. Sometimes I would wake up in the middle of the night in cold sweats, even though the room was warm. A sign of the evil spells they'd cast on me. Foulane said he didn't believe in such things, but I had proof that the women in his family were using sorcery against me. My *taleb* told me everything and I was fully aware of what they wanted to do to me and when. At first they tried to wreck our relationship, to force us to separate. My man stopped touching me or wanting to sleep with me. Then he became indifferent to my presence, as though he were allergic to the touch of my skin. Being close to me didn't arouse his desires. That wasn't normal. I later learned they'd been able to procure a lock of my hair and some of my sanitary napkins. I suffered, experienced sudden panic attacks, and would roam around the house in circles, incapable of calling for help, losing my strength and my sanity. During that time Foulane was nevertheless able to work, go out, and travel, completely at peace.

I followed the *taleb*'s instructions and cleaned the house from top to bottom. My friends helped me and we found little packets wrapped in tinfoil all over the house, tucked under each bed and inside the toilets. The house was overrun by spells designed to make me ill.

That day I discovered that I was in danger, under surveillance, and that I had to act in order to protect myself. My *taleb* wasn't up to such a task. He told me about an old, powerful woman in Marrakech who would be able to help. He also told me I should slaughter a ram on the threshold of my house and burn some incense to repel their spells.

I went to Marrakech. I had to wait for days to secure a meeting with Wallada—people called her that because she'd been a midwife in her youth. As soon as she saw me, Wallada said: "My poor girl, I'm glad you've finally come to see me; good, come and sit right there in front of me and give me a little something so we can begin our session." I pulled out a two-hundred-dirham note and placed it next to her. She was a very powerful woman. She wasn't a clairvoyant, but she could read people's faces and was adept in palmistry. She told me all about my life as though she'd been there every step of the way. She knew everything and described the malevolent people in my life. I was impressed with her talents because she could tell who I was just by looking at me, and figured out the root of my unhappiness. Wallada came from the countryside and was illiterate, but she could write incomprehensible signs endowed with magical powers. I could see she was already hard at work while she was still talking to me. She dipped her reed into some sepia ink and drew a series of mysterious symbols, each more cryptic than the last, that I would be able to use to ward off evil spells.

My session cost me a thousand dirhams, but it brought me some relief, and I left equipped with the means to counteract all that Foulane's sisters had dared to inflict on me. It helped me to give up on my husband's family. I was polite to them whenever I saw them, and I would mouth my insincere *As-Salaam-Alaikums*. The woman from

Marrakech and my *taleb* continued to work to ensure I was protected. I remained on my guard. I carried my *taleb*'s talismans with me at all times. Once every six months, the *taleb* would melt some bronze in a saucepan and mix it with a brew made of water and herbs that came from various places, which he would put in a bottle and hand over to me. I would use some of that yellowish liquid on my body before showering. During the worst of their attacks, I felt as though I was losing my mind, and surrounded by Evil, by powers that wanted to harm and destroy me. I could see it in Zoulekha's eyes. She was Foulane's nastiest and most envious sister, filled with absolute hatred. She looked at me as though she wanted to set fire to everything I did. One day she gave me a ring made of gold and silver. When I showed it to the *taleb*, he ordered me to take it off and give it to him. It was a booby-trapped ring, which had been made to counteract all the protective spells that he'd prepared for me. When I gave it back to her, she looked all surprised. I told her it was too tight for me and that I was allergic to gold. She smiled at me and pouted, as if to say, "Don't worry, you'll get what's coming to you!"

This is how I put up a fight against his family.

Foulane was right when he said my family often came to see me. They protected me and I could count on them. He was also right that a few girls from my village came to live with us so they could help out with the children. Yes, my family always came first, and no, I never liked any of his relatives. I had my reasons but he didn't want to understand them. I refused to let any of his nephews and nieces come over, because they were brattish and disrespectful. On one occasion when one of his nieces—a fat, stupid girl who'd failed her exams—was staying with us, I refused to let her loaf around the house, so I asked her to help me clean the children's bedrooms. She refused, so I asked her to leave. Her reply was: "You don't have the right to boss me around, I'm at home here, this is my uncle's house, you can't kick me out." So I threw all her belongings out onto the street and she went running to her uncle's arms. Foulane heaped a bunch of abuse at me that night.

His family always hated me. But I eventually stopped caring. It didn't get to me anymore, but he was the one who refused to see them for who they really were. He didn't believe me when I told him about all the amulets I'd found scatted around the house. "You're sick," he told me, "you're just making it all up."

Our Friends

We didn't frequent the same people, partly because of the age differ-ence, but also for class reasons. My friends were mostly immigrants. His were intellectuals, internationally renowned artists, writers, pol-iticians, and they were all full of themselves. They looked at me con-descendingly, often with the sort of kindness with which adults treat children.

I remember how, right at the beginning of our relationship, an Algerian woman—or was she Tunisian?—who was ugly and vulgar and married to a much older French man had screwed her face up so that she looked even uglier and said: "You've won the jackpot!"

"You're an idiot!" I'd replied.

The jackpot! Yes, a jackpot of troubles and contempt. I was al-ways suspicious of the people around him, but he stood up for them and preferred their company to mine. But when they screwed him over, he always came crying to me, at which point I would happily tell him to get lost.

After all those years of married life, we only managed to have a few mutual friends. There weren't many of them and I was never fully at east with them because they had such admiration for the great painter whom the king had bestowed his honors on after purchasing a dozen of his paintings at full retail value. What truly bothered me was that nobody gave me any recognition for always being right there for him, pushing him to work, and taking care of all of life's essentials in order to free him from all responsibilities.

I raised our children on my own. I would tell them that their father needed to work and that he couldn't be disturbed. I spared him all the hassles. Which explained why I always told his friends—whether they were his real friends or so-called friends—that I was one of the big reasons behind his success, but that my efforts went unrecognized, which was the fate that befell the wives of famous men, especially artists' wives.

As we didn't have the same friends, I told him to leave me alone whenever I went out with mine from time to time. I usually only hung out with girls, because we had more fun that way, we spilled our guts, swapped gossip, jokes, laughed, let ourselves go, and hardly noticed how the time flew by. But Foulane would always call me and ask me to come back home. I would tell him to leave me alone: "I'll come back when I feel like it!" He hated me for saying that. Whenever I returned, he wouldn't be able to sleep and would blame his insomnia on me. At which point he would go sleep in another room under the pretext that I stank of booze.

His friends often meddled in our business. They would call me and ask me to come see them because they had something important to tell me. Once I got there, they would lecture me: "Don't you know how lucky you are to share your life with such a great artist? People both admire him and are jealous of him, you must help make his life easier and not bother him with such silly things. He gets easily depressed, and he only wants a little peace so he can work. You see, he feels overwhelmed by your family, he can't put up with them."

On one occasion, instead of replying, I just shouted at them to stay out of our lives.

At which point Foulane lectured me: "How could you treat my childhood friends like that? They're only trying to help."

There were always misunderstandings, whether with him or with his friends.

Until the day I met Lalla, which changed everything. Foulane's jealousy for her gnawed away at him and made him furious and violent. He refused to speak while at the dinner table, but simply gave commands with his hands. All because I'd finally found someone who understood me, who helped me endure all the things he or his family and friends did to me. I was tired of being seen simply as a mother. I wanted to fulfill myself, to have a life of my own, and overcome all the defeats I'd suffered. When I met Lalla, I had the strange feeling that I'd met my soul mate, someone who knew the contents of my heart and my mind. She possessed a natural sweetness that she'd acquired during those years she'd spent in India studying with a guru whose name I've forgotten. She'd given me his books and we spent a lot of time discussing them. She opened my eyes and showed me a path, teaching me that I was a sensitive person endowed with incredible potential that my husband had always stifled. She helped me to see the wounds that my marriage had dealt me. She had a positive outlook on life. New horizons opened up before me. I felt like a child who'd been introduced to the school of life while in her presence. I realized how much time I'd wasted trying to fix things. Lalla held out her hand to me, and I will never forget that. In her, I'd finally met someone who was interested in me but asked for nothing in return. I spent hours at her place and we'd talk ourselves to sleep. Foulane immediately suspected we were lovers. Men are crazy! As soon as two women get together they suspect them of being lesbians. Lalla wasn't a lesbian. She liked men and made no secret of it. I even suspect she had lovers, but we never talked about that. Her reputation completely distorted who she really was. Men envied her freedom, beauty, and generosity. She was someone who spent all her time helping others.

Foulane's jealousy wasn't incomprehensible. I certainly spent more time with Lalla then I did with him or the children. Which was not unusual considering that every time he saw her he would start shouting at her and insulting her, which I couldn't stand. He was just like all those other bourgeois men he frequented, who were all prejudiced against her because she'd dared to divorce her husband because he didn't satisfy her and was almost always absent. They had managed to separate without any acrimony and were still friends. I too would have liked for my marriage to end like that. But my husband was a grotesque man who thrived in conflicts and wanted to control everything to suit his own ends. Lalla had understood all that. More perceptive than any psychiatrist, she had seen through to our biggest mistake: that we'd decided to continue our relationship which had actually been doomed from the start.

I wasn't the only one who thought Lalla was wonderful. There were five other women, all of whom had been disappointed by marriage and betrayed by their chauvinistic husbands. All of these women were looked down on by Casablanca's petty-bourgeois society. We would meet and share our problems, trying to analyze them. Lalla would burn some incense, put some nice Indian music on the stereo, and we would sit there contemplating one another in the warm glow of our friendship.

Lalla, who'd been born into a large family that could claim its descent from the Prophet Mohammed, had a gift for eloquence and knew how to open up our senses. We would sit in a circle around her and listen to her in silence, pierced by the truth that rang out of her words:

We are here to allow our energies to combine, to merge, to channel what is best in our souls into our collective soul so we can then walk hand in hand down the path of our primal wisdom, freeing our humanity from minds that no longer trouble us. We sit here in our purity, refusing to let in the weight of others' selfishness, those who see us as fields to plough, or incubators, or inferior beings who are meant to submit and resign themselves. Sisters, it's time for us to be free and we have to keep our ears pricked to listen to that freedom's rhythm and song. We are energy, and our positive waves can repel the negative ones cast out by our enemies. We are not objects enslaved to their desires, we are not objects at all, we are living energies climbing toward the summits of the highest mountains, where the air is as pure as the contents of our hearts and souls. We are on the right path, we won't submit ourselves any longer to men who think they are strong, we won't allow ourselves to be humiliated by their demands any longer, or to be sacrificed on the altars of their ambitions. The freedom of our energy is in our hands, the sensuality of our energy is in our hands, the beauty of truth is in our hands, so let us take charge of them and use them to eradicate our fears, our shame, our submission, our resignation, our conformity. Our energies will meet, converse, and propel us forward in a liberating momentum. Yes, we've freed ourselves, freed ourselves for good. Let us walk ahead without looking back, because the men who exploit us know we've become stronger than them and are ready to take our destinies, lives, and energies into our own hands.

Let us climb the mountain of our positive energies. Let us leave them our negative energies and let them bury their heads in the sand. Let us refuse to have anything else to do with those who hound us like shadows hoping to see us stumble and fall. We're not crazy, we're wise, freethinking women guided by the echo of our primal scream, we're clearheaded, an unfathomable

*sea, we draw our energy from the fire of life, and amidst the
trees and forests of life. We are strong and united, and we refuse
to be anyone's victim.*

This is the truth, and this truth helped to free me from that roy-
ally selfish man. All this I owe to Lalla, the only friend I ever had who
was always by my side when I needed someone to lean on. Thank you,
Lalla. Thank you for saving me and opening my eyes.

My Husband Is . . .

Foulane found a thousand reasons to explain why we fell out of love. Here are mine:

My husband has many positive qualities, but I've only ever seen his flaws.

My husband is an old bachelor at heart, selfish and fussy.

My husband eats really quickly, and that annoys me.

My husband heads to the airport three hours before his flight.

My husband is bad-tempered and nervous when he's with me, but charming with others.

My husband is impatient.

My husband snores and shifts around in bed.

My husband doesn't like to drive and hates the way I drive.

My husband is a misanthrope and would rather be on his own.

My husband is naïve, weak, and indecisive.

My husband is a sucker. He's been betrayed by his closest friends (women could always disarm him with their smiles, and his agents always stole from him).

My husband hates physical activity, doesn't go to the gym, and has a belly.

My husband loves black-and-white films and always quotes lines from their dialogue, which pisses me off!

My husband is two-faced (I love this expression and it really upsets him).

My husband is a loser and only made money because he was lucky.

My husband doesn't like to fight; he claims he hates conflict.

My husband has often been an absent father.

My husband doesn't have any dreams or fantasies (his paintings are evidence of this).

My husband's never smoked hash or drunk any vodka.

My husband's never gotten drunk or lost his composure.

My husband harangues me whenever I smoke a cigarette or drink some wine.

My husband is an Arab, and shares all their defects and archaisms.

My husband sings out of tune.

My husband doesn't believe in spirits, ghosts, and energies carried by waves.

My husband isn't generous. Every time he gives someone one of his paintings as a present, they're always small and he never signs them.

My husband is a hypochondriac.

My husband is a gutless chauvinist.

My husband is like a tree with a dead hollow trunk.

My husband is so clumsy that one of my friends has kept a list of his gaffes.

My husband pretends to read when he doesn't paint, but reading always puts him to sleep.

My husband doesn't know how to lie.

My husband is the worst kind of cheater.

My husband doesn't act like a husband.

My husband claims he loves women too much, which is a lie, he can't even love his wife.

Hate

It seems that in order to hate someone, you have to really love them first. Maybe that applied to me too. I loved Foulane, but very reluctantly. My mother once told me: "Love comes with time, little one, I only met your father on our wedding night, I learned how to live with him, to get to know him, and we gradually realized we were made to be with one another. So be patient, my daughter, love is life, and it's better for life to be calm and pleasant." Like all girls my age, I believed her. I idolized him, thought of him as a prince, a strong man I could rely on, someone I could lean on. At first, we had some truly happy times. He took care of me, was attentive, especially when I got pregnant. He was fantastic. Those are some of the happiest memories I have of us. He was loyal, never left me alone for a minute, took care of all the errands, and when the maid didn't come, he did all the dishes, took the laundry to the dry cleaner's, vacuumed, and left me all the time to relax. I would look at him and tell myself: "Now look at that, the famous artist washing the floor, I should take a picture of him and send it to the newspapers!" I'm kidding, of course. He was like a different man. I later understood that he'd been so nurturing during my pregnancy because he and his family simply saw me as an incubator. Besides, his family always looked at me as though I were a stranger. I was told that one of his sisters had said: "You should pay her to leave and we'll take care of the little one!" I wanted to throw acid in her face. But I cooled off. "It'll pass," I told myself. Not, "It'll get better." No, I knew it would never get better. He just let them talk and never stood up for me. I'm certain of that.

But nowadays I hate him, I admit it. I don't just want to hurt him, I want to do more than that. I'm only calm when he isn't there. The moment I can feel his presence, even in his current condition, I get all tense and nervous. One day he told me: "Hate is easy, love is more complex, we must lower our guard and just let it happen." What a bunch of mumbo jumbo. He always used those kinds of explanations to belittle me, as though he just wanted to remind me that he'd studied philosophy whereas I hadn't. Just like that story about the embroidered tablecloth he'd insisted on covering the round table in the living room with. I'm not as stupid as he thinks I am. If I took it away it's because I knew that it was so precious that it deserved to be framed, and not left on top of a table where it could get dirty or torn to pieces. If he wants proof he can go look inside the big chest in our bedroom and see for himself how carefully I stored it away.

I started to wish he would just disappear. We've all felt those kinds of desires at one point or another, if only for a few seconds. But once, during a party when he wouldn't stop buzzing around a flirty blonde, I suddenly realized I couldn't stand him anymore. I picked up my purse and left the party. He followed me out into the parking lot, grabbed the door handle, and wouldn't let go. I sped off and he fell, but I didn't stop, I just kept driving. If there had been a car behind me, he would have been run over. He got up and his face was covered in blood. Nothing serious, just a few scrapes, I later found out. I still remember that evening down to its slightest detail. He reproached me for it for a long time afterwards, blaming me for not having taken him to the hospital and for having left him behind. But after all I'd had to endure from him, I certainly wasn't going to let him open the door and talk with him as though nothing had happened. It wasn't that dissimilar to when I refused to be his chauffeur on his return from China. I had wanted to punish him for refusing to take me with him. I suspected he'd gone there with someone else. So, sick or not, I wasn't in the mood to drive him around.

I admit it, I'm a violent woman. So if he knew that, why would he keep provoking me?

He often reproached me for not admiring him. He was right. How could I possibly admire such a mean-spirited man, such a mediocre husband? As for his being an artist, I couldn't have cared less, it was useless to me. Being Foulane's wife might have been a stroke of good luck as far as others were concerned, but it made my life a living hell. He identified with Picasso and the way the latter coarsely went about making his romantic conquests. We'd even seen a film about Picasso where Foulane had openly confessed to admiring him. But I didn't admire my husband, I hated him, and seeing him enfeebled by his stroke did not inspire the slightest pity in me. Every time I looked at him, I couldn't help but see the monster who'd taken the best years of my life and then abandoned me. He claimed it was all my fault. It's easy to blame his stroke on me. The doctor had warned him to stick to a diet and to stop smoking and drinking. But he continued to live as though he were thirty years old. He was always stressed and anxious whenever we went abroad. He would show up at the airport incredibly early, hated taking care of the luggage, couldn't stand to wait in line, and would rush onto the plane as though someone was going to steal his seat. He'd already been a very stressed man by the time I met him. Thus it was that his stress, the lack of a healthy lifestyle, and the nights he went out carousing with his friends—who adored him because he always picked up the tab—all contributed to his stroke. If I had any responsibility, it was that I helped precipitate the situation. He eventually recovered a little, thanks to Imane, or so he claimed, who pretended that she was his nurse even though she slept with him despite the state he was in. She was just an ambitious girl who was taking advantage of an old man. The truth was that I was the one who looked after him. Which is something that I bitterly regret to this day.

I'll never leave Foulane, I'll never leave him alone. He has to assume his responsibilities. I couldn't care less about his health, mood, or state of mind. I'll never stop hating him so long as my thirst for revenge isn't quenched. One day I'll rebuild my life, but not before he's paid the price. So long as he refuses to atone for what he's done to me, or publicly confess in front of everyone, I'll refuse to let go! I'm too proud to leave him. I'm full of hate, and if anyone were to shake me, drops of poison would inevitably fall out.

I hate his smell.

I hate his charm.

I hate the smell of his breath.

I hate his mouth.

I hate his smirk.

I hate his hypocrisy.

I hate his friends.

I hate how quickly he eats and how he slobbers all over himself.

I hate his stress and his anxiety.

I hate his insomnia, which prevents me from sleeping.

I hate how weak he is and how he refuses to react.

I hate his hearty laughter.

I hate his single malt whisky.

I hate his Cuban cigars, which he guards jealously.

I hate his collection of luxury watches.

I hate the way he makes love.

I hate his pregnant silences.

I hate his indifference.

I hate his hypocritical outlook on religion.

I hate his long absences.

I hate his selfishness.

I hate his love handles.

I hate his passion for the cinema.

I hate the jazz he listens to at high volumes.

I hate all the women he met before me.

I hate and despise all the women he was with after me.

I hate how passive-aggressive he is.

I hate his mannerisms (he always bites his lower lip when he's angry).

I hate the way he used to call me just before he went to fuck someone else (he would always call me on the landline to make sure I was home).

I hate his paintings, his studio, his bed, his sofa, his pajamas, his toothbrush, his comb, his razor, I hate all his toiletries, his luggage, and especially that little leather suitcase that follows him everywhere.

I dream of destroying him, of seeing him at my mercy, on his knees, stripped of all his goods and assets, naked and ready to slide into the funerary shroud that I gave him on our wedding day.

I also began suffering from insomnia; after all, it's not like the artist exercised a monopoly on that. So I would examine my life and put things in perspective. Then I would amuse myself by thinking up ways to get to him, to hurt him. My need for revenge would become twice as ferocious during those sleepless nights:

- Burn his collection of ancient manuscripts, which I stole from his studio. I know, that's criminal, but if it makes him suffer, then that's what I'll have to do.
- Stalk the mistresses of his I've been able to track down and keep Foulane apprised of my actions and the reactions of the women who wrecked my life.

- Take advantage of his guard being momentarily lowered to get him to sign over power of attorney (I already have the letter) so I can transfer all his assets into my bank account. As he loves money, this will drive him crazy.
- Have medical experts declare him of unsound mind and thus have him placed under my tutelage.
- He'll only piss when I let him. He'll call and call but I won't come to help him to the bathroom. I love thinking about him feeling his hot piss run down his legs. He'll be so humiliated.

I've got plenty of other ideas. But I'm going to do this step by step. No sudden, impromptu moves.

Love

Sometimes I still ask myself: did I ever love this man? Perhaps I didn't love him as I should have done, but these days, after having gotten everything off my chest, and after having talked about it and reflected on it, I can safely say I was only ever spurred by love. Not just any kind of love. The sort of love that had neither rhyme nor reason to it. Something different. I loved him because I had no other choice. I came from a faraway place, a land few people knew much about. One day, when my family had been celebrating an engagement, I'd gotten very troubled. I looked around myself and everything seemed so unlike the life I led with Foulane. I felt I was utterly unlike those people: the women were satisfied, the men looked happy and comfortable, and the children were allowed to run loose around a dusty, filthy courtyard. I looked at my aunt, whose daughter had just given birth to a baby, and asked myself: "Do she and her husband love each other?" I observed them in their respective nooks: my aunt busy preparing dinner while my uncle played cards with the other men. Love, the real kind of love that sweeps everything in its path, was nowhere to be seen anywhere around me, and was certainly not to be found in that house in the middle of that desolate bled where everything was neatly arranged and in its place. Not the slightest trace of conflict . . . the women knew their place, and the men knew theirs. Nature and traditions followed their own logic, while I felt out of place in that gathering where everyone was happy and content. I had to make sure I didn't disturb it. I stepped away and observed that happiness following its own rhythm, adhering to a ritual I could not understand. I had become a stranger in my own homeland. My father had told me on numerous occasions that our roots were always a part of us, and I could see his point, but it felt as though mine hadn't followed, or better yet, that they had abandoned me; and when I went to look for them, all I found were the ridiculous traces of a crude, impoverished peasantry.

I learned about love by reading novels and watching a handful of films while I lived in Marseilles. I would identify with the heroine, who would eventually triumph and fall happily into the leading man's arms. I still couldn't tell the difference between romantic love and real love.

By the time I turned eighteen, I was still asking myself: who should I love? Who should I turn to? I wasn't attracted to anyone around me. I was ready to fall in love and was waiting for a man to burst into my life like an actor onto a stage. I longed for him, drew a picture of him in my head, conjured him out of thin air, and visualized him: tall, blue-eyed, elegant, handsome, and more importantly, kindhearted. I was ready for him. I struggled through my classes and waited for my lover to show up at night.

I was distant and absentminded the day I met Foulane, I was looking elsewhere and he was the one who approached me and started asking me a bunch of questions about my background, my life, and my future. He grabbed hold of my right hand and pretended to read the lines on my palm, then did the same with my left hand. He said all the right things. He was insightful. He talked a lot about Morocco, France, art, and his desire to go on holiday, a long holiday. I thought he was handsome but something about him unsettled me. He kept looking at other women while he was talking to me. His eye would wander around the exhibition hall and come to rest on other women's bodies. I pointed out that one of those women was returning his glance. "He's a ladies' man, forget about him!" I told myself. At which point he asked for my phone number and said he wanted me to go see him so he could show me something important. When I asked him to elaborate, he said he wanted to paint my portrait, which was how he lured women to his studio. I couldn't tell whether he was being serious or not. I turned him down politely and fate had it that our paths crossed again not long after at a party hosted by the professor who taught my course on the history of modern art. He wouldn't leave me alone all night. He walked me home to the little studio apartment in the banlieues where I was living at the time.

Thus our love was born. I couldn't get him out of my head and caught myself hoping for a sign from him, a telephone call, a postcard, or an impromptu visit.

Coming Alive

Voilà, I've gotten it all out of my system, and unlike him, I kept it brief and to the point. Regardless, I know that you'll believe his version of events rather than mine, because his work will outlive our miserable love story. After all, I'm just the country girl who entered his life and wrecked everything. He never made me happy and yet I still made many efforts to ensure his life was pleasant. I regret having turned a blind eye to many things. Seeing him now in his wheelchair with half his body paralyzed fills my heart with pity. Pity isn't a wonderful sentiment; however, I have no wish to see him regain his health so he can start betraying me again. From now on I'll take care of him, be his nurse, his mother, his wife, perhaps even his friend. I've put a stop to the divorce proceedings. I'm going to change my behavior and alter my tactics, which will surprise him and he'll realize he cannot do without me. I'm going to love him like I did in our early days, I'm going to love him and keep him close. I'm going to rid myself of my nastier urges; I'll give up on exacting my revenge, I'll be good to him and put myself at his disposal. I'll stop asking myself whether I love him or not because I know he's utterly incapable of love, or of giving and receiving. I'm not a monster, even though he's depicted me as a harbinger of death and disease.

My first gesture will be to bring him some broth, and then I'll give him a nice long massage just like his beautiful Imane used to do. She's now living just a few miles away from here. One day around the beginning of August I went to see her and brought her a present, a pretty dress that I haven't worn in a long time, and invited myself over to the tiny apartment in a poor neighborhood that she shares with her mother and brother. I was blunt with her and said: "I'm going to look after my husband myself, he needs me. I want him to get better so that he'll get back to his paintings thanks to me, because I'm his wife. He's a great artist, and so I'm asking you not to look after him anymore, I can see that this bothers him and it's affected his blood pressure, which is dangerous. I know I'm asking you for a favor, so I'm going to offer you something in exchange: I'll get your brother a visa so he can go to Spain and I'll keep paying you until you leave for Belgium. It can all be easily arranged, you can teach me how to give him his injections and to help him with his physical therapy. You'll also need to appease him and tell him that you can't come anymore because you're going to get married and your fiancé is on his way to take care of all the arrangements. I'll handle all the paperwork and I don't think it'll be complicated because your situation falls under the "right to family reunification" category. As for your brother, I'm sure it'll be easy, I know the Spanish consul well and Javier never says no to me. He's a good friend of my husband's too."

Imane was initially shocked by my visit and my proposal, but she had a good heart and thought it was normal for a wife to want to look after her sick husband. She told me she thought of Foulane as an uncle or father, that she'd just been doing her job, and that she loved her fiancé. I pretended to agree with her and stuck to practical questions. She showed me how to give him his injections, taught me how to massage him and revitalize his muscles. It was a very informative afternoon. She gave me her brother Aziz's passport and handed over her visa application to live in Belgium, which had been turned down. We hugged and I left, feeling proud of myself.

I'd gotten my plan off the ground and the trap was closing around him. All that was left to do was to approach Foulane and sweetly explain to him how his new life was going to unfold. I would have to practice in order to do that. Lalla helped me. She played the part of my husband, while I played myself. It was fun. At one point we burst out laughing. Lalla even said that our plan was going to be far more successful than all the incense the *taleb* from the mountains could provide. We opened a good bottle of wine to celebrate.

I'll be at his beck and call day and night. I'll offer him a truce for the sake of our children. It's the best way to avoid him slipping out of my grasp, so that he can finally become the man I always dreamed he could be. I'll look after him and become indispensable to him. I'll love him for what he is and I'll never try to change him again. I'm not a monster; I have feelings too. I can be a little wild and brutal, it's my nature. I hate all the playacting and hypocrisy that's so common in his family. I'll love him and give him everything I didn't during those years of disagreements, and I'm also going to admire him, even though I've always done all I could to prevent him from seeing how proud I was of him. I want him to see how much I love him, and to realize that I'm not his enemy, and that I'm the only woman who actually loves him, especially now that he's an invalid and his life has been stunted by his illness and its ramifications. I've acquainted myself with his condition and I'm told he'll make a full recovery. But will he recover full possession of his motor skills? Will he ever be able to paint like he used to? The doctors can't say for sure. There's nothing to do apart from watch his progress and be happy that he's able to pick up a brush again. I'll keep him close, no other woman will ever be able to get near to him, I'll be right here and he won't be able to budge from his wheelchair. The Twins, as he calls them, will help me when he needs to go to the bathroom or to go out. But from now on I'll be the one who washes him, so I can see him be utterly dependent on me, just like a child, and he won't be able to grumble, threaten me, or insult me like he used to do in the past. I'll be out of his reach. I'll sleep beside him, make him herbal tea, give him his medication, and even slip him some sedatives, so that he'll be able to sleep properly. The time has come for me to prove I'm a good selfless wife who's ready to sacrifice her youth yet again so that he can have a good life. I'll be attentive and never leave him alone. I spoke to his doctors and they think this is a good idea. After all, we promised ourselves to be good to one another, "in sickness and in health" as the traditional Christian vows say. In our country, people promise to help one another through illness, and that's what I'm going to do.

I'm going to take charge, but I'll do so with such tenderness that he'll be surprised, and it'll make it easier to handle him. I've already put all of his affairs in order. No documents can be signed without my consent. I've hidden a few of his paintings in the basement and locked the door with a padlock and I'm the only one with the key. He won't be able to give them away to people anymore. I called his agent who immediately told me that the price of his paintings had shot up and that it would be a good idea not to sell any for the time being. He explained that the fewer of his canvases are in circulation, the more prized they'll become. So regardless of what Foulane thinks, his painting days are over. In any case, he'll never be able to execute the kind of large paintings that go for such large sums. It's done, *fini*! He's mine now and I can do what I like with him, and I want him to be calm, obliging, maybe even happy.

There's still an important detail that I need to take care of: ensuring he hasn't fathered any other children. I found a photo in his chest that depicted a little boy in the arms of a blonde woman . . .

The meek wife who endured all those slaps is a thing of the past.

I, Amina Wakrine, penned this response to my husband's manuscript on the night of October 1, 2003, and I have decided to love him despite the state that he's in. My feelings won't wander down dead-end streets anymore. It was a carefully considered decision, which I came to largely thanks to Lalla. She was the one who came up with the idea that I should salvage the marriage. She's very clever. If it hadn't been for her, I would be moping around and crying in a corner. She even suggested I should bring him a woman from time to time if it would please him, but I don't know whether I'll be able to do that. No, I shouldn't exaggerate. This will be my revenge, and it will travel down the path of goodness, kindness, and generosity. It will be born out of love and redemption. I'll fill him with a deep, boundless love, a love that will leave him moonstruck, and envelop him with a sweetness that he doesn't even know can exist. I'll be docile, ask for his forgiveness, obey his every wish, and learn to anticipate his desires, to the point where he'll no longer be able to doubt my goodwill and desire to smooth out all his troubles and be his to command. Yes, I'll submit to him and resign myself, in the hopes of carving myself a permanent niche by his side. I'm grateful that fate has afforded me another chance to recover my place, which I should never have lost. Foulane won't be able to go back to his old ways once he understands what's going on. I'll do everything I can to make him into my object, my invalid, completely and utterly reliant on me and me alone. I will relish these moments. I'll revel in this blessing. Free at last, I'll finally be alive.

TAHAR BEN JELLOUN was born in Fez, Morocco, and immigrated to France in 1971. He is an internationally bestselling novelist, essayist, critic, and poet, and the winner of many of the world's most prestigious literary prizes, including the Prix Goncourt and the International IMPAC Dublin Literary Award. He lives in Paris.

ANDRÉ NAFFIS-SAHELY is a poet, critic, and translator from French and Italian.